This book belongs to

Daniel

# Listening with my Heart

**A STORY OF KINDNESS AND SELF-COMPASSION**

BY Gabi Garcia          Illustrated by Ying Hui Tan

Esperanza's tummy fluttered as she practiced her lines on the porch. Today was the class play! Waiting for Mama to walk with her to school, she paced back and forth when she spotted a heart-shaped rock.

Esperanza picked it up and showed it to Mama as soon as she stepped outside.
"I see you found a little treasure," said Mama.

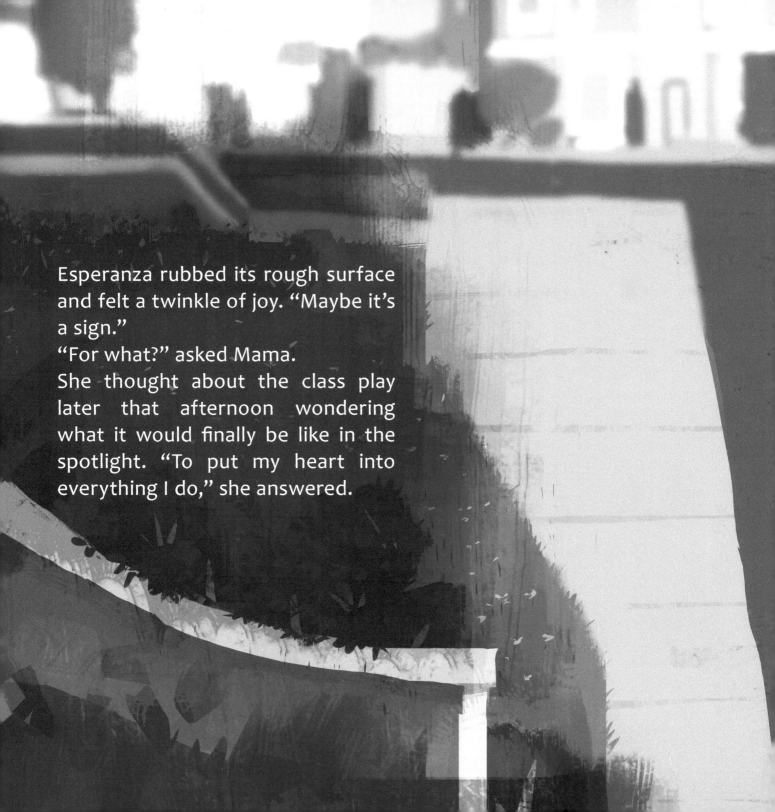

Esperanza rubbed its rough surface and felt a twinkle of joy. "Maybe it's a sign."

"For what?" asked Mama.

She thought about the class play later that afternoon wondering what it would finally be like in the spotlight. "To put my heart into everything I do," she answered.

At that moment, they heard scratching and a soft cry. Esperanza peeked under the stairs and spotted a kitty shaking and shivering. No mama in sight. She scooped the kitten onto her lap and cuddled her. "She's all alone. I think she's hungry." Esperanza reached for her lunch bag, pinched off a piece of chicken, and offered it to the kitty, who gobbled it up.

"Mama, I think the rock is a reminder to spread kindness and love. That's what we do when we listen with our hearts."

"I think you're on to something," said Mama.

"Can we keep Cleocatra? Please?" asked Esperanza, who'd already named the kitty.

"Queens are always welcome at our house," said Mama. "If she's still here after school, we'll take her in."

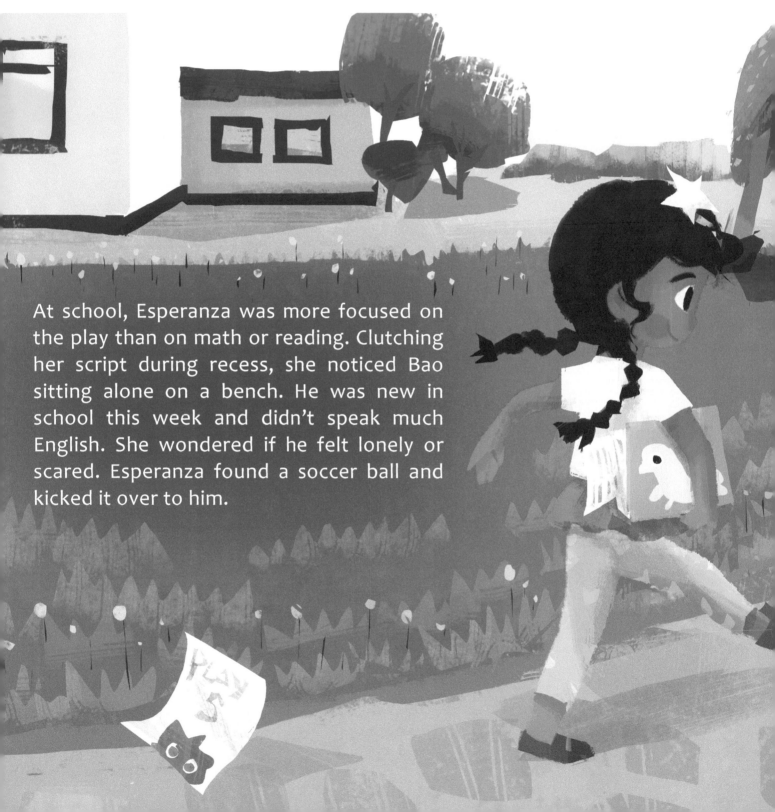

At school, Esperanza was more focused on the play than on math or reading. Clutching her script during recess, she noticed Bao sitting alone on a bench. He was new in school this week and didn't speak much English. She wondered if he felt lonely or scared. Esperanza found a soccer ball and kicked it over to him.

A smile spread across Bao's face. He stood, popped the ball in the air, then bounced it between his knee and his head a few times. "Dude's got moves!" thought Esperanza.

They spent recess giggling
and making up hand signals.

Afterwards, Esperanza borrowed Ms. Owen's English - Vietnamese dictionary. She wrote "friend" in Vietnamese, drew a picture of Bao and her, then put it on his desk. Esperanza rubbed the rock in her pocket. Listening with her heart made her feel peaceful inside.

Finally, it was time for the performance! It was too late for Bao to be in the play, but he stood at Ms. Owen's side as a stage-hand.

Excitement bubbled as Esperanza awaited her cue.

Esperanza walked on stage, tripped as she was about to say her first line, and splattered across the stage.

When she got up, she forgot her lines so Ms. Owen whispered them to her from backstage. Heat rushed through Esperanza's body as all eyes were glued to her. She wished she could disappear.

"I ruined the play!" thought Esperanza, rushing off stage as soon as she'd finished her part. "I messed up in front of everyone." She tucked herself in behind some props so no one would see her.

Esperanza noticed her body shaking and her face still burning. She took a deep breath and dug the rock out of her pocket. It was cracked and lopsided, just how she felt. Esperanza touched her hand to her heart and felt the disappointment.

Bao found Esperanza a few minutes later and handed her a drawing with the word friend written above it.

Esperanza nodded. She hadn't been treating herself like a friend.

Esperanza realized this wasn't the first time she'd been unkind to herself. At the soccer game last weekend, she'd missed the ball that swooshed by her head, and they lost the game.

"Nice work," a player from the other team yelled as the others laughed.

Esperanza thought she'd let her team down and was the worst soccer player in the world. Thinking those thoughts had made her feel worse.

At the curtain call, Esperanza reminded herself she hadn't ruined the play. She'd had an accident, and accidents happen to everyone.

Listening with her heart wasn't just about giving kindness and love to others, it was about giving it to herself, too. I can be a friend to myself, thought Esperanza.

When Esperanza got home she focused on her favorite things. She zipped down the hill on her bike then spent the afternoon painting at the kitchen table. She also got the hug she needed from Mama, and some cuddles from Cleocatra.

# LISTENING WITH YOUR HEART

Some days stink. Not everything will go the way you want. You'll get upset. When this happens, you can pause, take a few deep breaths, and practice listening with your heart. You can:

*Name what you are feeling.* Whatever you feel is okay.

*Listen to your body.* Notice the sensations you are having.

*Pay attention to your self-talk.* Are the words supportive and understanding or mean and rude? Are you being a friend to yourself?

When we treat ourselves with the same kindness and understanding we'd give to someone we care for, we are practicing **self-compassion.**

# BEING THE FRIEND I NEED

Wrap your arms around yourself and give yourself a gentle hug. Take a few deep breaths

When I feel sadness, may I treat myself like the friend I need. May I show love and kindness to myself.

When I feel anger, may I treat myself like the friend I need. May I show love and kindness to myself.

(Think of feelings you experience that are difficult for you and fill in the blank.)

When I feel _____, may I treat myself like the friend I need.

# KIND WORDS FOR MYSELF

Place both hands over your heart. Notice your hands touching each other and touching your heart. Take a few deep breaths and close your eyes if you'd like.

What loving and understanding words or phrases would you like to hear when you're having a tough time or feeling upset? What would feel good or comforting to hear? Take some time and see what words or phrases come up for you. Write them down below or in a notebook and read them to yourself whenever you need to hear them.

_____

_____

_____

_____

_____

_____

# WE ARE ALL CONNECTED

Everyone messes up, makes mistakes, and feels strong emotions-- it's normal. Everyone also wants to feel kindness and love. This is what connects us to each other.

Place your hands gently on your lap. Take a few deep breaths and close your eyes if you'd like. Say these words to yourself:

> I connect to myself through love and kindness.
> I connect to others through love and kindness.
> I connect to the world through love and kindness.

Notice how you feel after doing these activities. You can do them whenever you want. Listening with your heart feels good. It connects you  to others and reminds you to be a friend to yourself. **It helps grow a more peaceful world.**

In loving memory of Katherine, who brought so much love and light into the world. And thank you Ryan-- I couldn't have done this without your support.

# A NOTE TO PARENTS AND EDUCATORS

*In today's hypercompetitive world, children often internalize the message that their worth is attached to their accomplishments and that messing up is something to be ashamed of, rather than simply a normal part of life. This can lead to critical self-talk and them thinking they're not good enough. Listening with My Heart reminds us of the other golden rule– to treat ourselves like we would treat a friend. When we do this, we are practicing self-compassion.*

*Self-compassion can support our well-being by helping to build emotional resiliency. You can help your child cultivate self-compassion by:*

*Helping them become aware of their emotional experiences. Encourage them to name what they're feeling and pay attention to the physical sensations that accompany their feelings. Validate their experiences and let them know that whatever they're feeling is okay.*

*Reminding them that disappointment, setbacks, etc. are a part of growing up. It's important for children to understand that making mistakes is normal. This doesn't mean that they aren't responsible for their actions, but they can take responsibility compassionately.*

*Helping them become aware of their self-talk when things don't go the way they want or expect. Critical self-talk can leave kids feeling shame, embarrassment or believing that they're not good enough. If you notice this happening with your child, ask them to think about what they'd say to a friend having the same experience. Talk about the importance of treating themselves the way they'd treat someone they care for. You can also help them find words or phrases that would feel comforting to them when they're having a hard time.*

*Modeling self-compassion. Kids pay attention to how we deal with our own frustrations and shortcomings. Every mistake we make is an opportunity to model kindness and compassion for ourselves.*

Visit gabigarciabooks.com for FREE downloadable resources to accompany this book.

Warmly,
Gabi

Gabi Garcia is a mama, licensed professional counselor and picture book author. She spent the last 20 years learning from the children she served in the public schools, something she is immensely grateful for.

Gabi writes books that support parents, educators and caregivers in nurturing mindful, socially and emotionally aware children. She lives with her family in Austin, Texas.

Other books by Gabi Garcia
ALL TITLES AVAILABLE IN SPANISH

Ying Hui Tan is a children's book illustrator. You can see more of her work at yinghuitan.com.

skinned knee
publishing

902 Gardner Road no. 4
Austin, Texas 78721

Publisher's Cataloging-in-Publication data
Names: Garcia, Gabi, author. | Tan, Ying Hui, illustrator. Title: Listening with my heart : a story of kindness and self-compassion / by Gabi Garcia ; illustrated by Ying Hui Tan. Description: Austin, TX: Skinned Knee Publishing, 2017. Identifiers: ISBN 978-0-9989580-4-0 (Hardcover) | 978-0-9989580-3-3 (pbk.) | 978-0-9989580-5-7 (ebook) Summary: A young girl realizes that it is just as important to give love and kindness to herself as it is to give it to others.
Subjects: LCSH Emotions--Juvenile fiction. | Kindness--Juvenile fiction. | Friendship--Juvenile fiction. | Empathy--Juvenile fiction. | BISAC JUVENILE FICTION / Social Themes / Emotions & Feelings. Classification: LCC PZ7.G1556245 Li 2017 | DDC [E]--dc23

CPSIA information can be obtained
at www.ICGtesting.com
Printed in the USA
BVHW022152270620
582467BV00010BA/169

LEITH'S COMPLETE CHRISTMAS

# LEITH'S COMPLETE CHRISTMAS

Prue Leith,
Caroline Waldegrave and
Fiona Burrell

# Acknowledgements

This book has been written with much help from all our friends and families. We have also had much advice and recipes from the staff at Leith's School.

We would like to thank Judy van der Sande, Christine Shevlin and Sue Hooper for all their help in typing the often illegible manuscript.

We would also like to thank all those people who helped so much with the production of this book. Puff Fairclough and Janey Bevan cooked all the food for the photographs that were taken by Andrea Heselton and styled by Sue Russell. They were a great pleasure to work with, as were all the production team at Toucan Books. We would like to thank Carl Meek for his help, and I feel particularly grateful to Robert Sackville West who uncomplainingly accepted every major and minor alteration with calm and cheerfulness.

This book could not have been produced without the editorial expertise of Heather Thomas and the extra special editorial help from Roger Gough who provided sound advice, the occasional additional recipe and much applied logic.

Caroline Waldegrave

First published in Great Britain in 1992
Bloomsbury Publishing Limited, 2 Soho Square
London W1V 5DE

Copyright © 1992 by Leith's Farm Ltd

The moral right of the authors has been asserted

A CIP catalogue record for this book
is available from the British Library

ISBN 0 7475 1317 1

10 9 8 7 6 5 4 3 2 1

Edited and designed by
Toucan Books Limited, London

Photographer: Andrea Heselton
Assisted by: Sarah Mac
Stylist: Sue Russell
Home economists: Puff Fairclough, Janey Bevan

Printed in Great Britain by
The Bath Press, Avon

# CONTENTS

 = Vegetarian alternative

❄ ❄ ❄ ❄ ❄ ❄ ❄ ❄ ❄ ❄ ❄ ❄ ❄ ❄ ❄ ❄ ❄ ❄ ❄

# FOREWORD

❄ ❄ ❄ ❄ ❄ ❄ ❄ ❄ ❄ ❄ ❄ ❄ ❄ ❄ ❄ ❄ ❄ ❄ ❄

For the cook in the house Christmas is not always undiluted joy. We cherish the Victorian Christmas ideal of peace and plenty, goodwill to our fellow man, and good things to eat for everybody. But in reality the peace and goodwill are sometimes as hard to achieve as the bounty on the groaning board. We have an expression in our family: 'feeling Christmassy'. This does't mean loving and lovable. It means ratty, bad-tempered and probably tearful.

So, to state the obvious – the way to avoid stress and to ensure a happy and relaxed time (for the cook as well as for everyone else) is to plan things properly, to get as much done as possible in advance, to limit one's ambitions to the achievable, and above all to remember that no-one is coming to judge your cooking for the *Michelin Guide*. You are feeding your loving family and dear friends, not *Good Food Guide* inspectors. This book, we hope and trust, will be your friend and guide in the quest for a perfect, happy and delicious Christmas.

Prue Leith

❄ ❄ ❄ ❄ ❄ ❄ ❄ ❄ ❄ ❄ ❄ ❄ ❄ ❄ ❄ ❄ ❄ ❄ ❄

# INTRODUCTION

❄ ❄ ❄ ❄ ❄ ❄ ❄ ❄ ❄ ❄ ❄ ❄ ❄ ❄ ❄ ❄ ❄ ❄ ❄

The thought of the Christmas holiday period can be very daunting. Will I be able to get all the shopping done? Is the cooking of Christmas lunch very difficult? Will it all be too exhausting, will everyone get on well together? As usual if you're organized it's far easier to get through – also, it can end up being terrific fun.

This book is not meant to be a book of household management – it does not include lists of obvious things not to forget, such as wrapping paper and plenty of booze. It does, however, include the odd list of things that can be useful to remember, such as ingredients to have to hand for creative (i.e. leftover) cooking and lists of useful shops for specific ingredients.

We have assumed that you'll be coping with a household for about a 10-day period. If so, it is naturally wise to do an enormous shop of all your regular household requirements before the arrival of friends and family. It may well also be wise to do a bit of preparatory cooking and freeze suitable dishes.

The mixture of recipes may sound unusual in that some sound rather grand whereas others sound rather homely and cosy. This is because over any holiday period you are probably going to have the occasional dinner party, perhaps a buffet party and a drinks party. However, having had that number of parties, what most of us need in the evening is that universal comfort – food that you can eat with a fork as you slump exhausted in front of the television.

Relevant information for each recipe is given. If a recipe is for a party dish, we have given it in suitable quantities. If it's just for normal home use, then the quantities are for 4 people. For party dishes we have indicated how much of the dish can be prepared in advance, and whether or not it can be frozen. As you will see there is not a vegetarian section, but included in the first courses and main courses are various vegetarian recipes.

We have assumed that alcohol will be an important feature over the Christmas period and so have indicated what style of wine we would serve with each first course and main course. This is meant to be helpful rather than daunting – do look at the chapter on wine (see page 210) before setting out to buy lots of different types of wine.

I do hope that you enjoy cooking from this book and that it helps make for a very happy Christmas holiday.

Caroline Waldegrave

# Conversion Tables

The tables below are approximate, and do not conform in all respects to the official conversions, but we have found them convenient for cooking.

## Weight

| Imperial | Metric | Imperial | Metric |
|---|---|---|---|
| 1/4oz | 7-8g | 1/2oz | 15g |
| 3/4oz | 20g | 1oz | 30g |
| 2oz | 55g | 3oz | 85g |
| 4oz (1/4lb) | 110g | 5oz | 140g |
| 6oz | 170g | 7oz | 200g |
| 8oz (1/2lb) | 225g | 9oz | 255g |
| 10oz | 285g | 11oz | 310g |
| 12oz (3/4lb) | 340g | 13oz | 370g |
| 14oz | 400g | 15oz | 425g |
| 16oz (1lb) | 450g | 11/4lb | 560g |
| 11/2lb | 675g | 2lb | 900g |
| 3lb | 1.35 kg | 4lb | 1.8 kg |
| 5lb | 2.3 kg | 6lb | 2.7 kg |
| 7lb | 3.2 kg | 8lb | 3.6 kg |
| 9lb | 4.0 kg | 10lb | 4.5 kg |

## Liquid measures

| Imperial | ml | fl oz |
|---|---|---|
| 13/4 pints | 1000 (1 litre) | 35 |
| 1 pint | 570 | 20 |
| 3/4 pint | 425 | 15 |
| 1/2 pint | 290 | 10 |
| 1/3 pint | 190 | 6.6 |
| 1/4 pint (1 gill) | 150 | 5 |
| | 56 | 2 |
| 2 scant tablespoons | 28 | 1 |
| 1 teaspoon | 5 | |

## Lengths

| Imperial | Metric |
|---|---|
| 1/2in | 1cm |
| 1in | 2.5cm |
| 2in | 5cm |
| 6in | 15cm |
| 12in | 30cm |

## Oven temperatures

| °C | °F | Gas mark |
|---|---|---|
| 70 | 150 | 1/4 |
| 80 | 175 | 1/4 |
| 100 | 200 | 1/2 |
| 110 | 225 | 1/2 |
| 130 | 250 | 1 |
| 140 | 275 | 1 |
| 150 | 300 | 2 |
| 170 | 325 | 3 |
| 180 | 350 | 4 |
| 190 | 375 | 5 |
| 200 | 400 | 6 |
| 220 | 425 | 7 |
| 230 | 450 | 8 |
| 240 | 475 | 8 |
| 250 | 500 | 9 |
| 270 | 525 | 9 |
| 290 | 550 | 9 |

# Approximate American/European conversions

| Commodity | USA | Metric | Imperial |
|---|---|---|---|
| Flour | 1 cup | 140g | 5oz |
| Caster and granulated sugar | 1 cup | 225g | 8oz |
| Caster and granulated sugar | 2 level tablespoons | 30g | 1oz |
| Brown sugar | 1 cup | 170g | 6oz |
| Butter/margarine/lard | 1 cup | 225g | 8oz |
| Sultanas/raisins | 1 cup | 200g | 7oz |
| Currants | 1 cup | 140g | 5oz |
| Ground almonds | 1 cup | 110g | 4oz |
| Golden syrup | 1 cup | 340g | 12oz |
| Uncooked rice | 1 cup | 200g | 7oz |

Note: In American recipes, when quantities are stated as spoons, 'level' spoons are meant. English recipes (and those in this book) call for rounded spoons except where stated otherwise. This means that 2 American tablespoons equal 1 English tablespoon. Standard spoon measures are available from kitchen equipment shops.

# Useful measurements

| Measurement | Metric | Imperial |
|---|---|---|
| 1 American cup | 225ml | 8 fl oz |
| 1 egg | 56ml | 2 fl oz |
| 1 egg white | 28ml | 1 fl oz |
| 1 rounded tablespoon flour | 30g | 1oz |
| 1 rounded tablespoon cornflour | 30g | 1oz |
| 1 rounded tablespoon sugar | 30g | 1oz |
| 2 rounded tablespoons breadcrumbs | 30g | 1oz |
| 2 level teaspoons gelatine | 8g | $^{1}/_{4}$oz |

(However, in hot weather, or if the liquid is very acid, like lemon juice, or if the jelly contains solid pieces of fruit or meat and is to be turned out of the dish or mould, 20g/$^{3}/_{4}$oz should be used.)

# Wine quantities

| Imperial | ml | fl oz |
|---|---|---|
| Average wine bottle | 730 | 25 |
| 1 glass wine | 100 | 3 |
| 1 glass port or sherry | 70 | 2 |
| 1 glass liqueur | 45 | 1 |

✳✳✳✳✳✳✳✳✳✳✳✳✳✳✳✳✳✳✳

# CATERING QUANTITIES

✳✳✳✳✳✳✳✳✳✳✳✳✳✳✳✳✳✳✳

*Few people accurately weigh or measure quantities as a control-conscious chef must do, but when catering for large numbers it is useful to know how much food to allow per person. As a general rule, the more people you are catering for the less food per head you need to provide, e.g. 225g/8oz stewing beef per head is essential for 4 people, but 170g/6oz per head would feed 60 people.*

## SOUP

Allow 290ml/½ pint soup a head, depending on the size of the bowl.

## POULTRY

**Chicken and turkey** Allow 450g/1lb per person, weighed when plucked and drawn. An average chicken serves 4 people on the bone and 6 people off the bone.

**Duck** A 3kg/6lb bird will feed 3-4 people; a 2kg/4lb bird will feed 2 people. 1 duck makes enough pâté for 6 people.

**Goose** Allow 3.4kg/8lb for 4 people; 6.9kg/15lb for 7 people.

## GAME

**Pheasant** Allow 1 bird for 2 people (roast); 1 bird for 3 people (casseroled).

**Pigeon** Allow 1 bird per person.

**Grouse** Allow 1 young grouse per person (roast); 2 birds for 3 people (casseroled).

**Quail** Allow 2 small birds per person or 1 large boned stuffed bird served on a croûton.

**Partridge** Allow 1 bird per person.

**Venison** Allow 170g/6oz lean meat per person; 2kg/4lb cut of haunch weighed on the bone for 8-9 people.

**Steaks** Allow 170g/6oz per person.

## MEAT

### LAMB OR MUTTON

**Casseroled** 285g/10oz per person (boneless, with fat trimmed away).

**Roast leg** 1.35kg/3lb for 3-4 people; 2kg/4lb for 4-5 people; 3kg/6lb for 7-8 people.

**Roast shoulder** 2kg/4lb shoulder for 5-6 people; 3kg/6lb shoulder for 7-9 people.

**Roast breast** 450g/1lb for 2 people.

**Grilled best end cutlets** 3-4 person.

**Grilled loin chops** 2 per person.

### BEEF

**Stewed** 225g/8oz boneless trimmed meat per person.

**Roast (off the bone)** If serving men only, 225g/8oz per person; if serving men and women, 200g/7oz per person.

Roast (on the bone) 340g/12oz per person.

Roast whole fillet 2kg/4lb piece for 10 people.

Grilled steaks 200-225g/7-8oz per person depending on appetite.

PORK

Casseroled 170g/6oz per person.

Roast leg or loin (off the bone) 200g/7oz per person.

Roast leg or loin (on the bone): 340g/12oz per person.

2 average fillets will feed 3-4 people.

Grilled 1 x 170g/6oz chop or cutlet per person.

VEAL

Stews or pies 225g/8oz pie veal per person.

Fried 1 x 170g/6oz escalope per person.

MINCED MEAT

170g/6oz per person for shepherd's pie, hamburgers, etc.

110g/4oz per person for steak tartare.

85g/3oz per person for lasagne, cannelloni etc.

110g/4oz per person for moussaka.

55g/2oz per person for spaghetti.

FISH

Whole large fish (e.g. sea bass, salmon, whole haddock), weighed uncleaned, with head on: 340-450g/12oz-1lb per person.

Cutlets and steaks 170g/6oz per person.

Fillets (e.g. sole, lemon sole, plaice): 3 small fillets per person (total weight about 170g/6oz).

Whole small fish (e.g. trout, slip soles, small plaice, small mackerel, herring) 225-340g/8-12oz weighed with heads for main course; 170g/6oz for first course.

Fish off the bone (in fish pie, with sauce, etc) 170g/6oz per person.

SHELLFISH

Prawns 55-85g/2-3oz per person as a first course; 140g/5oz per person as a main course.

Mixed shellfish 55-85g/2-3oz per person as a first course; 140g/5oz per person as a main course.

VEGETABLES

Weighed before preparation and cooking, and assuming 3 vegetables, including potatoes, served with a main course: 110g/4oz per person, except (per person):

French beans 85g/3oz.

Peas 85g/3oz.

Spinach 340g/12oz.

Potatoes 3 small (roast); 170g/6oz (mashed); 10-15 (Parisienne); 5 (château); 1 large or 2 small (baked); 110g/4oz (new).

RICE

Plain, boiled or fried 55g/2oz (weighed before cooking) or 1 breakfast cup (measured after cooking).

In risotto or pilaf 30g/1oz per person (weighed before cooking) for first course; 55g/2oz per person for main course.

Note: As a general rule men eat more potatoes and less 'greens' than women!

SALADS

Obviously, the more salads served, the less guests will eat of any one salad. Allow 1 large portion of salad, in total, per head – e.g. if only one salad is served make sure there is enough for 1 helping each. Conversely if 100 guests are to choose from 5 different salads, allow a total of 150 portions – i.e. 30 portions of each salad.

Tomato salad 450g/1lb tomatoes (average 6 tomatoes), sliced, serves 4 people.

Coleslaw. 1 small cabbage, finely shredded, serves 10-12 people.

Grated carrot salad 450g/1lb carrots, grated, serves 6 people.

Potato salad 450g/1lb potatoes (weighed before cooking) serves 5 people.

Green salad Allow a loose handful of leaves for

each person (i.e. a large Cos lettuce will serve 8, a large Webb's will serve 10, a Dutch hothouse 'butterhead' will serve 4).

## SANDWICHES

2 slices of bread make 1 round of sandwiches.

**Cucumber** 1 cucumber makes 15 rounds.

**Egg** 1 hardboiled egg makes 1 round.

**Ham** Allow ³/₄oz/20g for each round.

**Mustard and cress** For egg and cress sandwiches, 1 punnet makes 20 rounds.

**Tomatoes** 450g/1lb makes 9 rounds.

**Smoked salmon** Allow ³/₄oz/20g for each round.

## COCKTAIL PARTIES

Allow 10 cocktail canapés per head.

Allow 14 cocktail canapés per head if served at lunchtime when guests are unlikely to go on to a meal.

Allow 4-5 canapés with pre-lunch or pre-dinner drinks.

Allow 8 cocktail canapés, plus 4 miniature sweet cakes or pastries per head for a wedding reception.

## PUDDINGS

**Cooking apples** Allow 225g/8oz a head for puddings.

**Fruit salad** Allow 8 oranges, 2 apples, 2 bananas and 450g/1lb grapes for 8 people.

**Mousses** Allow 290ml/¹/₂ pint double cream inside and 290ml/¹/₂ pint to decorate a mousse for 8 people.

**Strawberries** Allow 110g/4oz a head.

## MISCELLANEOUS

**Brown bread and butter** 1¹/₂ slices (3 triangular pieces) per person.

**French bread** 1 large loaf for 10 people; 1 small loaf for 6 people.

**Cheese** After a meal, if serving one blue-veined, one hard and one cream cheese: 85g/3oz per person for up to 8 people; 55g/2oz per person

for up to 20 people; 30g/1oz per person for over 20 people.

At a wine and cheese party : 110g/4oz per person for up to 8 people; 85g/3oz per person for up to 20 people; 55g/2oz per person for over 20 people. Inevitably, if catering for small numbers, there will be cheese left over but this is unavoidable if the host is not to look mean.

**Biscuits** 3 each for up to 10 people; 2 each for up to 30 people; 1 each for over 30 people.

**Butter** 30g/1oz per person if bread is served with the meal; 45g/1¹/₂oz per person if cheese is served as well.

**Cream** 15ml/1 tablespoon per person for coffee; 45ml/3 tablespoons per person for pudding or dessert.

**Milk** 570ml/1 pint for 18-20 cups of tea.

**Sliced bread** A large loaf, thinly sliced, generally makes 18-20 slices.

**Butter** 30g/1¹/₂oz soft butter will cover 8 large bread slices.

**Sausages** 450g/1lb is the equivalent of 32 cocktail sausages; 16 chipolata sausages; 8 pork sausages.

**Bouchées** 675g/1¹/₂lb packet puff pastry makes 60 bouchées.

**Chicken livers** 450g/1lb chicken livers will be enough for 60 bacon and chicken liver rolls.

**Dates** 50 fresh dates weigh about 450g/1lb.

**Prunes** A prune (with stone) weighs about 10g/¹/₃oz.

**Mushrooms** A button mushroom weighs about 7g/¹/₄oz.

**Bacon** A good sized rasher weighs about 30g/1oz.

**Button onions** A button onion weighs about 15g/¹/₂oz.

**Choux pastry** 6 egg choux paste makes 150 baby éclairs. They will need 570ml/1 pint cream and 225g/8oz chocolate.

**Short pastry** 900g/2lb pastry will line 150 tartlets.

❊❊❊❊❊❊❊❊❊❊❊❊❊❊❊❊❊❊❊

# FOOD SAFETY

❊❊❊❊❊❊❊❊❊❊❊❊❊❊❊❊❊❊❊

*These are the most important factors to take into account when thinking about food safety.*

*The important thing to remember is that bugs like warmth, moisture and time, so try not to give them their ideal conditions.*

*1. Keep cooking utensils and hands clean.*

*2. Store raw meat at the bottom of the fridge (so that any meat juices cannot drip on to cooked food).*

*3. Wrap food up loosely, let it breathe.*

*4. Don't put hot food into the refrigerator – it will raise the temperature of the fridge.*

*5. Get food to cool down as quickly as possible.*

*6. Never cover 'cooling hot food'.*

*7. Never cook large items (e.g. whole chickens) from frozen.*

*Ideally, don't stuff the turkey cavity as the stuffing may prevent the heat from penetrating the cavity and killing any bacteria present – you should just stuff the bird at the neck end. Once you have served the turkey, store the turkey and stuffing separately. This is especially important if by chance you have stuffed the cavity of the bird.*

*Try to avoid cross contamination of germs – store raw and cooked foods separately as far as possible. If you mix raw and cooked foods they should be mixed when they are both cold and then reheated thoroughly. Avoid keeping food warm – it should be hot or cold.*

❄❄❄❄❄❄❄❄❄❄❄❄❄❄❄❄❄❄❄

# COOKING CHARTS

❄❄❄❄❄❄❄❄❄❄❄❄❄❄❄❄❄❄❄

*We have put together this section of various cooking charts which we hope will be useful ready reckoners for roasting, grilling, frying and boiling most of the meats you will be cooking over the Christmas period.*

## Roasting Tables

If using a fan (convection) oven, reduce the cooking times by 15 per cent or lower the oven temperature by 20°C/40°F.

| Meat | | Temperature | | | Cooking time | |
|------|------|------|------|------|------|------|
| | | °C | °F | Gas | per kg | per lb |
| **Beef** | Brown | 220 | 425 | 7 | 20 mins + | |
| | Rare roast | 160 | 325 | 3 | 35 mins | 15 mins |
| | Medium roast | | | | 45 mins | 20 mins |
| **Pork** | Roast | 200 | 400 | 6 | 65 mins | 25 mins |
| **Veal** | Brown | 220 | 425 | 7 | 20 mins+ | |
| | Roast | 180 | 350 | 4 | 55 mins | 25 mins |
| **Lamb** | Brown | 220 | 425 | 7 | 20 mins | |
| | Roast | 190 | 375 | 5 | 45 mins | 20 mins |
| **Chicken** | | 200 | 400 | 6 | 35-45 mins | 15-20 mins |
| | NOTE: Few chickens, however small, will be cooked in much under an hour. | | | | | |
| **Turkey** | See chart on page 15. | | | | | |
| **Duck, goose** | Small  (under 2.5kg/5lb) | 190 | 375 | 5 | 45 mins | 20 mins |
| | Large | 190 | 375 | 5 | 33 mins | 15 mins |
| | | | | | + 15 mins over | |
| **Pigeon** | | 200 | 400 | 6 | 25-35 minutes | |
| **Grouse** | | 190 | 375 | 5 | 25-35 minutes | |

| Meat | Temperature | | | Cooking time | |
|---|---|---|---|---|---|
| | °C | °F | Gas | per kg | per lb |
| Guinea fowl | 190 | 375 | 5 | 70 minutes | |
| Partridge | 190 | 375 | 5 | 20-25 minutes | |
| Pheasant | 190 | 375 | 5 | 45-60 minutes | |
| Wild duck | 200 | 400 | 6 | 40 minutes | |
| Woodcock | 190 | 375 | 5 | 20-30 minutes | |
| Quail | 180 | 350 | 4 | 20 minutes | |
| Snipe | 190 | 375 | 5 | 15-20 minutes | |
| Teal | 210 | 425 | 7 | 25 minutes | |

## Thawing and cooking times for turkeys

Although the thawing time in this table can be relied, on the cooking times are dependent on an accurate oven. For safety's sake, plan the timing so that, if all goes right, the bird will be ready 1 hour before dinner. This will give you leeway if necessary. To test if the turkey is cooked, press a skewer into the thickest part of the thigh. The juices should run clear. When the bird is cooked, open the oven door to cool the oven, then put the turkey on a serving dish and put it back in the oven to keep warm.

Thawing in a warm room (over 18°C/65°F) or under warm water is not recommended, as warmth will encourage the growth of micro-organisms, which might result in food poisoning.

| Weight of bird when ready for the oven, regardless of whether it is boned, stuffed or empty | Thawing time at room temperature 18°C/65°F | Thawing time in refrigerator 5°C/40°F | Cooking time at 200°C/400°F Gas mark 6 | Cooking time at 180°C/350°F Gas mark 4 |
|---|---|---|---|---|
| | hours | hours | hours | hours |
| 4 -5 kilos/8-10lb | 20 | 65 | 2 $\frac{1}{2}$-3 hrs | - |
| 5 -6 kilos/10-13lb | 24 | 70 | 3-3 $\frac{3}{4}$ hrs | - |
| 6 -7 kilos/13-16lb | 30 | 75 | 30 minutes then | 3 $\frac{1}{4}$-4 |
| 8 -9 kilos/16-20lb | 40 | 80 | 30 minutes then | 4-4 $\frac{1}{2}$ |
| 9 -11 kilos/20-24lb | 48 | 96 | 1 hour then | 4-4 $\frac{1}{2}$ |

# Fried Steak

SERVES 4

*4 sirloin steaks cut 2cm/³/4 inch thick or 4 fillet*
*steaks cut 2.5cm/1 inch thick*
*freshly ground black pepper and salt*
*oil or dripping*
*maître d'hôtel butter (see page 199)*

1. Season the steaks with pepper. Leave to warm to room temperature if they have been chilled. Sprinkle lightly with salt just before cooking.
2. Brush a frying pan with a little oil or dripping and place over good heat until it is beginning to smoke.
3. Brown the steaks quickly on both sides. For a blue or rare steak, keep the heat fierce for the whole cooking time. For better done steaks, lower the temperature to moderate after the initial good browning. Length of cooking time varies according to the thickness of the meat, the type of steak, the degree of heat, the weight of the frying pan, etc. With experience it is possible to tell from the feel of the steak how well cooked it is – it feels very soft when blue; very firm when medium. But if you want to be certain, there is nothing for it but to cut a tiny slit in the fattest part of the meat, and take a look. Don't do this until you are fairly sure that the steak is ready – too many cuts will mean loss of juices. Cooking times, assuming a good hot pan, would be approximately as below:

| SIRLOIN | |
| --- | --- |
| Blue steak | 1 minute per side |
| Rare steak | 1½ minutes per side |
| Medium rare | 2 minutes per side |
| Medium steak | 2¼ minutes per side |
| FILLET | |
| Blue steak | 1½ minutes per side |
| Rare steak | 2¼ minutes per side |
| Medium rare | 3¼ minutes per side |
| Medium steak | 4½ minutes per side |

4. Serve the steaks topped with a slice of maître d'hôtel butter.

FULL RED

# Grilled Steak

SERVES 4

*4 fillet steaks, cut 2cm/³/4 inch thick, or 4 sirloin*
*steaks, cut 2.5cm/1inch thick*
*salt and freshly ground black pepper*
*butter, melted*
*maître d'hôtel butter (see page 199)*

1. Season the steaks with pepper. Leave to warm to room temperature if they have been chilled. Sprinkle lightly with salt just before cooking.
2. Heat the grill. Do not start cooking until it is at maximum temperature.
3. Brush the grill rack and steak with a little melted butter.
4. Grill the steak quickly on both sides. For a blue or rare steak, keep the heat fierce for the whole cooking time. For better done steaks, lower the temperature to moderate after the initial good browning. Length of cooking time varies according to the thickness of the meat, the type of steak, the efficiency of the grill, etc. With experience it is possible to tell from the

feel of the steak how well cooked it is – it feels very soft when blue, very firm when medium. But if you want to be certain, there is nothing for it but to cut a tiny slit in the fattest part of the meat and take a look. Do not do this until you are fairly sure that the steak is ready – too many cuts will mean loss of juices. Cooking times, assuming a good hot grill, would be approximately as below:

SIRLOIN

| Blue | $1^1/4$ minutes per side |
| Rare | $1^3/4$ minutes per side |
| Medium rare | $2^1/4$ minutes per side |
| Medium | $2^3/4$ minutes per side |

FILLET

| Blue | $2^1/4$ minutes per side |
| Rare | $3^1/4$ minutes per side |
| Medium rare | $4^1/4$ minutes per side |
| Medium | 5 minutes per side |

5. Serve each steak topped with a slice of maître d'hôtel butter.

FULL RED

# Boiling Times for Hams

A ham joint or gammon joint should be soaked overnight in cold water because you can never be sure if it is going to be salty or not.
Put the joint in a pan with clean cold water. Flavour with an onion, celery stick, a carrot and a bay leaf, bring up to the boil and allow 25 minutes per 450g/1 lb. For a larger joint, i.e. 3.5 kg/8 lbs and upwards, allow 20 minutes per 450g/1 lb.

GLAZES FOR HAM

1. *30g/1oz honey*
   *juice of 1 orange*
   *5ml/1 teaspoon English mustard*

Mix all the ingredients together. Remove the skin from the ham leaving some fat behind. Score the fat in a criss-cross pattern and coat with the runny glaze. Put in the preheated oven for 30 minutes.

2. *55g/2oz Demerara sugar*
   *15g/¹/₂oz English mustard*
   *cloves*

Mix the sugar and mustard together and rub into the scored fat of the ham. Stud with cloves. Put in the preheated oven for 30 minutes.

3. *55g/2oz Demerara sugar*
   *5ml/1 teaspoon ground cloves*

Mix together and rub into the scored fat of the ham. Place in the preheated oven for 30 minutes.

❄❄❄❄❄❄❄❄❄❄❄❄❄❄❄❄❄❄❄❄❄

# COUNTDOWN
# TO
# CHRISTMAS

❄❄❄❄❄❄❄❄❄❄❄❄❄❄❄❄❄❄❄❄❄❄❄

*Timeplan*

*Roast turkey*
*Sausagemeat and chestnut stuffing*
*Cream cheese and bacon stuffing*
*Sausagemeat and sage stuffing*
*Chestnut stuffing*
*Forcemeat balls*
*Cranberry and orange sauce*
*Bread sauce*
*Roast potatoes*
*Brussels sprouts and chestnuts*
*Christmas pudding*
*Brandy butter*
*Rum butter*
*Rum sauce*
*Mince pies*

VEGETARIAN ALTERNATIVE
*Aubergine and chestnut pie*

❄❄❄❄❄❄❄❄❄❄❄❄❄❄❄❄❄❄❄❄❄❄❄

# TIMEPLAN

*To enable you to enjoy Christmas Day with the rest of the family and not to spend all of it in the kitchen, it is very helpful to get as much as possible prepared in advance. If you also write a timetable for the day it will help to ensure that nothing is forgotten and everything arrives, hot, at the table at the same time.*

MENU

*Roast turkey*
*Stuffing*
*Bacon rolls*
*Sausages*
*Forcemeat balls*
*Bread sauce*
*Cranberry sauce*
*Roast potatoes*
*Brussels sprouts with chestnuts*
*Christmas pudding with brandy butter and/or*
*Rum sauce*
*Mince pies and cream*

Make a list of what can be done in advance and tick off each item as you go along. If you are freezing some items, e.g. stuffing, remember to defrost them in time.

The following can be made well in advance:

1. Christmas pudding
2. The stuffings (and then frozen)
3. The forcemeat balls (and then frozen)
4. The breadcrumbs for the bread sauce (and then frozen)
5. The mince pies (and then frozen)
6. The brandy butter (and then frozen)

You should make a really comprehensive shopping list. A couple of days before Christmas you should make the cranberry sauce. Also, if cooking a frozen turkey, check how long it will take to defrost and ensure that it has defrosted completely by Christmas Eve evening. For defrosting times see page 15.

CHRISTMAS EVE

1. Weigh the turkey to establish a rough cooking time. You will have to weigh it again once it's stuffed for the exact time (see page 15).

2. Make or defrost the stuffing and forcemeat balls, keep them chilled.

3. Put the cranberry sauce, brandy butter and cream into serving pots or jugs, cover and put into the fridge.

4. Make the rum sauce.

5. Make some turkey stock from the giblets. Do not use the liver as it makes it bitter. Drain, cool and then chill.

6. Make the bacon rolls and twist the sausages.

7. Make lots of ice.

8. Prepare the Brussels sprouts and peel the chestnuts.

9. Peel the potatoes – leave covered in water in a cool place .

10. Defrost or make the breadcrumbs.

11. Sharpen the carving knife.

12. Defrost the mince pies.

13. Sort out the dishes that are to be used.

14. Choose the wine and make sure someone has the job of dealing with it on Christmas Day.

CHRISTMAS DAY

NOTE: This assumes a 5.35kg/12lb turkey and that you will be eating at 1.30 pm.

| 9.15 am | Turn on the oven. Stuff the turkey and weigh it again to establish the precise cooking time (see page 15). |
| 9.30 am | Wrap the turkey in butter-soaked muslin and put in the oven. |
| 10.30 am | Lay the table. |
| 11.15 am | Fry the chestnuts. Set aside. |
| 11.30 am | Parboil the potatoes. |
| 11.45 am | Put the potatoes in the oven. |
| 12.00 pm | Put the pudding on to steam – keep checking the water level. |
| 12.05 pm | Put the sausages, bacon rolls and forcemeat balls in the oven. |
| 12.40 pm | Make the bread sauce. |
| 12.45 pm | Check the contents of the oven. When cooked, put them on serving dishes and replace, uncovered, in the turned-off oven, or keep warm in a low simmering or warming oven. |
| 1.00 pm | Make the gravy using the turkey stock. Strain into a saucepan for easy reheating. Put the water on for the sprouts. Do as much washing up and clearing up as possible. Warm the plates. |
| 1.15 pm | Cook the Brussels sprouts, reheat the chestnuts and mix together. Reheat the bread sauce and gravy. |
| 1.30 pm | Serve: checking: |

        1. Turkey, bacon rolls, sausages, forcemeat balls.

        2. Gravy

        3. Bread sauce

        4. Cranberry sauce

        5. Potatoes

        6. Sprouts

2.00 pm (or whenever) Put the mince pies in a very low oven to warm through. Warm through the rum sauce and serve up the pudding, brandy butter, mince pies and cream.

NOTE: To carve a turkey: if you are going to carve the turkey in the dining room simply carve it as normal, i.e. use a sharp carving knife and cut thin slices of breast meat and slightly thicker slices of brown meat from the legs and thighs. Don't forget to serve the stuffing. If you have a large turkey, you can carve half of it in the kitchen and carry it into the dining room uncarved side forwards so that it looks like a complete bird but is quick to serve.

To carve in the kitchen: remove the breast in one piece. Put the whole breast on a board and place the board on a clean tray (to catch all the juices – good for soup, prevents a mess). Slice into elegant slices and arrange down one side of a meat plate. Twist off the leg and drumstick from the same side and cut as elegantly as possible. Arrange down the other side of the meat plate. When you serve, give each guest a piece of brown and a piece of white meat. Again, don't forget the stuffing.

QUANTITIES

The turkey recipe is for 12 people but the rest of the recipes are for 8 people. We assume that most people like to have some leftover turkey for use later in the week.

❄ ❄ ❄ ❄ ❄ ❄ ❄ ❄ ❄ ❄ ❄ ❄ ❄ ❄ ❄ ❄ ❄ ❄ ❄ ❄ ❄ ❄ ❄

# Roast Turkey

A large square of fine muslin (butter-muslin) is needed for this recipe.

SERVES 12

5.35kg/12lb turkey

FOR THE SAUSAGEMEAT AND CHESTNUT STUFFING:

(for alternative stuffings see page 22)

*450g/1lb good-quality sausagemeat*

*450g/1lb unsweetened chestnut purée*

*110g/4oz fresh breadcrumbs*

*1 large egg, beaten*

*salt and freshly ground black pepper*

TO PREPARE THE TURKEY FOR THE OVEN:

*170g/6oz butter*

FOR THE GARNISH:

*1 chipolata sausage per person*

*1 streaky bacon rasher per person*

FOR THE GRAVY:

*10ml/2 teaspoons flour*

*turkey stock (see page 179)*

1. Make the sausagemeat and chestnut stuffing: mix together the sausagemeat, chestnut purée, breadcrumbs and beaten egg. Taste and season as required. Stuff this into the neck end of the turkey, making sure that the breast is well plumped. Draw the skin flap down to cover the stuffing. Secure with a skewer.
2. Weigh the turkey to establish cooking time (see page 14).
3. Set the oven to 180°C/350°F/gas mark 4.
4. Melt the butter and in it soak a very large piece of butter-muslin (about 4 times the size of the turkey) until all the butter has been completely absorbed.
5. Season the turkey well with salt and pepper. Completely cover the bird with the doubled butter-muslin and roast in the prepared oven for the time calculated (a 5.3kg/12lb turkey should take about 3½ hours).
6. Meanwhile, prepare the garnishes: make each chipolata sausage into 2 cocktail-sized ones by twisting gently in the middle. Take the rind off the bacon and stretch each rasher slightly with the back of a knife, cut into 2 and roll up. Put the sausages and bacon rolls into a second roasting pan, with the bacon rolls wedged in so that they cannot unravel. Forty-five minutes

before the turkey is ready, put the sausages and bacon in the oven.

7. When the turkey is cooked, the juices that run out of the thigh when pierced with a skewer should be clear. Remove the muslin and lift the bird on to a serving dish. Surround with the bacon and sausages and keep warm while making the gravy.

8. Lift the pan with its juices on to the top of the cooker and skim off the fat. Whisk in the flour and add enough turkey stock or vegetable water to make up to about 570ml/1 pint. Stir until boiling, then simmer for a few minutes. Taste and add salt and pepper if necessary. Strain into a warm gravy boat.

RED BURGUNDY OR
ANY LIGHT TO MEDIUM RED

❆ ❆ ❆ ❆ ❆ ❆ ❆ ❆ ❆ ❆ ❆ ❆ ❆ ❆ ❆ ❆ ❆ ❆ ❆ ❆

# ALTERNATIVE STUFFINGS FOR POULTRY

NOTE: These stuffings can be made well in advance and frozen. The bird should only be stuffed in the neck end, as placing stuffing in the cavity can mean that the centre of the bird takes longer to heat up and therefore bacteria can multiply rapidly.

## Cream Cheese and Bacon Stuffing

30g/1oz butter
1 onion, chopped
110g/4oz streaky bacon, chopped
225g/8oz cream cheese
85g/3oz fresh white breadcrumbs
salt and freshly ground black pepper

1. Melt the butter in a medium-sized saucepan and gently sweat the onion in it for about 5 minutes. Add the bacon and cook for a further minute.

2. Soften the cheese with a wooden spoon, add the breadcrumbs, onion and bacon. Mix well and season to taste with salt and pepper.

❆ ❆ ❆ ❆ ❆ ❆ ❆ ❆ ❆ ❆ ❆ ❆ ❆ ❆ ❆ ❆ ❆ ❆ ❆ ❆

# Sausage Meat and Sage Stuffing

*1 onion, finely chopped*
*225g/8oz good-quality sausagemeat*
*110g/4oz fresh white breadcrumbs*
*30ml/1 tablespoon chopped fresh sage*
*1 egg, beaten*
*salt and freshly ground black pepper*

Mix together the onion, sausagemeat, breadcrumbs and sage. Add the beaten egg and season carefully with salt and freshly ground black pepper.

❊ ❊ ❊ ❊ ❊ ❊ ❊ ❊ ❊ ❊ ❊ ❊ ❊ ❊ ❊ ❊ ❊ ❊ ❊ ❊

# Chestnut Stuffing

*225g/8oz chestnuts*
*30g/1oz butter*
*1 onion, chopped*
*1 turkey liver, chopped*
*110g/4oz fresh white breadcrumbs*
*15ml/1 tablespoon chopped fresh parsley*
*3 celery sticks, chopped*
*freshly ground nutmeg*
*salt and freshly ground black pepper*
*1 egg, beaten*

1. Make a slit in the shell of each chestnut. Place in a pan of boiling water and simmer for 10 minutes. Remove the outer and inner skins. Chop the chestnuts roughly.
2. Melt the butter in a saucepan, and add the onion and chestnuts. Cook gently for 5 minutes. Add the liver and cook for 2 minutes.
3. Transfer to a bowl and add the breadcrumbs, parsley, celery, nutmeg and seasoning. Bind together with an egg.

❊ ❊ ❊ ❊ ❊ ❊ ❊ ❊ ❊ ❊ ❊ ❊ ❊ ❊ ❊ ❊ ❊ ❊ ❊ ❊

# Forcemeat Balls

*55g/2oz cooked ham, minced or very finely chopped*
*110g/4oz sausagemeat*
*55g/2oz shredded suet*
*grated rind of 1 lemon*
*15ml/1 tablespoon chopped fresh parsley*
*15ml/1 tablespoon chopped mixed fresh herbs, e.g. thyme, sage, marjoram, basil, mint*
*170g/6oz fresh white breadcrumbs*
*salt and freshly ground pepper*
*pinch cayenne pepper*
*2.5ml/1/2 teaspoon ground mace*
*2 eggs*

1. Mix together the ham, sausagemeat, suet, lemon, parsley, herbs and breadcrumbs. Season with salt, freshly ground black pepper, cayenne pepper and mace.
2. Beat the eggs and gradually add to the breadcrumb mixture, beating until well mixed.
3. Using wet hands, roll the mixture into balls

slightly larger than a golf ball.

4. Put them in a roasting pan with the turkey or in a separate tin with a little oil or dripping.

5. They will take about 45 minutes to cook and should be turned once or twice.

NOTE: These are traditionally served with turkey but can also be served with roast chicken or roast pork.

❄ ❄ ❄ ❄ ❄ ❄ ❄ ❄ ❄ ❄ ❄ ❄ ❄ ❄ ❄ ❄ ❄ ❄ ❄ ❄ ❄

# SAUCES

## Cranberry and Orange Sauce

SERVES 8
*juice of 2 oranges*
*225g/8oz sugar*
*450g/1lb cranberries*

1. Put the orange juice and sugar together in a saucepan. Allow the sugar to dissolve over a gentle heat.

2. Add the cranberries and simmer very slowly until just tender.

3. Serve cold.

## Bread Sauce

SERVES 8
*1 large onion, peeled*
*12 cloves*
*570ml/1pint milk*
*2 bay leaves*
*10 peppercorns, or 1 pinch of white pepper*
*pinch of nutmeg*
*salt*
*110g/4oz fresh white breadcrumbs*
*110g/4oz butter*

*60ml/4 tablespoons cream (optional)*

1. Cut the onion in half. Stick the cloves into the onion pieces and put with the milk and bay leaf into a saucepan.

2. Add the peppercorns, nutmeg, and a good pinch of salt. Leave to stand for 30 minutes, then bring it to the boil very slowly.

3. Take the milk from the heat and strain it on to the breadcrumbs. Add the butter and cream. Mix and return to the saucepan.

4. Reheat the sauce carefully without boiling.

5. If it has become too thick, beat in more hot milk. It should be creamy.

# Roast Potatoes

SERVES 8
*12 medium-sized potatoes (about 1.8kg/4lbs)*
*salt*
*dripping or oil*

1. Wash and peel the potatoes and, if they are large, cut them into 5cm/2 inch pieces.
2. Bring them to the boil in salted water. Simmer for 5 minutes.
3. Drain them and shake them in the sieve to roughen and slightly crumble the surface of each potato. (This produces deliciously crunchy potatoes that can be kept warm for up to 2 hours without coming to any harm. Potatoes roasted without this preliminary boiling and scratching tend to become tough and hard if not eaten straight away.)
4. Heat the fat in a roasting pan and add the potatoes, turning them so that they are coated all over.
5. Roast, basting occasionally, and turning the potatoes over at half-time.

# Brussels Sprouts and Chestnuts

SERVES 8
*900g/2lbs very small Brussels sprouts*
*450g/1lb fresh chestnuts*
*55g/2oz butter*
*salt, freshly ground black pepper and nutmeg*

1. Wash and trim the sprouts, paring the stalks and removing the outside leaves if necessary.
2. Make a slit in the skin of each chestnut and put them into a pan of cold water. Bring to the boil, simmer for 10 minutes and then take off the heat. Remove 1 or 2 nuts at a time and peel. The skins come off easily if the chestnuts are hot but not too cooked.
3. Melt the butter in a frying pan, and slowly fry the chestnuts, which will break up a little until brown.
4. Bring a large pan of salted water to the boil, and tip in the sprouts. Boil fairly fast for 5-8 minutes until they are cooked, but not soggy: the flavour changes disastrously if boiled too long. Drain them well.
5. Mix the sprouts and chestnuts together gently, adding the butter from the frying pan. Season with salt, pepper and nutmeg.

# Christmas Pudding

MAKES 2.3kg/5lb
170g/6oz raisins
110g/4oz currants
200g/7oz sultanas
85g/3oz mixed peel, chopped
225g/8oz mixed dried apricots and figs, chopped
290ml/1/2 pint brown ale
30ml/2 tablespoons rum
grated rind and juice of 1 orange
grated rind and juice of 1 lemon
110g/4oz prunes, stoned and soaked overnight in
cold tea, then drained and chopped
1 dessert apple
225g/8oz butter
340g/12oz dark brown sugar
30ml/2 tablespoons treacle
3 eggs
110g/4oz self-raising flour
5ml/1 teaspoon mixed spice
2.5ml/1/2 teaspoon cinnamon
pinch of ground nutmeg
pinch of ground ginger
pinch of salt
225g/8oz fresh white breadcrumbs
55g/2oz chopped hazelnuts, toasted

1. Soak the dried fruit overnight in a mixture of the beer, rum, orange juice and lemon juice. Mix with the prunes.
2. Grate the apple, skin and all.
3. Cream the butter with the sugar. Beat until light and fluffy. Add the orange rind, lemon rind and treacle.
4. Whisk the eggs together and gradually add them to the mixture, beating well between each addition.
5. Fold in the sifted flour, spices, salt and breadcrumbs and stir in the dried fruit and soaking liquor.
6. Divide the mixture between greased pudding basins, cover with 2 layers of greaseproof paper and one piece of foil. Tie with string and steam for 10-12 hours.

NOTE: Christmas puddings can be kept for up to 1 year – after this period they begin to dry out. They can be frozen very successfully. Ideally a pudding should be made 3-4 months before Christmas. To store a pudding, recover it and keep in a cool dark place. You can give Christmas puddings 'a drink' – simply make small holes in the surface of the pudding with a cocktail stick and pour over a little brandy or rum as preferred. This can be done several times whilst it matures. To reheat, steam for 2-2 1/2 hours.

AUSTRALIAN LIQUEUR MUSCAT

❄ ❄ ❄ ❄ ❄ ❄ ❄ ❄ ❄ ❄ ❄ ❄ ❄ ❄ ❄ ❄ ❄ ❄ ❄ ❄ ❄

# Brandy Butter

225g/8oz unsalted butter
225g/8oz caster sugar
grated rind of 1 orange
60ml/4 tablespoons brandy

Cream the unsalted butter and sugar together until very light. Add the orange rind and brandy to flavour fairly strongly. Serve well chilled.

# Rum Butter

Rum Butter can be made using rum in place of the brandy. Omit the orange rind.

# Rum Sauce

(SERVE WITH CHRISTMAS PUDDING)

45g/1oz butter
30g/1oz flour
425ml/³/4 pint milk
30g/1oz caster sugar
45ml/3 tablespoons rum

1. Melt the butter in a saucepan, add the flour and cook slowly for 1 minute. Take the pan off the heat.
2. Gradually add the milk, stirring all the time. Replace on the heat and, still stirring, bring up to the boil. Simmer for 2 minutes.
3. Add the sugar and rum, adding more to taste if neccessary.

# Mince Pies

MAKES 20–24 TARTS
340g/12oz flour quantity well-chilled rich shortcrust pastry (see page 200)
450g/1lb mincemeat 1 or 2 (see page 65)

TO GLAZE:
beaten egg or milk

TO SERVE:
icing sugar

1. Set the oven to 190°C/375°F/gas mark 5.
2. Divide the pastry in half and roll one half out thinly and use it to line tartlet tins.
3. Fill each tartlet tin with enough mincemeat to come about three-quarters of the way up the pastry.
4. Roll out the remaining pastry and either stamp into shapes, such as stars, dampen lightly with water and press firmly but gently on top of the mincemeat or cut into circles to fit the tarts as lids. Dampen the pastry edges and press the tops down lightly, sealing the edges carefully.
5. Brush your chosen glaze on the lids – the milk will give a matt finish, and the beaten egg a shiny finish.
6. Snip the lids with a pair of scissors or sharp knife to make a small slit for the steam to escape, leaving the shapes untouched.
7. Bake for 20 minutes until light golden brown.
8. Cool on a wire rack.
9. Serve warm sprinkled with icing sugar.

NOTE: Once completely cold, mince pies can be frozen or stored in an airtight container.

LIQUER MUSCAT SUCH AS
BEAUMES DE VENISE

# Aubergine and Chestnut Pie ✔

This wonderful moist layered pie would make a perfect dish for any vegetarian's Christmas day.

FOR THE AUBERGINE LAYER:

1 medium-sized aubergine, cut into cubes
85ml/3fl oz olive oil
3 tomatoes, roughly chopped
30ml/2 tablespoons tomato purée
1 garlic clove, crushed
15ml/1 tablespoon fresh basil, chopped
15ml/1 tablespoon fresh marjoram, chopped
salt and freshly ground black pepper

FOR THE NUT LAYER:

1 small onion, finely chopped
2 sticks celery, finely chopped
55ml/4 fl oz water
110g/4oz walnuts, roughly chopped
110g/4oz unsweetened chestnut purée
55g/2oz peeled and cooked chestnuts, roughly
    chopped (see note)
30g/1oz fresh wholemeal bread cubes

FOR THE COURGETTE LAYER:

225g/8oz courgettes, sliced
1 small bunch chives, finely chopped
15ml/1 tablespoon single cream
salt and freshly ground black pepper

TO FINISH:

45ml/3 tablespoons oil
7 sheets filo pastry
15g/1 tablespoon sesame seeds

1. Put the aubergines into a colander. Sprinkle with salt and leave to stand for 20 minutes.
2. Preheat the oven to 200°C/400°F/gas mark 6.
3. Rinse the aubergines and pat dry. Fry them in three-quarters of the oil until beginning to soften, add the tomatoes, tomato purée, garlic, basil and marjoram. Season with salt and pepper and cook gently until tender.
4. Make the nut layer. Cook the onions and celery in the oil until soft. Add the water, walnuts, chestnut purée, chestnuts, bread cubes, salt and pepper. Cook for 2-3 minutes.
5. Sauté the courgettes in the remaining oil. When tender add the cream, chives, salt and pepper.
6. Layer the fillings up in a large dish, starting with the aubergines and finishing with the courgettes.
7. Cover the pie with 7 layers of filo pastry, brushing each layer with oil. Brush the top with oil and sprinkle with the sesame seeds.
8. Bake for 20 minutes or until the top is golden brown.

NOTE: To get 55g/2 oz of peeled cooked chestnuts you will need to buy about 170g/6oz of fresh chestnuts. To cook them, make a slit in the skin of each chestnut, and put them into a pan of cold water. Bring to the boil, simmer for 10 minutes, and then take off the heat. Remove 1 or 2 nuts at a time and peel – the skins come off quite easily – if the chestnuts are hot but not overcooked.

MUSCAT DE BEAUMES DE VENISE

✳ ✳ ✳ ✳ ✳ ✳ ✳ ✳ ✳ ✳ ✳ ✳ ✳ ✳ ✳ ✳ ✳ ✳ ✳ ✳ ✳

✳✳✳✳✳✳✳✳✳✳✳✳✳✳✳✳✳✳✳✳✳✳✳

# PLANNING
# A PARTY

✳✳✳✳✳✳✳✳✳✳✳✳✳✳✳✳✳✳✳✳✳✳✳

*Menu planning*
*Cooking for larger numbers*
*Food presentation*

*Boeuf Philippe*
*Smoked haddock koulibiac*
*Squid salad with cucumber and cumin*
*Venison terrine and Cumberland sauce*
*Game pie*
*Flat ham pie*
*Monkfish salad with exotic sauce*
*Cold Christmas turkey stuffed with ham*
*Tandoori chicken breasts*
*Smoked haddock Florentine*
*Seafood salad*

*Pasta and grilled pepper salad*
*Barley salad*
*Quinoa and lime salad*
*Fennel and walnut salad*

*Chocolate pecan pie*
*Creamed cheese with fresh fruit*
*Tarte tatin*

✳✳✳✳✳✳✳✳✳✳✳✳✳✳✳✳✳✳✳✳✳✳✳

❉ ❉ ❉ ❉ ❉ ❉ ❉ ❉ ❉ ❉ ❉ ❉ ❉ ❉ ❉ ❉ ❉ ❉ ❉ ❉

# MENU PLANNING

❉ ❉ ❉ ❉ ❉ ❉ ❉ ❉ ❉ ❉ ❉ ❉ ❉ ❉ ❉ ❉ ❉ ❉ ❉ ❉

*Once a menu is planned, cooking becomes much easier. It is making the decisions that can be so daunting. Here are a few hints that may help.*

*One of the most important things is to make the menu relevant to the people for whom you are cooking; giving a rugger XV grilled aubergines with pesto would be as absurd as giving a ladies' lunch party carbonnade of beef with savoury crumble. The menu should stay in style throughout. The figurative leap from the South of France, with aubergine flan, to the Nursery, with steak and kidney pudding, apart from being badly balanced, will also give your guests an uncomfortable culture shock. If you are cooking for old-fashioned friends we would not recommend giving them the Quinoa and lime salad. One of the many skills of cooking is to think of the people for whom you are cooking and choose a menu that you know they would like.*

*Here are a set of guidelines that can help:*

1. Never repeat the same basic ingredients in a menu – for example, do not have pastry in two courses or serve smoked salmon in the first and main courses. However, it is perfectly acceptable to have a fish first course, such as a seafood salad, followed by a fish main course.

2. Try to devise a menu that is full of colour. This is particularly important when planning a buffet party (see page 32). For a conventional lunch or dinner party, always think about the appearance of the main course plate.

3. Think about the balance of the menu. Do not be so inclined to generosity that you daunt your guests. If there is to be a great number of courses then serve a sorbet halfway through to refresh the palette. If you decide to serve a very rich pudding, always offer a light alternative.

4. The texture of a meal is important – it should vary.

5. Try not to have too many exciting and exotic tastes in one menu. If you get carried away, sometimes the basic flavour of a delicious ingredient can be drowned. If the menu is to include a highly seasoned dish, don't follow it with a subtle dish – your guests simply won't be able to appreciate it.

6. Most people love sauces, so if you serve a sauce be generous.

7. We would always recommend serving a salad with any rich meal.

At Leith's there is always much discussion about the order of a meal. In England we conventionally serve the pudding followed by the cheese. In France it is more normal to serve the cheese before the pudding – the theory being that the red wine is finished with the cheese and then the pudding is served with a sweet white wine. We rather like the French approach for both its wine appreciation factor and also for its practicality in that it means that the host or hostess can nip off to the kitchen and do any last minute cooking necessary for the pudding.

Finally, we would say don't overtax yourself. A dinner party is meant to be fun. Don't try to cook three hot courses and sit down to each successive course feeling slightly more flushed. Prepare as much as you can in advance – work out a timetable of how you are going to cope and enjoy the meal.

FIRST FOOTING

In many parts of Britain, not just Scotland, there is a tradition of 'First Footing'. The New Year should be brought into the house by a tall dark stranger, a man, who brings symbolic gifts of food, drink and warmth. These might be salt, oatcakes or mince pies, whisky and coal.

The 'First Footer' should then pass on through the house. This stranger will then bring good fortune to the house for the rest of the year. However, if the first person to cross the threshold is fair or a female, fair or dark, then ill fortune will follow. Nowadays, it is often used as an excuse to visit friends as the year changes.

In Scotland, New Year's Eve is called Hogmanay and has many traditions attached to it. The food that is served at midnight is usually shortbread, black bun, mince pies and served with whisky Atholl Brose or Het Pints (Hot Pints), which is a spiced ale mixed with eggs and whisky.

Atholl Brose is a warming drink of oatmeal, honey and whisky. This is more usually served, nowadays, as a pudding with cream to bind it all together (see page 125).

✳ ✳ ✳ ✳ ✳ ✳ ✳ ✳ ✳ ✳ ✳ ✳ ✳ ✳ ✳ ✳ ✳ ✳ ✳ ✳

# COOKING FOR LARGER NUMBERS

✳ ✳ ✳ ✳ ✳ ✳ ✳ ✳ ✳ ✳ ✳ ✳ ✳ ✳ ✳ ✳ ✳ ✳ ✳ ✳

*If you are going to be cooking for a buffet party, we have included in the next section various recipes that people can eat as they balance their glasses, forks, bags and occasional cigarettes rather precariously over your carpet that you were hoping not to have to get cleaned! Here are a few hints that may be helpful when planning your menu and arranging your food.*

The larger the choice of dishes, the more generous you have to be, and therefore if you are cooking for a small number the increased costs can be significant.

Think about ease of both serving and eating – if there are not many places for guests to sit down it should be a fork buffet.

Think about what the food will look like once people have started to fill their plates. We decorate the underplates with fresh flowers and leave the dishes themselves very simply garnished. Do not put too many flowers on the table – let the food speak for itself.

Have more than one service point with only about 16 sets of knives, forks and plates out at any one time – the crockery must not dominate the table. If you are cooking for 100 people, you will need at least 4 service points. Think carefully about the appearance of the food – it should be a good mixture of colours.

Try and make the table look attractive by using height. Place the food on cake stands and put boxes under the tablecloths.

Don't decorate the front of the tablecloth with garlands of flowers – they'll be crushed and look untidy.

Always think about what the buffet will look like at the end of the meal.

If possible change the tablecloth in between courses – if not, then certainly after coffee.

Use linen napkins to hide spills.

Never underestimate number of helpers you'll need – people helping themselves often have eyes bigger than their stomachs. For 100 people you will need 4 people serving the food.

Make sure that there is easy access to all service points and that there is a choice of all the dishes beside each pile of plates.

ABOVE: MINCE PIES.    OVERLEAF: CHRISTMAS DAY SPREAD

GLAZED HAM

CHRISTMAS PUDDING

AUBERGINE AND CHESTNUT PIE

TANDOORI CHICKEN BREASTS

CREAMED CHEESE WITH FRESH FRUIT

It is possible to buy (from disposable products suppliers) little plastic holders so that the wine glasses can be attached to plates.

Don't use linen napkins – they are too cumbersome at a buffet.

Precut and slice most of the food but for the sake of appearance leave some whole.

Never put out all the food – keep some back so that the last shall be first. Always hide the vegetarian dishes – you could run out and genuine veggies may not be able to have any.

Try to avoid individual dishes as they dictate how many people can have how much of a certain dish – you may well calculate tastes incorrectly.

If people have to queue you'll find that only about two-thirds of the guests will come back for puddings, and only about half will come back again for coffee. Obviously you have to cater for full take up but don't be over generous.

## FOOD PRESENTATION

If food looks delicious, people are predisposed to think that it tastes delicious. If you have spent a long time cooking, it is a shame just to dump the food on a plate. At Leith's School we have gradually developed a set of rules which can be used as guidelines when presenting food. Fashion may dictate the method – be it stylish nouvelle cuisine or chunky real food – but the guidelines are the same.

### 1. KEEP IT SIMPLE
Over-decorated food often looks messed about – no longer appetizing, but like an uncertain work of art. The more cluttered the plate, the less attractive it inevitably becomes.

### 2. KEEP IT FRESH
Nothing looks more off-putting than tired food. Salad wilts when dressed in advance; sautéed potatoes become dull and dry when kept warm for hours, and whipped cream goes buttery in a warm room, so don't risk it.

### 3. KEEP IT RELEVANT
A sprig of fresh watercress complements lamb cutlets nicely. The texture, taste and colour all do something for the lamb. But scratchy sprigs of parsley, though they might provide the colour, are unpleasant to eat. Gherkins cut into fans do nothing for salads; tomato slices do not improve the look of a platter of sandwiches – they rather serve to confuse and distract the eye. It is better to dish up a plate of chicken mayonnaise with a couple of suitable salads to provide the colour and contrast, than to decorate it with undressed tomato waterlilies or inedible baskets made out of lemon skins and filled with frozen sweetcorn.

### 4. CENTRE HEIGHT
Dishes served on platters, such as chicken sauté, meringues, profiteroles or even a bean salad, are best given 'centre height' – arranged so the mound of food is higher in the middle with sides sloping down. Coat carefully and evenly with the sauce, if any. Do not overload serving platters with food, which makes dishing up difficult. Once breached, an over-large pile of food looks unattractive.

### 5. CONTRASTING ROWS
Biscuits, petits fours, little cakes and cocktail canapés all look good if arranged in rows, each row consisting of one variety. Pay attention to contrasting colour, taking care, say, not to put two rows of chocolate biscuits side by side or two rows of white sandwiches.

### 6. DIAGONAL LINES

Diamond shapes and diagonal lines are easier to achieve than straight ones. The eye is more conscious of unevenness in verticals, horizontals and rectangles.

### 7. NOT TOO MANY COLOURS

As with any design, it is easier to get a pleasing effect if the colours are controlled – say, just green and white, or just pink and green, or chocolate and coffee colours or even two shades of one colour. Coffee icing and hazelnuts give a cake an elegant look. Adding multi-coloured icings to a cake, or every available garnish to a salad, tends to look garish. There are exceptions of course: a colourful salad Niçoise can be as pleasing to the eye as a dish of candy-coated chocolate drops.

### 8. CONTRASTING THE SIMPLE AND THE ELABORATE

If the dish or bowl is elaborately decorated, contrastingly simple food tends to show it off better. A Victorian fruit epergne with ornate stem and silver carving will look stunning filled with fresh strawberries. Conversely, a plain white plate sets off pretty food design to perfection.

### 9. UNEVEN NUMBERS

As a rule, uneven numbers of, say, rosettes of cream on a cake, baked apples in a long dish, or portions of meat on a platter look better than even numbers. This is especially true of small numbers. Five and three invariably look better than four, but there is little difference in effect between eleven and twelve.

### 10. A GENEROUS LOOK

Tiny piped cream stars, or sparsely dotted nuts, or mean-looking chocolate curls on a cake look amateurish and stingy.

### 11. AVOID CLUMSINESS

On the other hand, the temptation to cram the last spoonful of rice into the bowl, or squeeze the last slice of pâté on to the dish leads to a clumsy look, and can be daunting to the diner.

### 12. OVERLAPPING

Chops, steaks, sliced meats, even rashers of bacon, look best evenly overlapping. This way, more of them can be fitted comfortably on the serving dish than if placed side by side.

### 13. BEST SIDE UPPERMOST

Usually the side of a steak or a cutlet that is grilled or fried first looks the best, and should be placed uppermost. Bones are generally unsightly and, if they cannot be clipped off or removed, should be tucked out of the way.

# Boeuf Philippe

FOR 4 PEOPLE
*450g/1lb fillet of beef (ends will do)*
*Worcestershire sauce*
*freshly ground black pepper*
*15ml/1 tablespoon beef dripping*
*1/4 cauliflower*
*110g/4oz French beans*
*2 tomatoes*
*French dressing (see page 195)*
*2.5ml/1/2 teaspoon horseradish sauce*
*1 garlic clove, crushed*
*8 black olives*
*bunch of watercress*

FOR 8 PEOPLE
*790g/1 3/4 lb fillet of beef (ends will do)*
*Worcestershire sauce*
*freshly ground black pepper*
*15ml/1 tablespoon beef dripping*
*1/2 cauliflower*
*225g/8oz French beans*
*4 tomatoes*
*2.5ml/1/2 teaspoon horseradish sauce*
*1 garlic clove, crushed*
*French dressing (see page 195)*
*12 black olives*
*bunch of watercress*

FOR 12 PEOPLE
*1.2kg/2 1/2 lb fillet of beef (ends will do)*
*Worcestershire sauce*
*freshly ground black pepper*
*30ml/2 tablespoons beef dripping*
*1 cauliflower*
*340g/12oz French beans*
*6 tomatoes*
*5ml/1 teaspoon horseradish sauce*
*1 large garlic clove, crushed*

*French dressing (see page 195)*
*18 black olives*
*bunch of watercress*

ADVANCE PREPARATION
The beef can be cooked the day before but
must be cut up at the last minute. All the
vegetables can be blanched and refreshed the
day before. The salad must be put together at the
last minute.

FREEZABILITY
This dish does not freeze

1. Set the oven to 200°C/400°F/gas mark 6.
2. Season the meat with Worcestershire sauce
and black pepper. Heat the beef dripping in a
roasting pan over the cooker ring and add the
beef. Brown evenly on all sides. The beef
should be cooked in the oven for 10-15 minutes
for every 450g/1lb. Long thin pieces will take
less time to cook than short fat pieces.
Allow to cool.
3. Wash the cauliflower and cut into florets.
Plunge these into a pan of boiling water for 4-5
minutes. Drain. Rinse under cold water to
prevent further cooking. Drain again.
4. Wash and tail the beans. Cook in boiling
salted water for 5 minutes, then rinse under cold
water and drain.
5. Plunge the tomatoes into boiling water for 5
seconds and skin. Cut into quarters.
6. Add the horseradish sauce and crushed
garlic to the French dressing. The salad is now
ready for assembly but this should not be
done until just before serving. The beef will
lose its colour if dressed too soon, and the
salad will look tired if left to stand for any
length of time.
7. Cut the beef into thin slices and then into

thin strips, cutting across the grain of the meat. Place in a basin with the other ingredients, reserving some tomatoes and olives for decoration.

8. Using your hands, mix in almost all the French dressing and pile into a serving dish.

Place the reserved tomatoes and olives on top of the dish and brush with the remaining French dressing. Garnish with a bunch of watercress.

CLARET

❄ ❄ ❄ ❄ ❄ ❄ ❄ ❄ ❄ ❄ ❄ ❄ ❄ ❄ ❄ ❄ ❄ ❄ ❄ ❄ ❄

# Smoked Haddock Koulibiac

The quantity called for in this recipe will serve 10-12 people.

*30ml/2 tablespoons olive oil*
*1 small onion, chopped*
*140g/5oz long grain rice*
*290ml/¹/2 pint fish stock (see page 179)*
*1 sprig thyme*
*1 bay leaf*
*salt and freshly ground black pepper*
*140g/5oz button mushrooms, wiped and sliced*
*55ml/2 fl oz dry white wine*
*225ml/8 fl oz double cream*
*2 tablespoons finely chopped chives*
*450g/1lb quantity brioche dough (see page 45)*
*1 egg, beaten*
*5 medium hardboiled eggs, sliced*
*800g/1lb 12oz skinned smoked haddock fillet*

ADVANCE PREPARATION

The filling can be made the day before.

The brioche dough can be made to stage 4 and then refrigerated overnight. The next day remove it from the refrigerator and leave at room temperature until it reaches blood heat and then knock back.

FREEZABILITY

The whole koulibiac can be frozen if you don't use the hardboiled eggs in the filling. Defrost to room temperature, re-glaze and bake (note that it won't be as perfect as a freshly made koulibiac).

1. Heat half the olive oil in a large saucepan, add the onion and cook gently without colouring for two minutes.

2. Add the rice, fish stock, thyme and bay leaf, and season with salt and pepper. Bring to the boil, reduce the heat and cover. Cook for 15 minutes or until the stock is absorbed and the rice cooked. Remove the herbs and leave the rice to cool.

3. Meanwhile, heat the remaining oil in a frying pan. Add the mushrooms and cook until they are soft and any liquid has evaporated. Add the wine and cream and reduce, by boiling rapidly, to half its original quantity.

4. Mix the rice and cream mixture together. Add the chives and taste for seasoning.

5. Preheat the oven to 190°C/375°F/gas mark 5.

6. Roll out one-third of the brioche dough to a rectangle 25cm x 35cm/10in x 14in. Place on a greased baking sheet without a lip. (If your baking sheet has a lip simply turn it over.) Brush a little beaten egg over the surface of the dough.

7. Spread one-third of the rice mixture over the dough leaving a 3cm/1¹/4in border all the way

round. Put half of the sliced eggs on top and then half of the fish. Put another third of the rice mixture on top of the fish and continue to layer up as before, finishing with the rice.

8. Roll out the remaining piece of dough to approximately 1½ times the size of the original piece. Brush the border of the brioche with beaten egg. Lift the top piece with a rolling pin and lay it carefully over the filling. Press down gently to seal and trim off the excess dough. Crimp the edges with thumb and forefinger. Brush with the beaten egg and decorate the top with leftover brioche dough.

9. Bake in the preheated oven for 35-40 minutes until golden brown. Serve immediately.

SPICY DRY WHITE WINE

# Savoury Brioche Dough

*15g/½oz fresh yeast*
*5ml/1 teaspoon honey*
*100ml/3½ fl oz lukewarm water*
*450g/1lb strong plain flour*
*5ml/1 teaspoon salt*
*4 eggs, beaten*
*140g/5oz softened unsalted butter*

1. Cream the yeast with the honey and add the lukewarm water.

2. Sift the flour and salt together into a bowl. Make a well in the centre.

3. Add the beaten eggs, the yeast mixture and the softened butter. Mix to form a dough and knead on an unfloured surface for about 5 minutes until smooth, elastic and shiny. Place in a clean bowl and cover with a piece of greased polythene.

4. Leave to rise for 30-40 minutes.

5. Knock back the dough by removing it from the bowl and kneading for about 5 minutes. Use as required.

# Squid Salad with Cucumber and Cumin

60ml/4 tablespoons olive oil
5ml/1 teaspoon cumin
salt and freshly ground black pepper
juice of 2 limes
30ml/2 tablespoons chopped mint and chives

FOR 4 PEOPLE
450g/1lb squid
150ml/¹/4 pint water
150ml/¹/4 pint dry white wine
1 onion, chopped
1 bay leaf

FOR THE SALAD:
1 cucumber
6 spring onions, finely sliced

FOR THE DRESSING:
5ml/1 teaspoon Dijon mustard
30ml/2 tablespoons crème fraiche, or Greek yoghurt
30ml/2 tablespoons olive oil
2.5ml/¹/2 teaspoon cumin
salt and freshly ground black pepper
juice of 1 lime
15ml/1 tablespoon chopped mint and chives

FOR 8 PEOPLE
900g/2lb squid
290ml/¹/2 pint water
290ml/¹/2 pint dry white wine
2 onions, chopped
1 bay leaf

FOR THE SALAD:
1¹/2 cucumbers
9 spring onions, finely sliced

FOR THE DRESSING:
10ml/2 teaspoons Dijon mustard
60ml/4 tablespoons crème fraiche, or Greek yoghurt

FOR 12 PEOPLE
1.35kg/3lb squid
290ml/¹/2 pint water
290ml/¹/2 pint dry white wine
2 onions, chopped
1 bay leaf

FOR THE SALAD:
2 cucumbers
12 spring onions, finely sliced

FOR THE DRESSING:
10ml/2 teaspoons Dijon mustard
60ml/4 tablespoons crème fraiche, or Greek yoghurt
60ml/4 tablespoons olive oil
5ml/1 teaspoon cumin
salt and freshly ground black pepper
juice of 2 limes
30ml/2 tablespoons chopped mint and chives

ADVANCE PREPARATION
The squid can be cooked the day before the party.
The cucumber should not be prepared more
than 2 hours in advance.
The dressing can be made the day before the party.
It should not be tossed together in advance.

FREEZABILITY
This dish does not freeze.

1. Clean the squid (see opposite). Chop the
tentacles into 2.5cm/1 inch lengths.
2. Place the water, wine, onion and bay leaf in a
saucepan, bring to the boil and simmer for

10 minutes. Allow to cool, then add the squid and bring to the boil again. Remove from the heat, leave to stand for 5 minutes and then lift out the squid and allow to cool.

3. Peel the cucumber and cut into 4. Using an apple corer, remove the seeds and then slice the cucumber into rings about the same size as the squid rings.

4. Make the dressing by mixing all the ingredients together, and check the seasoning.

5. Toss the squid, cucumber, and spring onion in the dressing.

VERY DRY WHITE

❋ ❋ ❋ ❋ ❋ ❋ ❋ ❋ ❋ ❋ ❋ ❋ ❋ ❋ ❋ ❋ ❋ ❋ ❋ ❋ ❋

# To Clean a Squid

1. Remove the blood (ink) and the entrails under cold running water – they will come out easily.

2. Remove the clear plastic-like piece of cartilage that runs the length of the body on the inside.

3. Cut off and throw away the head (it is the round middle bit with two large eyes).

4. Scrape off the pinkish-purple outside skin – a fine membrane from the body and tentacles. Don't worry if you cannot get all the tentacles completely clear of it.

5. Wash the body and tentacles to remove all traces of ink: you should now have a perfectly clean, white, empty squid.

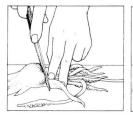 

*Remove the entrails and cartilage*

*Cut off the head and scrape away the membrane*

*Body, fins and tentacles*

❋ ❋ ❋ ❋ ❋ ❋ ❋ ❋ ❋ ❋ ❋ ❋ ❋ ❋ ❋ ❋ ❋ ❋ ❋ ❋ ❋

# Venison Terrine and Cumberland Sauce

This quantity makes a terrine that will serve about 8 people.

*225g/8oz back pork fat*
*225g/8oz lean pork*
*225g/8oz lean venison*
*1 onion, finely chopped*
*1 garlic clove, crushed*
*8 juniper berries, crushed*
*2.5ml/<sup>1</sup>/2 teaspoon ground mace*
*2.5ml/<sup>1</sup>/2 teaspoon ground allspice*
*60ml/4 tablespoons red wine*
*30ml/2 tablespoon brandy*
*salt and freshly ground black pepper*
*2 eggs*
*285g/10oz streaky bacon, cut very thin and*
  *stretched with a knife*

To serve
*Cumberland sauce (see page 198).*

ADVANCED PREPARATION
This is best made 2 or 3 days in advance.

FREEZABILITY
It can be frozen.

1. Cut half the pork fat into small dice. Mince the pork, remaining fat and venison and mix with the onion, garlic, cubed fat, juniper berries, spices, wine, brandy, seasoning and eggs. Beat very well, and check the seasoning.
2. Line a 1 litre/1¾ pint terrine with streaky bacon and fill with the mixture. Cover with the remaining bacon rashers.
3. Leave in a cool place for at least 3 hours for the flavour to develop – the longer the better.
4. Preset the oven to 170°C/325°F/gas mark 3.
5. Put the covered terrine in a bain-marie (a roasting pan half filled with boiling water). Cook in the preheated oven for 1½-2 hours. The terrine is cooked when it shrinks away from the side of the dish and no pink juices run out when it is pierced with skewer.
6. Keep the terrine in the refrigerator for a couple of days to allow the flavours to mature.
7. Serve alone or with Cumberland sauce.

MEDIUM RED

# Game Pie

The quantities called for in this recipe will make a pie that will serve 6-8 people.

FOR THE FORCEMEAT:

*110g/4oz poultry livers*

*1 pheasant, boned and skinned (see page 209)*

*450g/1lb pork belly, derinded*

*3 shallots, finely chopped*

*2 sage leaves, finely chopped*

*5ml/1 teaspoon chopped thyme*

*1 garlic clove, crushed*

*10ml/2 teaspoons salt*

*5ml/1 teaspoon coarsely ground black pepper*

*15ml/1 tablespoon brandy*

*45ml/3 tablespoons dry white wine*

FOR THE JELLY:

*1 stick celery*

*1 carrot, sliced*

*1 slice of onion*

*1 bay leaf*

*sprig of parsley*

*sprig of marjoram*

*bones, giblets (except the liver) and skin of the pheasant*

*15g/¹/₂oz gelatine*

FOR THE PASTRY CRUST:

*pâte à pâté made with 450g/1lb flour (see page 204)*

*piece of pig's caul about 30cm/12 inch square*

*beaten egg*

ADVANCED PREPARATION

Preparation for this dish must start 2-3 days in advance

FREEZABILITY

The pie can be frozen at stage 12. Defrost it thoroughly and re-glaze with egg before baking.

1. Trim any discoloured parts and sinew from the livers.

2. Reserve 1 pheasant breast, the pheasant liver and 1 other poultry liver. Mince the rest of the pheasant meat with the remaining livers and the pork belly. Add the shallot, sage, thyme, garlic, salt, pepper, brandy and wine. Mix well and place in a deep bowl.

3. Lay the breast meat and livers on top, and cover. Refrigerate for 24 hours.

4. Make up the pâte à pâté.

5. Use two-thirds of it to line a 20cm/8 inch raised pie mould or a loose-bottomed cake tin.

6. Line the empty pie shell with the pig's caul, allowing the sides to hang down over the edge.

7. Put half the minced mixture into the mould. Cut the pheasant breast into strips and lay them on top of the forcemeat.

8. Lay the livers on top of the pheasant strips. Cover with the rest of the forcemeat, pressing down well to eliminate any air pockets.

9. Draw the caul up over the forcemeat to envelop it.

10. Preheat the oven to 190°C/375°F/gas mark 5.

11. Use the remaining pastry to cover and elaborately decorate the top of the pie. Press the edges of the top firmly to the base pastry. Make a hole in the middle of the pastry top to allow steam to escape.

12. Brush with beaten egg.

13. Bake the pie for 15 minutes, then turn the oven down to 150°C/300°F/gas mark 2, for a further 1³/4 hours. Allow to cool overnight.

14. Make the stock by simmering the jelly ingredients (except the gelatine) in 1 litre/1³/4 pints water for 2 hours. Strain through muslin or a double 'J' cloth and chill overnight.

15. Remove all traces of fat from the stock. Pour it into a saucepan and sprinkle on the gelatine. Leave to soak for 10 minutes,

then bring slowly to the boil. Boil until there is approximately 290ml/½ pint of liquid left.

16. Leave until cold but not set – it should be syrupy. Carefully pour, little by little, into the pie, through the hole in the pastry. A small funnel will make this operation easier. Continue until the liquid level is visible and will no longer gradually sink. If, by some mischance, the pastry case has a hole in it allowing the liquid to leak out, plug the hole with softened butter.

17. Chill the pie until the liquid is set – about 2 hours.

NOTE: If pouring the liquid into the pie proves difficult, carefully make, with the tip of a knife, another hole in the cooked pastry towards the edge, and pour the liquid through this.

CLARET

❋ ❋ ❋ ❋ ❋ ❋ ❋ ❋ ❋ ❋ ❋ ❋ ❋ ❋ ❋ ❋ ❋ ❋ ❋ ❋

# Flat Ham Pie

FOR 6 PEOPLE
*pâte à pâté made with 450g/1lb flour (see page 204)*
*55g/2oz Gruyère or Cheddar cheese, grated*
*30g/1oz grated Parmesan cheese*
*45g/1½oz butter, melted*
*55g/2oz fresh white breadcrumbs*
*225g/8oz ham*
*30ml/2 tablespoons chopped dill or chives*
*1 large garlic clove, crushed*
*150ml/¼ pint soured cream*
*freshly ground black pepper*
*juice of ½ lemon*
*beaten egg*

FOR 12 PEOPLE
*pâte à pâte made with 900g/2lb flour (see page 204)*
*110g/4oz Gruyère or Cheddar cheese, grated*
*55g/2oz grated Parmesan cheese*
*55g/2oz butter, melted*
*110g/4oz fresh white breadcrumbs*
*450g/1lb ham*
*60ml/4 tablespoons chopped dill or chives*
*2 garlic cloves, crushed*

*290ml/½ pint soured cream*
*freshly ground black pepper*
*juice of 1 lemon*
*beaten egg*

If making this for 12 people you might find it easier simply to make 2 pies, but if you feel brave make one gigantic pie. The pastry is very crumbly so don't worry if you have to patch it a little bit – it will still taste delicious.

ADVANCE PREPARATION
The whole pie can be assembled the day before the party. Re-glaze with egg prior to baking.

FREEZABILITY
The whole pie can be frozen before baking. Re-glaze once thoroughly defrosted and bake as instructed.

1. Make up the pâte à pâté and roll out into rectangles, one to fit a Swiss roll tin, the other slightly larger.
2. Set the oven to 200°C/400°F/gas mark 6.
3. Lightly grease and flour the base of a Swiss roll

tin or a rectangular baking sheet. Put the smaller rectangle of pastry on it and prick all over with a fork. Bake for 15 minutes and leave to cool.

4. Mix together the Gruyère or Cheddar, the Parmesan, the melted butter and the breadcrumbs. Scatter half of this all over the half-cooked pastry, leaving a good 1cm/½ inch clear all round the edge.

5. Chop the ham into small pieces and scatter it on top of the cheese mixture. Then scatter over the dill or chives.

6. Mix the garlic with the soured cream and spread all over the ham. Season well with pepper but no salt.

7. Sprinkle evenly with the lemon juice and top with the rest of the cheese mixture. Wet the edge of the bottom piece of pastry with lightly beaten egg and put the top sheet of pastry in place, pressing the edges to seal it well.

8. Use any pastry trimmings to decorate the pie and brush all over with beaten egg.

9. Bake until the pastry is crisp and pale brown. Serve hot or cold.

NOTE: This recipe can also be made with leftover trimmings of smoked salmon.

LIGHT RED/ROSE

# Monkfish Salad with Exotic Sauce

This recipe has been adapted from *The Josceline Dimbleby Collection* published for Sainsbury's. It is one of our most popular recipes and is ideal for a cold buffet.

SERVES 10
*2.3kg/5lb monkfish, skinned and cubed*
*120ml/8 tablespoons olive oil*
*4 large green chillies, deseeded and chopped*
*900g/2lb tomatoes, skinned and chopped*
*3-4 garlic cloves, finely chopped*
*10ml/2 teaspoons ground cardamom*
*20ml/4 teaspoons caster sugar*
*30ml/2 tablespoons tomato purée*
*juice of 1 lemon*

*salt*
*a good bunch of fresh coriander leaves*
*225g/8oz button mushrooms, finely sliced*

ADVANCE PREPARATION
This dish can be made several hours in advance

FREEZABILITY
The dish as a whole does not freeze well but the exotic sauce, if made separately, freezes very well indeed.

1. Heat the oil in a large frying pan and cook the fish over a medium heat for 5-7 minutes, turning gently. Turn off the heat, remove the fish with a slotted spoon and leave on one side in a mixing bowl. Leave the fish juices in the frying pan.

2. Pour any juices that have drained from the fish into the mixing bowl back into the frying pan. Bring the juice to the boil and add the chillies, tomatoes, garlic, cardamom, sugar,

tomato purée and lemon juice. Stir and allow to simmer over a low heat for 7-10 minutes until the tomato is soft. Season to taste with salt and turn off the heat.

3. Chop about three-quarters of the coriander and stir into the hot sauce. Pour the sauce over the fish in the bowl and gently mix in. Stir the sliced mushrooms into the mixture. Leave until cold.

4. When the salad has cooled, pile it into a clean dish. Pull the whole leaves off the remaining sprigs of coriander and scatter them over the fish.

NOTE: This recipe can be very easily adapted for use with other ingredients, such as chicken, shellfish, tofu or veal.

AUSTRALIAN/CALIFORNIAN
CHARDONNAY

✳ ✳ ✳ ✳ ✳ ✳ ✳ ✳ ✳ ✳ ✳ ✳ ✳ ✳ ✳ ✳ ✳ ✳ ✳ ✳

# Cold Christmas Turkey Stuffed with Ham

This is a perfect party dish. It serves at least 20 people. It can be made a day or two in advance but does not freeze well. It is good served with any of the fruit pickles (see pages 69-70) or with a herby mayonnaise.

*2.3kg/5lb piece of boiled bacon or ham, skinned*
*6.7kg/15lb turkey, boned (see note on page 209)*

FOR THE STUFFING:
*30g/1oz butter*
*1 large onion, finely chopped*
*900g/2lb pork belly, minced*
*450g/1lb unsweetened tinned chestnut purée or*
   *mashed cooked fresh chestnuts*
*225g/8oz fresh white breadcrumbs*
*2 eggs, lightly beaten*
*5ml/1 teaspoon dried sage*
*30ml/2 tablespoons chopped parsley*
*salt and freshly ground black pepper*

FOR THE ROASTING:
*55g/2oz butter*

TO GARNISH:
*bunch of watercress*

1. Set the oven to 200°C/400°F/gas mark 6.
2. To make the stuffing: melt the butter, add the onion and cook until soft but not coloured.
3. When cold, mix with all the other stuffing ingredients.
4. Open the turkey out flat on a board, skin side down. Spread the stuffing on the turkey and put the ham or bacon on top.
5. Draw up the sides and sew together with a needle and fine string. Turn the bird right side up and try to push it into an even, rounded shape. Weigh the turkey (probably using the bathroom scales!) to establish the cooking time – see the chart on page 15.
6. Smear the butter all over the turkey and put it into a roasting tin. If the turkey looks too flat, wedge the sides with bread tins to hold it in shape.
7. Roast the bird for 1 hour, lower the temperature to 180°C/350°F/gas mark 4 and roast for a further 4-5 hours (see page 15).

Baste occasionally as it cooks and cover with foil or greaseproof paper if it is browning too much.

8. When the turkey is cooked, a skewer will glide through the thigh easily and the juices should run clear.

9. Leave to get completely cold.

10. Garnish the turkey with the watercress.

NOTE: When you remove the turkey from the roasting pan do not throw away the juices.

Tip them into a glass bowl and leave to get cool. Lift off the fat and use as required in sauces, gravies and soups.

BEAUJOLAIS

❀ ❀ ❀ ❀ ❀ ❀ ❀ ❀ ❀ ❀ ❀ ❀ ❀ ❀ ❀ ❀ ❀ ❀ ❀

# Tandoori Chicken Breasts

This recipe assumes that you are going to mix all the spices yourself. We have all used tandoori spice mix in our time but it really is worth giving the real thing a go.

FOR 4 PEOPLE

*4 chicken breasts, boned and skinned*
*3 garlic cloves, crushed*
*290ml/1/2 pint low fat yoghurt*
*1 heaped teaspoon of the following:*
    *ground coriander*
    *ground cumin*
    *ground fenugreek*
    *sweet paprika*
    *ground ginger*
*1.25ml/1/4 teaspoon chilli powder*
*1.25ml/1/4 teaspoon dry English mustard*

FOR 8 PEOPLE

*8 chicken breasts, boned and skinned*
*5 garlic cloves, crushed*
*570ml/1 pint low fat yoghurt*
*2 heaped teaspoons of the following:*
    *ground coriander*

    *ground cumin*
    *ground fenugreek*
    *sweet paprika*
    *ground ginger*
*2.5ml/1/2 teaspoon chilli powder*
*2.5ml/1/2 teaspoon dry English mustard*

FOR 12 PEOPLE

*10 chicken breasts, boned and skinned*
*6 garlic cloves, crushed*
*860ml/1 1/2 pints low fat yoghurt*
*3 heaped teaspoons of the following:*
    *ground coriander*
    *ground cumin*
    *ground fenugreek*
    *sweet paprika*
    *ground ginger*
*5ml/1 teaspoon chilli powder*
*5ml/1 teaspoon dry English mustard*

TO SERVE:
*yoghurt*
*lemon wedges*

TO GARNISH:
*1 bunch watercress*

ADVANCE PREPARATION
The chicken can be marinated in the yoghurt and spices once it has been cut into strips, and kept refrigerated overnight. Make sure that the bowl is tightly covered.

FREEZABILITY
This dish does not freeze.

1. Mix the garlic, yoghurt and spices together in a large bowl.
2. Cut the chicken breasts into strips.
3. Marinate the chicken breasts in the yoghurt and spices for 1 hour.
4. Preheat the grill.
5. Line the grill pan with aluminium foil. Put the chicken strips on to the grill pan and grill for 10 minutes.
6. Pile on to a large plate. Serve garnished with watercress and hand the yoghurt and lemon wedges separately.

LOIRE RED

# Smoked Haddock Florentine

FOR 4 PEOPLE
*4 x 170g/6oz smoked haddock fillets*
*290ml/½ pint milk*
*20g/¾oz butter*
*450g/1lb fresh spinach, washed, cooked & chopped*
*salt and freshly ground black pepper*
*pinch of nutmeg*
*30ml/1 tablespoon dried breadcrumbs*

FOR THE CHEESE SAUCE:
*20g/¾oz butter*
*20g/¾oz flour*
*pinch of dry English mustard*
*pinch of cayenne pepper*
*55g/2oz Gruyère or strong Cheddar cheese, grated*

FOR 8 PEOPLE
*8 x 170g/6oz smoked haddock fillets*
*570ml/1 pint milk*
*45g/1½oz butter*
*900g/2lb fresh spinach, washed, cooked and chopped*
*salt and freshly ground black pepper*
*pinch of nutmeg*
*60ml/2 tablespoons dried breadcrumbs*

FOR THE CHEESE SAUCE:
*45g/1½oz butter*
*45g/1½oz flour*
*pinch of dry English mustard*
*pinch of cayenne pepper*
*110g/4oz Gruyère or strong Cheddar cheese, grated*

FOR 12 PEOPLE
*12 x 170g/6oz smoked haddock fillets*
*860ml/1½ pints milk*
*60g/2¼oz butter*
*1.35kg/3lb fresh spinach, washed, cooked and chopped*
*salt and freshly ground black pepper*
*pinch of nutmeg*
*60ml/2 tablespoons dried breadcrumbs*

FOR THE CHEESE SAUCE:
60g/2¼oz butter
60g/2¼oz flour
pinch of dry English mustard
pinch of cayenne pepper
110g/4oz Gruyère or strong Cheddar
   cheese, grated

ADVANCE PREPARATION
The dish can be completely assembled and then
chilled until ready for thorough reheating.

FREEZABILITY
This dish freezes very well.

1. Set the oven to 180°C/350°F/gas mark 4.
2. Wash and season the fillets.
3. Lay the fish skin side up in an ovenproof
dish. Pour over the milk, cover and bake for
15 minutes.
4. Take out the fish, skin, drain and remove any
bones. Reserve the milk for the sauce.

5. Make the cheese sauce. Melt the butter and
stir in the flour, mustard and cayenne pepper.
Cook for 30 seconds. Draw the pan off the heat.
Pour in the milk and mix well.
6. Return the pan to the heat and stir until
boiling. Simmer, stirring well, for 2 minutes.
Add all but a tablespoon of the grated cheese,
and mix well, but do not re-boil. Season as
required and set aside.
7. Toss the spinach in the butter in a pan.
Season with salt, pepper and nutmeg.
8. Pile the spinach into an ovenproof dish.
Spread it reasonably flat. Arrange the fish
on top of the spinach. Reheat the cheese
sauce and pour it evenly on top of the fish.
Sprinkle with the reserved cheese and dried
breadcrumbs.
9. Reheat until bubbly and hot and then grill to
brown the top if necessary.

ALSACE WHITE

# Seafood Salad

SERVES 10

FOR THE COURT BOUILLON:
290ml/½ pint white wine
290ml/½ pint water
2 green chillies, finely chopped
5 shallots, finely chopped
2 bay leaves
2 limes, pared rind and juice
6 black peppercorns
pinch of salt

450g/1lb monkfish, trimmed and cut into medallions
340g/12oz scallops, cleaned and split in half
   widthways if large
225g/8oz large shelled raw prawns
225g/8oz large shelled raw scampi
12 raw oysters
450g/12oz raw mussels
200ml/7 fl oz Greek yoghurt
1 x 450g/1lb cooked lobster

TO GARNISH:
sprigs of dill

ADVANCE PREPARATION

All the ingredients can be prepared the night before and then arranged just before serving.

FREEZABILITY

This recipe does not freeze well.

1. First make the court bouillon: put the wine, water, chillies, shallots and bay leaves into a large shallow pan. Add the pared rind and juice from one lime and season with the peppercorns and salt. Bring to the boil – simmer for 10 minutes and remove the bay leaves, pared lime rind and peppercorns. Bring back to the boil.
2. Add the monkfish and scallops to the pan, cover with a lid and turn the heat down to very low. After 2 minutes, add the prawns, scampi, oysters and mussels, and bring back to a simmer. Replace the lid and turn the heat off.
Leave covered until all the fish is cooked.
3. Strain the fish and reserve the liquor. Put it back in the pan and reduce, by boiling rapidly, to 2 tablespoons. Allow to cool.
4. When the reduced fish stock is cold add it to the Greek yoghurt. Taste and add salt, white pepper and lime juice to taste.
5. Remove the lobster meat from its shell. Slice up the tail meat into medallions and, if possible, keep the claw meat whole.
6. Arrange the mixed cold seafood on a large plate, reserving the claw meat. Coat with the sauce and garnish with the lobster claws and sprigs of dill.

CRISP DRY WHITE,
SUCH AS SAUVIGNON

# Pasta and Grilled Pepper Salad

SERVES 4

*225g/8oz pasta, preferably spirals*
*2 red peppers*
*110g/4oz broccoli*
*French dressing (see page 195)*
*chopped sage*

SERVES 8

*450g/1lb pasta, preferably spirals*
*4 red peppers*
*225g/8oz broccoli*
*French dressing (see page 195)*
*chopped sage*

SERVES 12

*675g/1 1/2lb pasta, preferably spirals*
*5 red peppers*
*340g/12oz broccoli*
*French dressing (see page 195)*
*chopped sage*

ADVANCE PREPARATION

The pasta can be cooked the day before the party. The peppers can be completely prepared the day before the party. The broccoli can be blanched and refreshed. The French dressing can be made well in advance. The sage must not be chopped in advance.

FREEZABILITY

This recipe does not freeze.

1. Cook the pasta in plenty of boiling salted water with 15ml/1 tablespoon oil. When tender, drain well and leave to cool.

2. Cut the peppers into quarters and remove the stalk, inner membrane and seeds. Heat the grill to its highest temperature.

3. Grill the peppers, skin side uppermost, until the skin is black and blistered. With a small knife, remove all the skin. Cut into strips.

4. Cook the broccoli in boiling salted water. Refresh under cold running water. Drain well and leave to cool.

5. Toss the pasta, pepper, broccoli, French dressing and sage together.

# Barley Salad

SERVES 4
*30g/1oz pearl barley*
*1 large beetroot, cooked and chopped*
*1/2 green apple, cored and chopped*
*French dressing (see page 195)*

SERVES 8
*55g/2oz pearl barley*
*2 large beetroot, cooked and chopped*
*1 green apple, cored and chopped*
*French dressing (see page 195)*

SERVES 12
*85g/3oz pearl barley*
*3 large beetroot, cooked and chopped*

*1 1/2 green apples, cored and chopped*
*French dressing (see page 195)*

ADVANCE PREPARATION
The barley can be cooked in advance.
The beetroot should not be chopped until the day of the party.
The apple must not be chopped in advance.
The French dressing can be prepared in advance.

FREEZABILITY
The barley can be cooked and frozen.

1. Boil the barley in plenty of salted water for about 1 hour, until tender. Drain well.

2. Toss the barley with the beetroot and apple in the French dressing.

# Quinoa and Lime Salad

Quinoa is a grain similar to tapioca. It is available in large supermarkets and health food shops. The quantity called for seems odd but it is simply because most supermarket versions seem to come in 255g/9oz packs. This recipe will be sufficient for 8 people. The sauce is also very good served with pasta. It calls for Szechuan peppercorns – if they are not available use freshly ground black pepper. If you can buy them, simply dry-fry them for 2 minutes. Leave to cool. Dry well and then grind as black pepper.

*255g/9oz quinoa*
*720ml/1¼ pints water*
*salt*

FOR THE DRESSING:
*juice of 6 limes*
*125ml/4 fl oz groundnut oil*
*salt and freshly ground black pepper*
*15ml/1 tablespoon dry-roasted Szechuan*
*    peppercorns, ground*
*4 small garlic cloves, crushed*
*15ml/1 tablespoon each flat parsley, basil and*
*    coriander, roughly chopped*

TO SERVE:
*10 Kalamata olives, stoned and slivered*
*140g/5oz cooked kidney beans*
*1 radicchio*
*small bunch basil or coriander*

ADVANCE PREPARATION
The quinoa can be cooked a day in advance. Unfortunately the sauce loses its brilliant green if made in advance – it should not be kept for more than 8 hours.

FREEZABILITY
This dish does not freeze.

1. Rinse and drain the quinoa well before use to remove any bitterness. It can then be lightly roasted in oil to enhance the flavour, if you wish.
2. Put the quinoa in a pan with the water and salt, bring to the boil, then reduce the heat, cover and cook for 15-20 minutes or until the liquid had been absorbed and the quinoa looks transparent. If all the liquid has not been absorbed, drain well.
3. Remove from the heat and fluff up with a fork. Allow to cool.
4. Make the dressing: put the ingredients in a liquidizer and blend until smooth, then season well to make a strong dressing.
5. Mix the dressing with the quinoa and mix in most of the olives and kidney beans, reserving a few for the garnish.
6. Line a serving bowl with the radicchio leaves, spoon in the quinoa, scatter over the reserved olives and kidney beans and garnish with either fresh basil or coriander.

❄ ❄ ❄ ❄ ❄ ❄ ❄ ❄ ❄ ❄ ❄ ❄ ❄ ❄ ❄ ❄ ❄ ❄ ❄

# Fennel and Walnut Salad

Allow half a small bulb of fennel per head – this recipe serves 6.

*3 small bulbs of fennel*
*110g/4oz fresh shelled walnuts, coarsely chopped*
*15ml/1 tablespoon chopped marjoram*
*French dressing made with hazelnut oil (see page 195)*

ADVANCE PREPARATION
The fennel can be blanched and refreshed the night before.
The walnuts can be chopped the night before.
The French dressing can be made in advance.
The salad should be assembled at the last minute, as should the chopped marjoram and fennel top.

FREEZABILITY
This dish does not freeze.

1. Remove the feathery green tops of the fennel and put aside. Wash, then finely slice the fennel heads, discarding any tough outer leaves or discoloured bits.
2. Blanch the fennel in boiling water for 3-4 minutes to soften slightly. Refresh by running under cold water until cool. Drain well on absorbent paper, or dry in a teatowel.
3. Mix together the fennel, nuts and marjoram and moisten with a little French dressing. Pile into a salad bowl.
4. Chop the green leaves of the fennel and scatter them over the salad.

# Chocolate Pecan Pie

This recipe is enough for 6-8 people and should be made in a 23cm/9 inch flan case. It is very rich indeed!

*225g/8oz shortcrust pastry (see page 199)*
*200g/7oz pecan nuts, roughly chopped*
*85g/3oz dark chocolate, roughly chopped*
*2 eggs*
*110g/4oz caster sugar*
*55g/2oz golden syrup*
*55g/2oz honey*
*30g/1oz unsalted butter, melted*

ADVANCE PREPARATION
This can be completed the day before the party.

FREEZABILITY
This pudding does not freeze well – however the pastry can be made and frozen.

1. Set the oven to 200°C/400°F/gas mark 6.
2. Roll out the pastry and line a 23cm/9 inch flan case. Chill in the refrigerator and bake blind in the preheated oven.
3. Put the pecans and chopped chocolate into the baked flan case.
4. Mix together the eggs, sugar, syrup, honey and butter, and pour over the nuts and chocolate.
5. Reduce the oven temperature to

180°C/350°F/gas mark 4 and place the pie in the centre of the oven for 40-45 minutes or until the filling is just set.

NOTE: to bake blind, line the raw pastry case with a piece of foil or a double sheet of greaseproof paper and fill it with dried lentils, beans, rice or even pebbles or coins. This is to prevent the pastry bubbling up during cooking. When the pastry is half cooked (about 15 minutes) the 'blind beans' can be removed and the empty pastry case further dried out in the oven. The beans can be re-used indefinitely.

❄ ❄ ❄ ❄ ❄ ❄ ❄ ❄ ❄ ❄ ❄ ❄ ❄ ❄ ❄ ❄ ❄ ❄ ❄ ❄ ❄

# Creamed Cheese with Fresh Fruit

The quantity called for will serve 4-6 people. Simply double all the ingredients for 12.

*225g/8oz cottage cheese*
*290ml/1/2 pint double cream, lightly whipped*
*55g/2oz icing sugar, sifted*
*2 drops vanilla essence*
*3 figs, quartered*
*3 kiwis, peeled and sliced*
*4 oranges, peeled and segmented*

ADVANCE PREPARATION
The creamed cheese can be prepared the night before the party. The fruit should not be prepared too far in advance but the oranges can be peeled and segmented the night before, if pushed.

FREEZABILITY
The creamed cheese mixture freezes well.

1. Put the cottage cheese into a sieve and drain very well.
2. Push the cheese through the sieve (or process briefly in a processor) and fold in the lightly whipped double cream. Sweeten with icing sugar and add the vanilla essence.
3. Pile on to a large oval dish and shape into a shallow mound. Arrange the fruit attractively on top of the cheese.

LIGHT SWEET WHITE

❄ ❄ ❄ ❄ ❄ ❄ ❄ ❄ ❄ ❄ ❄ ❄ ❄ ❄ ❄ ❄ ❄ ❄ ❄ ❄ ❄

# Tarte Tatin

This recipe makes enough for 6 people – if you are cooking for more people simply make several pies.

FOR THE PASTRY:
*170g/6oz plain flour*
*55g/2oz ground rice*
*140g/5oz butter*
*55g/2oz caster sugar*
*1 egg, beaten*

FOR THE TOPPING:
*110g/4oz butter*
*110g/4oz granulated sugar*
*900g/2lb cooking apples*
*grated rind of 1 lemon*

ADVANCE PREPARATION
The whole pie can be assembled in advance (if you do this, make sure that the apples are cold before you put the pastry on top) and then baked as and when required.

FREEZABILITY
This dish will freeze completely prepared for baking but the apples will go a little soft. Ideally only the pastry should be made and frozen.

1. Set the oven to 190°C/375°F/gas mark 5.
2. To make the pastry: sift the flour and ground rice into a large bowl. Rub in the butter until the mixture resembles breadcrumbs. Stir in the sugar. Add the egg and bind the dough together. Chill while you prepare the top.
3. To make the topping: melt the butter in a 25cm/10 inch frying pan with a metal handle. Add the granulated sugar and remove from the heat. Peel, core and thickly slice the apples. Arrange the apple slices over the melted butter and sugar in the base of the frying pan. Sprinkle the grated lemon rind over the top.
4. Place the frying pan over a high flame until the butter and sugar start to caramelize. It may take 6-7 minutes and you will be able to smell the change – it is essential that the apples get dark. Remove from the heat.
5. Roll the pastry into a circle, 5mm/$^1$/4 inch thick, to fit the top of the pan. Lay it on top of the apples and press down lightly. Bake in the oven for 25–30 minutes.
6. Allow to cool slightly, turn out on to a plate and serve warm.

NOTE: If you do not have a frying pan with a metal handle, cook the apples in an ordinary frying pan. Let the butter and sugar become well caramelized and tip into an ovenproof dish. Cover with the pastry and then bake in the oven on a hot baking sheet. It can also be made in a shallow cast-iron dish – if it has handles (or flanges) turning out the Tarte Tatin is quite difficult, but not impossible.

SWEET WHITE

❋❋❋❋❋❋❋❋❋❋❋❋❋❋❋❋❋❋❋❋❋❋

✾✾✾✾✾✾✾✾✾✾✾✾✾✾✾✾✾✾✾✾✾✾

# EDIBLE PRESENTS

✾✾✾✾✾✾✾✾✾✾✾✾✾✾✾✾✾✾✾✾✾✾✾

*Spiced tomato chutney*
*Hot piccalilli*
*Spiced fruit pickle*
*Mincemeat (1)*
*Mincemeat (2)*
*Apple and sage jelly*
*Rowan jelly*
*Lemon curd*

FLAVOURED OILS AND VINEGARS
*Spiced vinegar*
*Spiced pears*
*Pickled peaches*
*Pickled red cabbage*
*Pickled lemons*
*Devilled nuts*
*Marinated olives*

*Candied orange peel*
*Candied orange peel dipped in chocolate*
*Venetian biscuits*
*Shortbread*
*Flavoured shortbreads*
*Old-fashioned gingerbread*
*Peanut butter fudge*
*Chocolate truffles*

✾✾✾✾✾✾✾✾✾✾✾✾✾✾✾✾✾✾✾✾✾✾

# Spiced Tomato Chutney

MAKES 1.35 kg/3lb

900g/2lb tomatoes

1 green chilli

3 onions, chopped

2 garlic cloves, crushed

225ml/8 fl oz wine vinegar

2.5ml/$^1$/2 teaspoon ground cinnamon

5ml/1 teaspoon salt

5ml/1 teaspoon ground ginger

6 cloves

225g/8oz soft dark brown sugar

30ml/2 tablespoons chopped fresh parsley

100ml/3$^1$/2fl oz oil

30ml/2 tablespoons mustard seeds, white or black

1. Skin and chop the tomatoes, keeping the seeds.
2. Chop the chilli finely, discarding the seeds.
3. Put the tomatoes, onions, chilli, garlic, vinegar, cinnamon, salt, ginger, cloves, sugar and parsley in a pan and bring up to the boil. Simmer over a low heat, stirring all the time for 10 minutes.
4. Heat the oil in a frying pan and add the mustard seeds. Fry for 1 minute, stirring all the time. They will appear to be almost deep-frying. Leave to cool for a few minutes and then add the seeds and oil to the tomato mixture. Stir well.
5. Continue to simmer until the mixture begins to thicken, stirring occasionally. This may take 30–50 minutes.
6. Meanwhile, prepare the preserving jars by rinsing out with boiling water and then placing in a very low oven until they are required.
7. Fill the jars with the hot chutney and seal well.

NOTE: This is delicious when it is just made but will have matured well after 3 months. If the chutney is to be stored for any length of time, un-lacquered metal lids should be avoided as they will be attacked by the vinegar. Porosan skin tied over each jar makes a good cover.

✳ ✳ ✳ ✳ ✳ ✳ ✳ ✳ ✳ ✳ ✳ ✳ ✳ ✳ ✳ ✳ ✳ ✳ ✳ ✳

# Hot Piccalilli

MAKES 2.7kg/6lb

450g/1lb salt

4.6 litres/8 pints boiling water

675g/1$^1$/2lb cauliflower, broken into small florets

450g/1lb cucumber, diced with the skin left on

675g/1$^1$/2lb pickling onions, skinned

450g/1lb green beans, topped and tailed and cut in 2.5cm/1 inch lengths

450g/1lb marrow, diced

45g/1$^1$/2oz dry English mustard

15g/$^1$/2oz turmeric

45g/1$^1$/2oz ground ginger

1$^1$/2 level tablespoons flour

170g/6oz caster sugar

1.1 litres/2 pints distilled vinegar

1. Mix together the salt and boiling water. Leave to cool.
2. Prepare the vegetables and cover with the brine (salt and water). Leave for 24 hours.
3. Drain and rinse the vegetables.
4. Mix the mustard, turmeric, ginger, flour and

sugar together and mix to a smooth liquid with 570ml/1 pint vinegar.

5. Pour the other 570ml/1 pint vinegar into a large saucepan. Add the prepared vegetables, and simmer until tender but still crisp. Stir in the spiced flour mixture. Cook, stirring continuously, until the pickles come to the boil and the sauce thickens. Simmer for 3 minutes. Leave to go cold.

6. Pack into jars and cover when cold.

❄ ❄ ❄ ❄ ❄ ❄ ❄ ❄ ❄ ❄ ❄ ❄ ❄ ❄ ❄ ❄ ❄ ❄ ❄ ❄ ❄

# Spiced Fruit Pickle

MAKES 1.35kg/3lb

900g/2lb mixed fresh fruit, e.g. plums, apricots, peaches, rhubarb

450g/1lb sugar

425ml/³⁄4 pint cider vinegar

grated rind and juice of 1 orange

5ml/1 teaspoon ground ginger

20ml/4 teaspoons mustard seeds

6 cloves

1 cinnamon stick

1. Prepare the fruit by removing the stones and cutting into 1cm/¹⁄2 inch pieces – leave the skins on.

2. Dissolve the sugar in the vinegar, add the orange rind and juice, ginger, mustard seeds, cloves and cinnamon stick.

3. Add the fruit and bring to the boil. Simmer carefully for 15 minutes.

4. Strain the fruit and reduce the liquid by boiling until it is syrupy. Mix it with the fruit.

5. Pour the pickle into clean, sterilized jam jars and seal with jam seals.

NOTE: This can be used straight away but is better if left to mature for at least a month. Store in a cool, dark place.

❄ ❄ ❄ ❄ ❄ ❄ ❄ ❄ ❄ ❄ ❄ ❄ ❄ ❄ ❄ ❄ ❄ ❄ ❄ ❄ ❄

# Mincemeat (1)

This mincemeat does not keep well – if you want to preserve it, omit the banana and add it just before using the mincemeat.

MAKES JUST OVER 450g/1lb

1 small cooking apple, washed and cored
55g/2oz butter
85g/3oz sultanas
85g/3oz raisins
85g/3oz currants
45g/1 1/2oz mixed peel, chopped
45g/1 1/2oz chopped almonds
grated rind of large lemon
2.5ml/1/2 teaspoon mixed spice
15ml/1 tablespoon brandy
85g/3oz brown sugar
1 banana, chopped

Grate the apple, skin and all. Melt the butter and add it, with all the other ingredients, to the apple. Mix well.

# Mincemeat (2)

This recipe is from Fiona Burrell's grandmother. It makes 6 x 450g/1lb jars of mincemeat.

3 lemons
450g/1lb raisins
450g/1lb sultanas
280g/10oz mixed peel
450g/1lb cooking apples, washed and cored
450g/1lb currants
450g/1lb brown sugar
450g/1lb shredded suet
5ml/1 teaspoon ground ginger
5ml/1 teaspoon ground cinnamon
5ml/1 teaspoon grated nutmeg
55ml/2 fl oz whisky
55ml/2 fl oz rum

1. Wash the lemons and boil them for approximately 1 hour or until soft. Allow to cool and cut in half, reserving the juice but throwing away any pips.
2. Mince (or put through a food processor) the lemon flesh and rind, raisins, sultanas, mixed peel, apples (skin and all). Do not mince the currants.
3. Tip the contents of the mincer or food processor into a bowl, add any lemon juice, and the currants, sugar, suet and spices. Mix well and soak with the whisky and rum.
4. Place in jars, a large crock or plastic container. Stir occasionally and add a little whisky and rum if it becomes dry. It will keep well over two Christmases.

NOTE: This makes a mincemeat which is more like a paste than a conventional mincemeat.

# Apple and Sage Jelly

MAKES 1.8kg/4lb

*2kg/4<sup>1</sup>/2lb cooking apples (see note)*
*1.1 litre/2 pints water*
*150ml/<sup>1</sup>/4 pint cider vinegar*
*450g/1lb sugar to each 570ml/1 pint juice*
*55g/2oz sage leaves, finely chopped*

1. Wash the apples and cut them into thick pieces without peeling or coring.
2. Put the apples and water into a saucepan, bring up to the boil, cover and simmer for about 1 hour. Add the vinegar and boil for a further 5 minutes.
3. Meanwhile, scald a jelly bag twice with boiling water.
4. Hang the jelly bag from the legs of an upturned stool and place a bowl underneath it.
5. Pour the apple pulp and juice into the jelly bag and allow to drip steadily for about 1 hour or until the bag has stopped dripping. Do not squeeze the bag.
6. Measure the juice and pour into the preserving pan. Add 450g/1lb sugar to every 570ml/1 pint of juice. Put the jam jars to warm.
7. Bring up to the boil gradually, ensuring that the sugar has dissolved before the juice has boiled, and stirring constantly.
8. Boil briskly, uncovered, for about 10 minutes, and skim frequently. Test for setting point. When this has been reached, allow the jelly to cool slightly and stir in the sage.
9. Pour into the warm jam jars and cover.

NOTE: This recipe can also be made using crab apples, with or without the sage as preferred.

# Rowan Jelly

The rowan tree or mountain ash produces clusters of bright scarlet berries in August. They are inedible as they are so acidic but they do produce a lovely, slightly smoky jelly, which goes very well with venison or as an addition to sauces and gravies instead of redcurrant jelly.

*900g/2lb rowan berries*
*900g/2lb cooking apples*
*juice of 2 lemons*
*1.5 litres/2<sup>1</sup>/2 pints water*
*granulated sugar*

1. Strip the rowan berries from their stalks with a fork and wash them well. Wash the apples and remove any bruises.
2. Cut up the apples roughly with the skin and pips and put them into a saucepan with the rowan berries, lemon juice and water. Bring to the boil and simmer very gently uncovered until absolutely tender.
3. Strain the mixture through a jelly bag and leave to drip for several hours or overnight.
4. Measure the juice and to each 570ml/1 pint add 450g/1lb granulated sugar. Put the juice and sugar in a preserving pan, bring up to the boil, stirring all the time and making sure no sugar sticks to the bottom of the pan and burns.

Boil fast until a set is reached. To test for this put a little of the jelly onto a chilled saucer, leave for a minute and push through it with a finger. If there is a skin on top which wrinkles, it will set.

5. Remove any scum from the surface and pour into sterilized jam jars. Cover, label and store in a dark cupboard.

❋ ❋ ❋ ❋ ❋ ❋ ❋ ❋ ❋ ❋ ❋ ❋ ❋ ❋ ❋ ❋ ❋ ❋ ❋ ❋ ❋

# Lemon Curd

MAKES 450g/1lb
*2 large lemons*
*85g/3oz butter*
*225g/8oz granulated sugar*
*3 eggs*

1. Grate the rind of the lemons on the finest gauge of the grater, taking care to grate the rind only, not the pith.
2. Squeeze the juice from the lemons.

3. Put the rind, juice, butter, sugar and lightly beaten eggs into a heavy saucepan or double boiler and heat gently, stirring all the time until the mixture is thick.
4. Strain into jam jars and cover.

NOTE I: This curd will keep in the refrigerator for about 3 weeks.

NOTE II: If the curd is boiled, no great harm is done, as the acid and sugar prevent the eggs from scrambling.

❋ ❋ ❋ ❋ ❋ ❋ ❋ ❋ ❋ ❋ ❋ ❋ ❋ ❋ ❋ ❋ ❋ ❋ ❋ ❋ ❋

✻ ✻ ✻ ✻ ✻ ✻ ✻ ✻ ✻ ✻ ✻ ✻ ✻ ✻ ✻ ✻ ✻ ✻

# FLAVOURED OILS AND VINEGARS

✻ ✻ ✻ ✻ ✻ ✻ ✻ ✻ ✻ ✻ ✻ ✻ ✻ ✻ ✻ ✻ ✻ ✻

*These make beautiful presents at any time of year – not only at Christmas. Save any attractive oil and vinegar bottles, or, alternatively, you could buy the recycled glass bottles that are now on the market.*

## OILS

Olive oil is the best oil to use. Think about the flavours and appearance that you want.
The flavourings should sit in the oil for about 2-4 weeks before the oil is used although the colours will fade in time.

### SOME COMBINATIONS
Split red chilli peppers and peppercorns
Basil and slightly bruised garlic
Rosemary and pared lemon rind

### WARNING
If the oil is not strained before using, the herbs and some other flavourings can go mouldy when exposed to air.

## VINEGARS

White wine vinegar and cider vinegar are the best vinegars to use. You can add the following fruits and herbs:

Tarragon
Lemon rind and garlic
Raspberry
Blackcurrant
Chilli and garlic

These can stay in the vinegar as it gets used, but the last 1cm/$\frac{1}{2}$ inch may be a little cloudy.

# Spiced Vinegar

MAKES 2.3 litres/4 pints
2.3 litres/4 pints wine vinegar
30g/1oz blade mace
15g/¹/2oz root ginger
30g/1oz whole allspice berries
15g/¹/2oz whole cloves
1 large cinnamon stick

10 peppercorns
6 dried red chillies
1 bay leaf

1. Put the vinegar and spices into a saucepan, bring up to the boil and then transfer to a glass, or china bowl. Cover and leave for at least 2 hours.
2. Strain the vinegar and pour into sterilized bottles or jars.

# Spiced Pears

MAKES APPROXIMATELY 2 x 900g/2lb jars
1.35kg/3lb firm pears
20-30 cloves
425ml/³/4 pint distilled vinegar or white wine vinegar
425ml/³/4 pint water
400g/14oz granulated sugar
30g/1oz root ginger, peeled and sliced
pared rind of 1 lemon
1 stick cinnamon
2.5ml/¹/2 teaspoon grated nutmeg

1. Peel and halve the pears. Remove the stalks and cores. Stud the outside of each pear half with a clove.
2. Bring the vinegar and water to the boil and add the sugar, stirring until it dissolves. Remove the pan from the heat.
3. Carefully place the pears in the pan with the ginger, lemon rind, cinnamon and nutmeg. Cover the pan and simmer the pears until they are tender. This could take anything between 10 and 30 minutes.
4. Meanwhile, prepare the preserving jars by rinsing them out with boiling water and placing in a very low oven until ready for use.
5. Remove the pears from the syrup and place in the prepared jars. Boil the syrup for a couple of minutes until it becomes a little tacky. Pour over the pears, with the ginger, lemon rind and cinnamon stick. Seal the jars with non-metallic lids. Store in a dark place. Serve with cold meats or cheese.

# Pickled Peaches

*570ml/1 pint white wine vinegar*
*15g/¹/₂oz root ginger, bruised*
*10 cloves*
*1 cinnamon stick*
*10 allspice berries, lightly crushed*
*900g/2lb sugar*
*1.8kg/4lb peaches, just ripe*

1. Put the vinegar, ginger, cloves, cinnamon stick and allspice berries in a pan and bring to the boil. Simmer gently for 10 minutes. Strain.

2. Add the sugar to the spiced vinegar and bring slowly to the boil, making sure that the sugar has completely dissolved before the syrup boils. Simmer for 3 minutes.

3. Meanwhile, dip the peaches in boiling water and skin them. Cut them in half and remove the stones.

4. Add the fruit to the spiced syrup and poach gently until tender.

5. Put the peaches into clean, sterilized preserving jars and cover with the syrup. They are very good served with cold meats and cheese.

# Pickled Red Cabbage

*1.35kg/3lb firm red cabbage*
*55g/2oz salt*
*1.7 litres/3 pints spiced vinegar (see page 69)*
*30g/1oz soft dark brown sugar*

1. Shred the cabbage very finely, removing the central core and limp outer leaves.

2. Layer in a large non-metallic bowl with the salt. Cover and leave for 12 hours or overnight.

3. Rinse the cabbage well to get rid of any excess salt. Mix the sugar into the spiced vinegar.

4. Pack the cabbage into jars and pour over the sweetened spiced vinegar.

5. Cover and seal the jars.

NOTE: This should be used within 2-4 weeks as it tends to lose its crispness. If you like a slightly less sharp taste, more sugar can be added.

# Pickled Lemons

A few slices of these lemons can be added to meat casseroles at the end of cooking, to give a citrus flavour to the whole dish. They are particularly good with chicken and pork. The oil can also be used to fry meat and vegetables. Do not allow the lemons to be exposed to the air or they will go mouldy.

*6 lemons*
*5ml/1 teaspoon salt*

7.5ml/1½ teaspoons paprika
10 cloves
1 cinnamon stick
570ml/1 pint olive oil

1. Slice the lemons and place on a wire rack. Sprinkle with salt and allow to stand for 24 hours.

2. Layer the lemon slices in a preserving jar, sprinkling a little paprika between each layer. Add the cloves and cinnamon stick. Pour over the olive oil, making sure that the lemons are completely covered.

3. Seal the jar tightly and store for at least 3 weeks before using.

❋ ❋ ❋ ❋ ❋ ❋ ❋ ❋ ❋ ❋ ❋ ❋ ❋ ❋ ❋ ❋ ❋ ❋ ❋ ❋

# Devilled Nuts

2.5ml/½ teaspoon chilli powder
5ml/1 teaspoon caster sugar
10ml/2 teaspoons dry English mustard
5ml/1 teaspoon garam marsala
5ml/1 teaspoon curry powder
2.5ml/½ teaspoon salt
30g/1oz butter
375g/12oz blanched nuts, e.g. almonds, hazelnuts,
    brazil nuts etc.
375g/12oz roasted salted peanuts

1. Mix together the chilli powder, sugar, mustard, garam marsala, curry powder and salt.
2. Melt the butter in a frying pan and carefully fry the blended nuts until they are golden brown. Drain on kitchen paper.
3. Mix the hot nuts with the dry ingredients and add the peanuts. Allow to cool.

NOTE: These nuts should be stored in airtight containers and will keep for 1 month.

❋ ❋ ❋ ❋ ❋ ❋ ❋ ❋ ❋ ❋ ❋ ❋ ❋ ❋ ❋ ❋ ❋ ❋ ❋ ❋

# Marinated Olives

The large green or black olives can be used for this recipe. They are marinated for 2-3 weeks, packed into jam jars.

225g/8oz black or green olives
1 piece of pared lemon rind or orange rind
1 garlic clove, sliced
5ml/1 teaspoon crushed coriander seeds
5ml/1 teaspoon chopped oregano (you can used dried)
290ml/½ pint olive oil

1. Rinse any brine off the olives and dry them well.
2. Mix them with the lemon or orange rind, garlic, coriander and oregano. Add the oil and mix well.
3. Pack into a jar, seal and store in a cool place for 2-3 weeks before eating them.

# Candied Peel

This will take about a month from start to finish – however, if you like a chewy finish the peel need only be dried for a week.

*6 oranges, lemons, limes, grapefruit or a mixture of all these*
*370g/12oz granulated sugar*

1. Wash the fruit thoroughly and cut into quarters. Remove the peel. It is better to candy the peel in large pieces and then cut as required later.
2. Cover the peel in water and simmer for 1½-2 hours until it is quite tender. The water for cooking grapefruit peel must be changed twice.
3. Remove the peel and pour the liquid into a measuring jug. Make up to 290ml/½ pint with water.

4. Put the liquid back in the pan, add 225g/8oz of the sugar and heat it gently until the sugar dissolves. Bring to the boil and add the peel, remove from the heat and leave in a cool place for 2 days.
5. Drain the syrup into a clean pan and add the remaining sugar. Dissolve carefully and bring back to the boil. Add the peel and simmer gently until the peel is semi-transparent. This will take about 20-30 minutes. Pour into a bowl, allow to cool and cover. Keep in a cool place for 2-3 weeks.
6. Remove the peel from the syrup and place on a wire rack to dry out. This can be in an airing cupboard. The temperature must not exceed 50°C/120°F. When the peel is no longer sticky it can be stored, by packing between pieces of waxed paper, in a cardboard or wooden box. If put in a plastic airtight container it can go mouldy.
7. For a crystallized finish, dip the peel in boiling water briefly, drain well and roll in caster sugar.

❉ ❉ ❉ ❉ ❉ ❉ ❉ ❉ ❉ ❉ ❉ ❉ ❉ ❉ ❉ ❉ ❉ ❉ ❉ ❉

# Candied Orange Peel Dipped in Chocolate

These tangy orange sticks make a very good Christmas present. They are also delicious served with coffee.

*110g/4oz candied orange peel (see above)*
*110g/4oz dark chocolate*

1. Cut the orange peel into long strips of about ½ cm/ ¼ inch thickness.
2. Melt the chocolate, very carefully, in a bowl over a pan of gently simmering water. Do not allow it to get too hot.
3. Place a sheet of silicone paper or aluminium foil on a baking sheet or tray.
4. Dip each piece of peel into the chocolate covering it completely. Using two forks remove the peel from the chocolate and gently shake off any excess. Place it carefully on the prepared tray. Repeat with all the peel. Put aside to set at room temperature. Once set, store in a cardboard or wooden box lined with tissue paper.

NOTE: If preferred, the peel can be half dipped in chocolate to give a colour contrast.
Other peels can also be used, e.g. grapefruit, lemon or tangerine.

PICKLES

MONKFISH SALAD WITH EXOTIC SAUCE

TARTE TATIN

VENISON TERRINE AND CUMBERLAND SAUCE

VEGETARIAN LASAGNE

Biscuits

PETITS FOURS

FLAVOURED OILS AND VINEGARS

# Venetian Biscuits

MAKES 24

*110g/4oz blanched almonds*
*450g/1lb flour*
*pinch of salt*
*5ml/1 teaspoon baking powder*
*140g/5oz granulated sugar*
*85g/3oz plain chocolate, chopped into small pieces*
*4 large eggs, lightly beaten*
*1 egg white, to glaze*

1. Preheat the oven to 190°C/375°F/gas mark 5. Grease a baking sheet.
2. Place the almonds on the baking sheet and bake in the oven until golden brown. Cool. Chop two-thirds and grind the remaining third finely.
3. Sift the flour, salt and baking powder into a bowl. Add the sugar, chocolate and almonds. Mix well.
4. Make a well in the centre and add the beaten eggs. Gradually incorporate the dry ingredients with the eggs. The dough should be firm.
5. Divide the dough into 4 and roll each piece into a long thin sausage shape approximately 2cm/3/4 inch in diameter and 20cm/8 inches long.
6. Place the rolls on the baking sheet at least 5cm/2 inches apart. Lightly whisk the egg white until just frothy and brush over the tops of the rolls.
7. Place in the preheated oven and bake for 20 minutes.
8. Remove the rolls from the oven, reduce the heat to 105°C/225°F/gas mark 1/2. Cut the rolls at a 45-degree angle at 1cm/1/2 inch intervals and return them individually to the baking sheet. Put back in the oven for a further 30 minutes. Allow to cool completely before serving.

NOTE: Raisins or glacé fruit can be used in place of the chocolate. The biscuits are meant to be eaten after being dipped in a liqueur, e. g. Amaretto or Grappa.

# Shortbread

MAKES 6-8

*110g/4oz butter*
*55g/2oz caster sugar*
*110g/4oz plain flour*
*55g/2oz rice flour*

1. Set the oven to 170°C/325°F/gas mark 3.
2. Beat the butter until soft, add the sugar and beat until pale and creamy.
3. Sift in the flours and work to a smooth paste.
4. Place a 15cm/6 inch flan ring on a baking sheet and press the shortbread paste into a neat circle. Remove the flan ring and flatten the paste slightly with a rolling pin. Crimp the edges. Prick lightly.
5. Mark the shortbread into 6 or 8 wedges, sprinkle lightly with a little extra caster sugar and bake for 40 minutes until a pale biscuit colour. Leave to cool for 2 minutes and then lift on to a cooling rack to cool completely.

# Flavoured Shortbreads

Shortbread can be stamped into biscuits or made into petticoat tails and put into attractive tins. There are many variations that can be made by adding different ingredients to the basic recipe (see previous page).

### ALMOND SHORTBREAD

Add 85g/3oz ground almonds with the flour to the creamed butter and sugar.

### HAZELNUT SHORTBREAD

Add 110g/4oz roughly chopped, browned and skinned hazelnuts with the flour to the creamed butter and sugar.

### GINGER SHORTBREAD

Add 5ml/1 teaspoon of ground ginger and 55g/2oz chopped crystallized stem ginger with the flour.

### ORANGE SHORTBREAD

Add the finely grated rind of 2 oranges to the creamed butter and sugar before adding the flour.

# Old-Fashioned Gingerbread

These can be cut into different shaped biscuits and used as Christmas tree decorations. To do this, cut a hole in the baked biscuits while they are still hot. Leave to cool on a wire rack. When cool, thread through green and red ribbons and tie on to the Christmas tree.

MAKES ABOUT 120 SMALL BISCUITS
*340g/12oz plain flour*
*5ml/1 teaspoon baking powder*
*5ml/1 teaspoon salt*
*5ml/1 teaspoon grated nutmeg*
*5ml/1 teaspoon ground cloves*
*10ml/2 teaspoons ground cinnamon*
*10ml/2 teaspoons ground ginger*
*225g/8oz butter*
*225g/8oz caster sugar*
*170g/6oz dark brown sugar*
*2 eggs, beaten*

1. Set the oven to 180°C/350°F/gas mark 4.
2. Sift the flour, baking powder, salt and spices into a large bowl.
3. Melt the butter in a saucepan, add the caster sugar and dark brown sugar, mix well and allow to cool. Add the beaten eggs.
4. Make a well in the dry ingredients and gradually add the butter and sugar mixture. Place in the refrigerator until completely cold.
5. Cut into 4 pieces and roll each one out separately until the thickness of a pound coin. Stamp into different shapes, e.g. stars, balls, angels, Christmas trees. Place on a greased baking sheet and bake in batches in the preheated oven for about 10 minutes.

NOTE: This mixture should be made by hand. It is very easy to overwork.

# Peanut Butter Fudge

This fudge has a grainy texture and a slightly savoury taste.

*110g/4oz crunchy peanut butter*
*290ml/¹/2 pint milk*
*450g/1lb granulated sugar*
*30g/1oz butter*
*5ml/1 teaspoon vanilla essence*

1. Put the peanut butter, milk and sugar in a large saucepan. Dissolve the sugar over a gentle heat and then bring to the boil.
2. Simmer, stirring constantly, until a little of the mixture forms a soft ball when dropped into cold water (115°C/230°F on a sugar thermometer).
3. Remove from the heat, and add the butter and vanilla essence. Cool for a few minutes. Beat with a wooden spoon until creamy. Pour into a well-greased 30x20cm/12x8inch shallow tin and leave in a cool place.
4. When cool, cut into squares.

# Chocolate Truffles

MAKES 24
*255g/9oz chocolate couverture, coarsely chopped*
*100ml/3¹/2 fl oz double cream*
*vanilla pod*
*20g/³/4oz unsalted butter*
*cocoa powder*

1. Melt the chocolate in a bowl set over (not in) a pan of simmering water. Leave to cool.
2. Put the cream into a saucepan, add the vanilla pod and bring up to scalding point. Leave to cool. Remove the vanilla pod.
3. Beat the butter until very soft. Mix it into the chocolate, add the vanilla cream and leave to chill, until firm, in the refrigerator.
4. Shape into small balls and roll lightly in cocoa powder.

NOTE: The cocoa powder tends to become damp if the truffles are left for much longer than a couple of hours. They can also be finished off in a variety of different ways which will store better.

1. Cut up 110g/4oz plain, milk or white chocolate. Pace in a bowl over a pan of gently simmering water. Do not allow the chocolate to get too hot. Remove from the heat. When it is cool but still runny, place the cold truffles into the chocolate, remove with a fork and run them along the surface of a cooling rack. Leave to set on silicon paper. When set, melt a little of the contrasting choclate and using a fine piping bag or a fork, dribble lines across the chocolate.
2. Alternatively once the truffles have been dipped in the chocolate, they can be rolled on a plate covered with grated chocolate of a different colour if wished and then placed straight into petit four cases.

✳✳✳✳✳✳✳✳✳✳✳✳✳✳✳✳✳✳✳✳✳✳✳

# FIRST COURSES
# AND LIGHT
# LUNCHES

✳✳✳✳✳✳✳✳✳✳✳✳✳✳✳✳✳✳✳✳✳✳✳

*Grilled aubergines with pesto*
*Onion tart*
*Tuna fish and pasta salad*
*Stilton soup*
*Small pea and ham puddings*
*Aubergine flan*

✳✳✳✳✳✳✳✳✳✳✳✳✳✳✳✳✳✳✳✳✳✳✳

# Grilled Aubergines with Pesto

SERVES 4

*2 medium aubergines, sliced*
*salt*
*150ml/¹/4 pint French dressing (see page 195)*
*parsley pesto sauce (see page 195)*
*10ml/2 teaspoons French mustard*

1. Sprinkle the aubergine slices liberally with salt and leave in a colander for 30 minutes.

2. Make the French dressing and season with the mustard.

3. Rinse the aubergines, drain and dry well. Marinate in the French dressing for 2 hours. Drain well.

4. Heat the grill.

5. Grill the aubergines for about 10 minutes on each side, or until soft and pale brown.

6. Spread one side of the aubergine with the pesto sauce and return to the grill for 1 minute.

7. Arrange on a round plate and serve immediately.

LIGHT RED/ROSE

# Onion Tart ✔

SERVES 4

*rich shortcrust pastry made with 225g/8oz flour*
    *quantity (see page 200)*
*55g/2oz butter*
*15ml/1 tablespoon olive oil*
*675g/1¹/2lb onions, sliced*
*2 eggs*
*2 egg yolks*
*150ml/¹/4 pint single cream*
*salt and pepper*
*grated nutmeg*

1. Preheat the oven to 200°C/400°F/gas mark 6.

2. Roll out the pastry and line a 20cm/8 inch flan ring with it. Leave in the refrigerator to relax for 20 minutes.

3. Melt the butter, add the oil and onions and cook very slowly until soft but not coloured. This may take up to 30 minutes. Leave to cool.

4. Bake the pastry case blind, then turn the oven down to 180°C/350°F/gas mark 4.

5. Mix together the eggs, cream and onions. Season to taste with salt and pepper. Pour into the pastry case and sprinkle with nutmeg. Bake until golden and just set, about 20 minutes.

BEAUJOLAIS/ALSACE WHITE

# Tuna Fish and Pasta Salad

SERVES 8

*85g/3oz pasta shells*
*salt and freshly ground black pepper*
*oil and lemon, for cooking*
*150ml/¹/4 pint French dressing (see page 195)*
*1x200g/7oz tin flageolet beans, rinsed and drained*
*1x200g/7oz tin borlotti beans, rinsed and drained*
*1x200g/7oz tin red kidney beans, rinsed and drained*
*1 bunch spring onions, sliced diagonally*
*1 box mustard and cress*
*15ml/1 tablespoon chopped fresh chives*
*15ml/1 tablespoon finely chopped fresh parsley*
*1x200g/7oz tin tuna fish, drained and broken*
  *into chunks*

*squeeze of lemon juice*
*16 small black Niçoise olives*

1. Cook the pasta in plenty of boiling salted water, with 15ml/1 tablespoon oil and 1 slice of lemon, until just tender – about 10 minutes.
2. Drain and rinse under running cold water.
3. Soak the pasta in the French dressing for 30 minutes, seasoning well.
4. Mix the pasta with the beans, spring onions, half the mustard and cress, half the chives and parsley and the lemon juice.
5. Add the tuna fish and mix gently.
6. Pile into a serving dish and scatter over the remaining herbs, black olives and mustard and cress.

VERY DRY WHITE

# Stilton Soup

SERVES 4

*1 medium onion, finely chopped*
*2 sticks celery, finely choppped*
*55g/2oz butter*
*45g/1¹/2oz flour*
*75ml/5 tablespoons white wine*
*1 litre/1³/4 pints white stock (see page 178)*
*290ml/¹/2 pint milk*
*225g/8oz Stilton cheese, grated or crumbled*
*30ml/2 tablespoons cream*
*salt and pepper*

1. Soften the onion and celery in the butter over gentle heat. Add the flour and cook for 1 minute.
2. Take off the heat and stir in the wine and

stock. Return to the heat and bring slowly to the boil, stirring continuously until the soup thickens. Simmer for 25 minutes.
3. Add the milk and simmer for 2 minutes. Remove from the heat and whisk in the Stilton. Liquidize and push through a sieve.
4. Add the cream and salt and pepper. Reheat the soup, taking care not to let it boil, or it will curdle.

NOTE I: White port, well chilled, is delicious with this soup.
NOTE II: The soup can be served chilled. In this event streak the cream into the soup just before serving, giving it an attractive marbled appearance.

BEAUJOLAIS

# Small Pea and Ham Puddings

MAKES 8–10

*400g/14oz cooked green peas*
*small pinch of cayenne pepper*
*2 eggs*
*100ml/3¹/2 fl oz whipping cream*
*15ml/1 tablespoon Dijon mustard*
*70g/2oz diced ham*
*butter for greasing*
*salt and freshly ground black pepper*

FOR THE SAUCE:

*100g/3oz aduki beans (soaked in cold*
*    water overnight)*
*290ml/¹/2 pint white stock (see page 178)*
*10ml/2 teaspoons sherry*
*15ml/1 tablespoon soy sauce*
*5ml/1 teaspoon grated fresh ginger*
*1 sprig rosemary, bruised*
*1 garlic clove, crushed*
*2.5ml/¹/2 teaspoon arrowroot or cornflour*

1. Preheat the oven to 170°C/325°F/gas mark 3.
2. Place the peas, cayenne and eggs in a food processor and blend until smooth. Add the cream and blend once more. Pour the mixture into a bowl. Fold in the mustard and ham. Season to taste. Pour into 8 timbales or cups. Cover each with a piece of greased greaseproof paper.
3. Place in a bain-marie and bake in the oven for 15-20 minutes until firm to the touch. Allow to cool slightly.
4. Meanwhile, make the sauce: put the aduki beans in cold water. Bring to the boil and simmer for 30 minutes or until soft. Drain and keep warm.
5. Heat the stock, sherry, soy sauce, ginger, rosemary and garlic together. Cook for 5 minutes and then pass through a fine sieve into a clean pan. Slake the arrowroot with a little cold water and add to the sauce. Bring the sauce up to the boil, add the beans and season to taste.
6. Unmould the pea and ham puddings on to warm plates and pour a little aduki sauce around each pudding to serve.

LIGHT RED

# Aubergine Flan

SERVES 6

*Lemon shortcrust pastry made with 340g/12oz flour*
   *(see page 201)*

FOR THE FILLING:

*1 medium aubergine, sliced*
*90ml/6 tablespoons olive oil*
*2 medium onions, finely sliced*
*3 cloves garlic, crushed*

*6 large tomatoes, skinned and chopped*
*pinch of fresh thyme*
*pinch of fresh rosemary*
*pinch of cayenne pepper*
*salt and freshly ground black pepper*
*4 eggs*
*150ml/1/4 pint single cream*
*85g/3oz Cheddar cheese, grated*
*30g/1oz fresh Parmesan cheese, grated*
*12 black olives, pitted*

1. Sprinkle the aubergine slices with salt, and leave in a colander for 30 minutes to exude any bitter juices.

2. Roll out the pastry and line a loose bottomed flan ring about 26.5cm/11 inch diameter. Leave in the refrigerator for about 45 minutes to relax – this prevents shrinkage during cooking.

3. Preheat the oven to 200°C/400°F/gas mark 6.

4. Bake the pastry case blind for 10-15 minutes. Remove from the oven and reduce the heat to 180°C/350°F/gas mark 4.

5. Rinse the aubergines well and pat dry. Fry them in about 30ml/2 tablespoons of the oil until golden brown. Drain on absorbent kitchen paper.

6. Heat the remaining oil, add the onions and fry until lightly browned. Add the garlic and fry for a further 30 seconds. Add the tomatoes, thyme, rosemary, cayenne, salt and pepper. Cook for 5-6 minutes or until a rich pulp.

7. Beat the eggs, and stir in the cream and cheeses. Mix with the tomato mixture. Season to taste.

8. Spoon half into the baked flan case, cover with the fried aubergines and then spoon in the remaining tomato mixture with the black olives. Bake for 40 minutes until set and slightly risen.

LIGHT RED/ROSE

❆ ❆ ❆ ❆ ❆ ❆ ❆ ❆ ❆ ❆ ❆ ❆ ❆ ❆ ❆ ❆ ❆ ❆ ❆

# MAIN COURSES

*Spaghetti con vongole*
*Vegetarian lasagne*
*Green dragon walnut meatballs*
*Cheese and nut balls*
*Chicken fried rice*
*Rack of lamb with mustard and breadcrumbs*
*Steak and kidney pudding*
*Shoulder of lamb 'en ballon'*
*Leith's Good Food's boned duck*
*Mustard grilled chicken*
*Spiced beef*
*Venison casserole*
*Braised pork fillets with pickled lemons*
*Carbonnade de boeuf with savoury crumble topping*
*Roast goose with apple sauce*
*Roast goose Mary-Claire*
*Spicy grilled chicken*
*Boned stuffed chicken*
*Scallops with red pepper butter sauce*
*Polenta and aubergine cakes*
*Chicken curry with almonds*
*Leek, mushroom and chestnut filo pie*

# Spaghetti con Vongole

This recipe has been taken from *A Taste of Venice* by Jeanette Nance Nordio.

SERVES 4

*450g/1lb spaghetti*
*900g/2lb baby clams in their shells*
*90ml/6 tablespoons olive oil*
*2 garlic cloves, peeled and bruised*
*4 large tomatoes, skinned and chopped*
*salt and freshly ground black pepper*
*15ml/1 tablespoon chopped parsley*

1. Wash and scrub the clams thoroughly.
2. Heat 15ml/1 tablespoon oil in a saucepan, add the clams, cover and shake until the clams have opened. Discard any that have remained closed. Remove the clams and strain the juices. Reserve both.
3. Heat the remaining oil in a saucepan, add the garlic and cook until golden brown; remove and discard. Add the tomatoes, clam juice and seasoning and cook for about 30 minutes. Add the clams and cook gently for 1-2 minutes. Add the parsley.
4. Meanwhile, cook the spaghetti in plenty of boiling salted water to which 15ml/1 tablespoon of oil has been added. When *al dente*, drain and mix with the tomato sauce. Serve immediately and give the guests finger bowls.

DRY WHITE

❄ ❄ ❄ ❄ ❄ ❄ ❄ ❄ ❄ ❄ ❄ ❄ ❄ ❄ ❄ ❄ ❄ ❄ ❄ ❄

# Vegetarian Lasagne ✔

SERVES 4

*170g/6oz green lasagne*
*salt*
*30ml/2 tablespoons oil*
*7g/¼ oz butter, for greasing*
*12 basil leaves, roughly chopped*
*salsa pizzaiola (see page 196)*
*salt and freshly ground black pepper*
*225g/8oz ricotta cheese*
*55g/2oz fresh Parmesan cheese, grated*
*30g/1oz butter, softened*
*pinch of grated nutmeg*
*225g/8oz Mozzarella cheese*

1. Cook the lasagne: drop the pasta, a few pieces at a time, into a pan of fast boiling salted water to which the oil has been added. Cook for about 10 minutes. Rinse under boiling water and leave to dry – do not stack the pasta pieces on top of each other as they will stick together.
2. Add the basil leaves to the salsa pizzaiola, and season to taste.
3. Put the ricotta cheese into a bowl, and add the Parmesan and butter. Beat well and season with salt, pepper and freshly grated nutmeg.
4. Cut the Mozzarella into very fine dice.
5. Set the oven to 190°C/375°F/gas mark 5.
6. Butter an ovenproof dish and spoon over a thin layer of tomato sauce (salsa pizzaiola).
7. Arrange a layer of pasta on top of the sauce, then a layer of ricotta filling and then spoon

over a layer of tomato sauce. Continue layering in this way, and halfway through sprinkle over half of the Mozzarella cheese. Then continue to layer up, finishing with the tomato sauce. Sprinkle evenly with the remaining Mozzarella.

8. Bake for 20-25 minutes, until bubbling and lightly browned on top. Leave the lasagne to stand for 10 minutes before serving.

LIGHT RED/ROSE

❋ ❋ ❋ ❋ ❋ ❋ ❋ ❋ ❋ ❋ ❋ ❋ ❋ ❋ ❋ ❋ ❋ ❋ ❋ ❋

# Green Dragon Walnut Meatballs

This recipe has been taken from *Marvellous Meals with Mince* by Josceline Dimbleby.

SERVES 4

FOR THE MEATBALLS:
*1 large green pepper*
*450g/1lb minced beef or pork*
*2 garlic cloves, finely chopped*
*85g/3oz walnuts, chopped*
*15ml/1 tablespoon tomato purée*
*30ml/2 tablespoons soy sauce*
*5ml/1 teaspoon ground ginger*
*3-4 pinches of cayenne pepper*
*15ml/1 tablespoon caster sugar*
*salt*
*15ml/1 tablespoon sunflower oil for frying*

FOR THE SAUCE:
*22.5ml/1 1/2 tablespoons soy sauce*
*67.5ml/4 1/2 tablespoons water*
*15ml/1 tablespoon wine vinegar*
*7.5ml/1/2 tablespoon caster sugar*
*4-5 spring onions, finely chopped*

1. Cut the pepper in half and take out the seeds and stem. Bring a small pan of salted water to

the boil, put in the pepper, cover the pan and boil for 6-8 minutes, until soft. Drain and chop finely.

2. Put the mince in a bowl and add the chopped pepper, garlic, walnuts, tomato purée and soy sauce. Then add the ground ginger, cayenne pepper, sugar and a good sprinkling of salt.

3. Mix everything together very well with a wooden spoon. If you have a food processor the mixture can be whizzed together briefly: this prevents the meatballs from breaking up when they are cooked. Then, with wet hands, form the mixture into balls the size of a ping-pong ball.

4. Heat the sunflower oil in a large frying pan and fry the meatballs over a low to medium heat, turning to brown all over, for about 15 minutes. Transfer with a slotted spoon to a serving dish and keep warm in a low oven.

5. Pour most of the fat out of the pan but leave the residue of meat juices. Add the soy sauce, the water and the vinegar. Stir in the caster sugar and dissolve over a low heat. Then bubble fiercely for a minute or two until you have a thick, dark and syrupy sauce. Remove from the heat and stir in the chopped spring onions. Spoon the sauce over the meatballs and serve immediately.

FULL RED

# Cheese and Nut Balls ✔

SERVES 3-4

110g/4oz fresh brown breadcrumbs

85g/3oz chopped mixed nuts, e.g. hazelnuts,
    almonds, walnuts, toasted

15ml/1 tablespoon chopped mixed herbs, e.g.
    parsley, mint, thyme

1 large onion, finely chopped

5ml/1 teaspoon tomato purée

110g/4oz Cheddar cheese, grated

1 egg, lightly beaten

salt and freshly ground pepper

seasoned flour

oil for frying

1. Mix together all the ingredients except the flour. Season well with salt and plenty of freshly ground black pepper.
2. Using wet hands, shape the mixture into balls the size of a ping-pong ball, roll in seasoned flour and deep-fry in oil until brown. Serve with pasta.

LIGHT RED

❋ ❋ ❋ ❋ ❋ ❋ ❋ ❋ ❋ ❋ ❋ ❋ ❋ ❋ ❋ ❋ ❋ ❋ ❋ ❋ ❋

# Chicken Fried Rice

SERVES 4

4 chicken breasts, skinned and boned

oil

1 onion, chopped

1 garlic clove, crushed

2.5cm/1 inch piece root ginger, skinned and
    finely chopped

1 green chilli, finely chopped

170g/6oz basmati rice, soaked for 30 minutes

2.5ml/1/2 teaspoon ground turmeric

10ml/2 teaspoons dried lemon grass,
    or 5ml/1 teaspoon fresh lemon grass

290ml/1/2 pint chicken stock

salt and freshly ground black pepper

1. Cut away any fat from the chicken and cut into bite-sized pieces.
2. Fry the chicken lightly in a little oil in a large sauté pan. Remove from the pan. Add the onion and cook for 10 minutes. Add the garlic, ginger, chilli and rice and fry until the rice becomes a little opaque. Add the turmeric and cook for 1 minute.
3. Return the chicken to the sauté pan. Add the lemon grass and enough stock to just cover the rice. Season with salt and pepper.
4. Bring up to the boil and simmer slowly, adding more stock if necessary, until the rice is cooked. This will take about 30 minutes.

FULL DRY WHITE

# Rack of Lamb with Mustard and Breadcrumbs

SERVES 2

*10ml/2 teaspoons pale French mustard*
*15ml/1 tablespoon fresh white breadcrumbs*
*15ml/1 tablespoon chopped fresh herbs (mint,*
    *chives, parsley and thyme)*
*1.25ml/¹/4 teaspoon salt*
*2.5ml/¹/2 teaspoon freshly ground black pepper*
*10ml/2 teaspoons unsalted butter*
*1 x best end of neck, chined, trimmed and skinned*

1. Set the oven to 220°C/425°F/gas mark 7.
2. Trim off as much fat as possible from the meat.
3. Mix together the French mustard, breadcrumbs, herbs, salt, pepper and butter. Press a thin layer of this mixture over the rounded, skinned side of the best end.
4. Place it, crumbed side up, in a roasting pan and roast for 25-30 minutes for a 7-cutlet best end, less for a smaller one. This will give pink, slightly underdone lamb. Serve with the butter and juices from the pan poured over the top.

CLARET

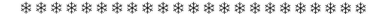

# Steak and Kidney Pudding

SERVES 4

*675g/1 ¹/2lb chuck steak*
*225g/8oz ox kidney*
*flour*
*suet pastry made with 340g/12oz flour*
    *(see page 94)*
*salt and pepper*
*1 onion, chopped*
*10ml/2 teaspoons chopped fresh parsley*

1. Cut the steak into cubes about 2.5cm/ 1 inch square.
2. Chop the kidney, discarding any sinews.
3. Place both steak and kidney in a large sieve. Pour over the flour and shake until the meat is lightly coated.

4. On a floured surface, roll out two-thirds of the suet pastry into a round about 1cm/¹/2 inch thick. Flour the surface lightly to stop it sticking together when folded. Fold the pastry over to form a half-moon shape. Place the pastry with the straight side away from you and roll it lightly so that the straight side becomes curved and the whole rounded again. Now separate the layers, and you should have a bag, roughly the shape of a 1kg/2lb pudding basin. Use it to line the basin, easing the pastry where necessary to fit, and trimming off the top so that 1cm/¹/2 inch sticks up over the edge.
5. Fill the lined basin with the meat, sprinkling plenty of seasoning, chopped onion and parsley in between the layers.
6. Add water to come three-quarters of the way up the meat.
7. Roll the remaining third of suet pastry 5mm/ ¹/4 inch thick, and large enough to just cover the

pudding filling. Put in place, wet the edges and press them together securely.

8. Cover the pudding with a double piece of greaseproof paper, pleated down the centre to allow room for the pastry to expand, and a similarly pleated piece of foil. Tie down with string.

9. Place in a saucepan of boiling water with a tightly closed lid, or in a steamer, for 5-6 hours, taking care to top up with boiling water occasionally so as not to boil dry.

10. Remove the paper and foil, and serve the pudding from the bowl.

NOTE I: Traditionally, steak and kidney puddings served from the bowl are presented wrapped in a white linen napkin.

NOTE II: As the filling of the pudding may, with long cooking, dry out somewhat, it is worth having a gravy boat of hot beef stock handy to moisten the meat when serving.

NOTE III: A delicious addition to steak and kidney pudding is to add a small can of smoked oysters to the meat filling.

FULL RED

# Suet Pastry

*butter for greasing*
*340g/12oz self-raising flour*
*salt*
*170g/6oz shredded beef suet*
*water to mix*

1. Grease a 1.1 litre/2 pint pudding basin.

2. Sift the flour with a good pinch of salt into a bowl. Stir in the shredded suet and add enough water to mix, first with a knife, and then with one hand, to a soft dough.

# Shoulder of Lamb 'en Ballon'

This dish is served with a sweet port gravy.

SERVES 6-8
1 boned shoulder of lamb
butter
salt and pepper
sprigs of rosemary
290ml/$\frac{1}{2}$ pint stock or water
2 glasses port (140ml/5 fl oz)
watercress to garnish (optional)

FOR THE STUFFING:
30ml/2 tablespoons parsley
85g/3oz smoked ham, chopped
salt and pepper

FOR THE GLAZE:
30ml/2 tablespoons redcurrant jelly

1. Set the oven at 190°C/375°F/gas mark 5.
2. Mix the stuffing ingredients together and push into the lamb, or, if the lamb has been opened out, spread it on one half and fold the other half over to cover it.
3. Using a long piece of string, tie the shoulder so that the indentations made by the string resemble the grooves in a melon or the lines between the segments of a beachball (see page 96).
4. Weigh the lamb.
5. Smear all over with butter and sprinkle with salt and pepper. Scatter a few rosemary leaves on top. Pour the stock into the pan.
6. Roast for 25 minutes per 450g/1lb. Half an hour before the cooking time is up, smear the lamb with 30ml/2 level tablespoons redcurrant jelly and return to the oven.
7. Remove the strings carefully and lift the lamb on to a warm serving dish. Leave to rest for 15 minutes before serving. It will retain heat even if not placed in a warming cupboard.
8. Meanwhile, make the gravy. Skim the fat from the juices in the pan. Add the port and bring to the boil. Boil vigorously until the sauce is syrupy and reduced to about one-third of a pint. Taste and add salt and pepper if necessary. Strain into a gravy boat. Garnish the lamb with watercress if wished.

CLARET

❄ ❄ ❄ ❄ ❄ ❄ ❄ ❄ ❄ ❄ ❄ ❄ ❄ ❄ ❄ ❄ ❄ ❄ ❄

# Lamb 'en Ballon'

This is a stuffed boned shoulder of lamb that is tied up to look like a balloon (see page 95 for the recipe). To reassemble the shoulder, spread the stuffing on one half of the boned lamb and fold the other half close up over to cover it. If the shoulder has been tunnel-boned, push the stuffing into it. Turn the shoulder over, skinned side up. Tie the end of a 3m/9ft piece of string firmly round the shoulder, making a knot in the middle at the top. Take the string around again, but this time at right angles to the first line, again tying at the first knot. Continue this process until the 'balloon' is trussed about 8 times. Tuck in any loose flaps of meat or skin.

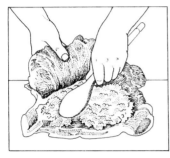 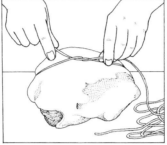 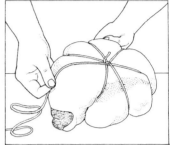

*To assemble lamb en ballon, stuff a boned shoulder and tie*

❊ ❊ ❊ ❊ ❊ ❊ ❊ ❊ ❊ ❊ ❊ ❊ ❊ ❊ ❊ ❊ ❊ ❊ ❊ ❊ ❊

# Leith's Good Food's Boned Duck

SERVES 4

*1 duck, boned*
*1 large chicken breast, boned and skinned*
*1/2 small onion, chopped*
*110g/4oz dried apricots, sliced*
*chopped tarragon and parsley*
*30g/1oz pistachio nuts*

1. Set the oven to 200°C/400°F/gas mark 6.
2. Carefully remove any excess fat from the duck, especially from the vent end.
3. Put the chicken breast and onion together in a food processor and whizz briefly. Add the apricots, tarragon, parsley and nuts. Mix well and season.
4. Stuff the duck and wrap it in a piece of muslin or a clean 'J' cloth and tie it at either end so that it looks like a Christmas cracker.
5. Put on a wire rack in a roasting pan. Prick lightly and rub with salt. Roast for 1¼ hours. Serve hot or cold with Cumberland sauce (see page 198).

RED BURGUNDY

❊ ❊ ❊ ❊ ❊ ❊ ❊ ❊ ❊ ❊ ❊ ❊ ❊ ❊ ❊ ❊ ❊ ❊ ❊ ❊ ❊

# Mustard Grilled Chicken

Although this is called grilled chicken it is partially baked to ensure that the chicken is cooked without becoming burnt.

SERVES 4

*30g/1oz butter*
*30ml/2 tablespoons French mustard*
*2kg/4¹/2lb chicken*
*juice of 1 lemon*
*15ml/1 teaspoon sugar*
*15ml/1 teaspoon paprika*
*freshly ground black pepper*
*few sprigs of watercress*

1. Mix together the butter and mustard.
2. Preheat the oven to 200°C/400°F/gas mark 6.
3. Joint the chicken into 8 (see page 208). Cut off the wing tips and the knuckles.

Remove any small feathers.
4. Spread each chicken joint on the underside with half the mustard mixture. Sprinkle with half the lemon juice, sugar and paprika. Season with pepper. Bake for 10 minutes.
5. Turn the chicken over and spread again with the mustard mixture. Sprinkle with the rest of the paprika, lemon juice and sugar. Season with pepper. Bake for a further 10 minutes.
6. Heat up the grill.
7. Arrange the joints under the grill in such a way that the larger joints are closest to the strongest heat and that the breast joints are near the edge of the grill.
8. Grill until dark and crisp but be very careful not to let the joints burn.
9. Arrange the joints neatly on a flat serving dish. Pour over the juices from the pan and garnish with watercress.

LIGHT RED

# Spiced Beef

This recipe takes 8 days to complete.

SERVES 8

*1 garlic clove*
*1.35kg/3lb boneless sirloin of beef*
*55g/2oz brown sugar*
*30g/1oz ground allspice*
*2-3 bay leaves, chopped*
*85g/3oz salt*
*about 450g/1lb plain flour*

1. Peel the garlic and cut it into thin slivers. Stick these into the beef flesh. Rub the surface of the joint with the sugar.
2. Leave in a cool place for 12 hours. Mix together the allspice, chopped bay leaves and salt.
3. Take a little of the salt mixture and rub it well into the meat.
4. Keep for a week in a refrigerator or cool place, turning and rubbing with more salt and spice each day.
5. Set the oven to 190°C/375°F/gas mark 5.
6. Make enough of a fairly thick doughy paste (by mixing flour and water together)

to completely envelop the beef.

7. Wrap the meat in the paste.

8. Put it, paste and all, into a roasting pan and pour in a small cup of water. Bake for 1¼ hours.

9. Remove and allow to cool. Snip off the crust and discard it before serving the beef.

NOTE : This is especially good eaten cold with Cumberland sauce (see page 198) or a sweet pickle.

CALIFORNIAN/AUSTRALIAN
CABERNET SAUVIGNON

✳ ✳ ✳ ✳ ✳ ✳ ✳ ✳ ✳ ✳ ✳ ✳ ✳ ✳ ✳ ✳ ✳ ✳ ✳ ✳ ✳

# Venison Casserole

SERVES 4

*675g/1¹/₂lb venison*

FOR THE MARINADE:

*1 onion, sliced*

*1 carrot, sliced*

*1 celery stick, sliced*

*1 garlic clove, crushed*

*6 juniper berries*

*slice of lemon*

*1 bay leaf*

*290ml/¹/₂ pint red wine*

*30ml/2 tablespoons wine vinegar*

*6 peppercorns*

FOR THE CASSEROLE:

*15ml/1 tablespoon oil*

*30g/1oz butter*

*110g/4oz onions, peeled*

*1 garlic clove, crushed*

*110g/4oz button mushrooms*

*10ml/2 teaspoons flour*

*150ml/¹/₄ pint beef stock*

*15ml/1 tablespoon cranberry jam*

*salt and freshly ground black pepper*

*55g/2oz fresh cranberries*

*15g/¹/₂oz sugar*

*110g/4oz cooked whole chestnuts*

*chopped parsley*

1. Cut the venison into 5cm/2inch cubes, trimming away any tough membrane or sinew.

2. Mix the ingredients for the marinade together and add the meat. Mix well, cover and leave in a cool place or in the refrigerator overnight.

3. Set the oven to 170°C/325°F/gas mark 3.

4. Lift out the venison cubes and pat dry with absorbent paper. Strain the marinade, reserving the liquid for cooking.

5. Heat half the oil in a heavy saucepan and brown the cubes of meat, frying a few at a time. Lay them in a casserole. If the bottom of the pan becomes brown or too dry, pour in a little of the strained marinade, swish it about, scraping off the sediment stuck to the bottom, and pour over the cubes of meat. Then heat a little more oil and continue browning the meat.

6. When all the meat has been browned, repeat the déglaçage (boiling up with a little marinade and scraping the bottom of the pan).

7. Now melt the butter and fry the onions and garlic until the onions are pale brown all over. Add the mushrooms and continue cooking for 2 minutes.

8. Stir in the flour and cook for 1 minute. Remove from the heat, add the rest of the

marinade and the beef stock, return to the heat and stir until boiling, again scraping the bottom of the pan. When boiling, pour over the venison.

9. Add the cranberry jam. Season with salt and pepper.

10. Cover the casserole and place in the heated oven for about 2 hours or until the meat is really tender.

11. Meanwhile cook the cranberries briefly with the sugar in 30-45ml/2-3 tablespoons water until just soft but not crushed. Strain off the liquor. Lift the venison pieces, mushrooms and onions with a perforated spoon into a serving dish.

12. Boil the sauce fast until reduced to a shiny, almost syrupy, consistency. Add the chestnuts and cranberries and simmer gently for 5 minutes.

13. Pour the sauce over the venison and serve garnished with chopped parsley.

FULL RED

# Braised Pork Fillets with Pickled Lemons

This recipe uses pickled lemons which take 3 weeks to mature. Lemon juice can be used instead but the flavour is not as good.

SERVES 6

*900g/2lb pork fillets*
*salt and freshly ground black pepper*
*15ml/1 tablespoon olive oil from the jar of*
    *pickled lemons*
*1 medium onion, cut in quarters*
*1 large or two small garlic cloves, cut in half*
*5ml/1 teaspoon cinnamon*
*5ml/1 teaspoon ground ginger*
*150ml/¼ pint red wine*
*290ml/½ pint chicken stock*
*10 slices of pickled lemon (see page 70)*
*10 black olives, pitted (optional)*

1. Heat the oven to 170°C/ 325°F/gas mark 3.

2. Trim the pork fillets of any fat and membrane but leave in whole pieces. Season with a little salt and pepper.

3. Heat the oil in a frying pan and brown the fillets all over. Lift into a casserole dish.

4. Add the pieces of onion and garlic to the frying pan and brown lightly. Place them, with the meat, in the casserole dish. Fry the cinnamon and ginger for 30 seconds, add the wine and stock and bring up to the boil. Pour over the meat and place the casserole in the oven for 30 minutes.

5. Lift the pork out of the casserole and liquidize all the remaining contents of the dish until smooth.

6. Pour back over the meat and add the lemon slices and olives, if using. Put back in the oven for 15 minutes.

7. To serve: slice the meat into 2cm/¾ inch slices and serve the sauce separately. Serve with Boulangère potatoes and parsnip purée.

MEDIUM RED

# Carbonnade de Boeuf with Savoury Crumble Topping

SERVES 4-6

900g/2lb chuck steak
15ml/1 tablespoon beef dripping
3 onions, finely sliced
1 garlic clove, crushed
10ml/2 teaspoons brown sugar
10ml/2 teaspoons flour
290ml/½ pint brown ale
290ml/½ pint brown stock
5ml/1 teaspoon wine vinegar
1 bay leaf
pinch of thyme
pinch of nutmeg
salt and freshly ground black pepper

FOR THE TOPPING:

55g/2oz butter
1 garlic clove, crushed
15ml/1 tablespoon grainy mustard
15ml/1 tablespoon Dijon mustard
170g/6oz fresh white breadcrumbs
15ml/1 tablespoon chopped fresh marjoram
15ml/1 tablespoon chopped fresh mixed herbs e.g.
    mint, thyme, rosemary and parsley
salt and freshly ground black pepper

1. Set the oven to 150°C/300°F/gas mark 2.
2. Cut the beef into small steaks, cutting across the grain of the meat. Melt half of the dripping in a large frying pan and fry the steaks, a few at a time, until browned all over, putting them into a flameproof casserole as they are browned. If the bottom of the pan becomes very dark or too dry, pour in a little of the stock, swish it about, scraping off the sediment stuck to the bottom, and pour over the meat. Heat up a little more fat and continue to brown the meat. When it is all brown, repeat the déglaçage (adding the stock and scraping the pan).
3. Fry the onions slowly and, when beginning to brown, add the garlic and sugar. Cook for a further minute or until nicely brown.
4. Stir in the flour and cook, stirring, over the heat for 1 minute. Remove from the heat and pour in the brown ale and the remaining stock.
5. Return to the heat and bring slowly to the boil, stirring continuously. Pour into the casserole and add the vinegar, bay leaf, thyme, nutmeg, salt and pepper.
6. Cover and bring to simmering point over direct heat, simmer for 5 minutes, then bake for 2-3 hours. Raise the oven temperature to 190°C/375°F/gas mark 5.
7. Meanwhile, make the topping: melt the butter in the small saucepan, add the garlic and cook over a gentle heat for 1 minute.
8. Put both mustards in a medium-sized bowl, add the butter and garlic and mix well. Stir in the breadcrumbs and herbs. Season to taste with salt and pepper.
9. When the carbonnade is cooked, sprinkle the topping mixture over the top of the casserole. Replace it, uncovered, in the oven for 25 minutes, or until it is brown and crunchy on the top.

FULL RED

❊ ❊ ❊ ❊ ❊ ❊ ❊ ❊ ❊ ❊ ❊ ❊ ❊ ❊ ❊ ❊ ❊ ❊ ❊

# Roast Goose with Apple Sauce

SERVES 6

4.5kg/10lb goose

salt and freshly ground black pepper

lemon

TO FINISH:

15ml/1 tablespoon honey

FOR THE GRAVY:

570ml/1 pint white stock (see page 178) or goose
    stock made from the giblets without the liver (see
    recipe for turkey stock (1) on page 179)

TO SERVE:

apple sauce (see page 198)

TO GARNISH:

1 small bunch of watercress

1. Wipe the goose all over. Season the inside
with salt and pepper and rub with a cut lemon.
2. Set the oven to 190°C/375°F/gas mark 5.
3. Weigh the goose and establish the cooking
time. Allow 15 minutes to the 450g/1lb and
15 minutes over.
4. Prick the goose all over and sprinkle with salt.
Place on a wire rack over a roasting pan.
Roast, basting occasionally, but do not worry if
you forget as goose is very fatty. Every so often
you will have to remove fat from the roasting
pan with a plastic baster. Do not throw it away
as it is wonderful for cooking. If the goose gets
too dark, cover it with aluminium foil.
5. Ten minutes before the bird is cooked, remove
from the oven and spread the honey evenly over
the skin – this will help to make it crisp. When
the goose is cooked, turn off the oven and place
the bird on a serving plate and return to the oven.
6. Make the gravy: carefully spoon off all the fat
in the roasting pan, leaving the cooking juices
behind. Scrape off and discard any burnt pieces
stuck to the bottom of the pan. Add the stock
and bring up to the boil, whisking well, and
simmer for about 15 minutes. Increase the heat
and boil until syrupy. Season to taste and boil
for 30 seconds. Strain into a warm gravy boat.
7. Garnish the goose with the watercress,
and serve the apple sauce and gravy separately.

RICH, FRUITY RED

❊ ❊ ❊ ❊ ❊ ❊ ❊ ❊ ❊ ❊ ❊ ❊ ❊ ❊ ❊ ❊ ❊ ❊ ❊ ❊

# Roast Goose Mary-Claire

A 4. 5kg/10lb goose may sound huge for 6 people
but most of a goose seems to be carcase!
Therefore this goose has a lot of delicious,
Middle Eastern-style stuffing. It is a similar
stuffing to that made by Leith's Good Food
for its famous roast stuffed duck. Be careful not
to overcook the goose or it will become dry
and tough.

SERVES 6

*4.5kg/10lb goose*

*salt and freshly ground black pepper*

*1/2 lemon*

FOR THE STUFFING:

*30g/1oz butter*

*1 onion, finely chopped*

*285g/10oz chicken breast, minced (or cut in 4 if*
*    using a food processor)*

*15ml/1 tablespoon sage, lightly chopped*

*340g/12oz dessert apples, peeled, cored and chopped*

*10 dried apricots, soaked for 2 hours, drained*
*    and chopped*

*55g/2oz unsalted pistachio nuts, lightly chopped*

*55g/2oz shredded beef suet*

*85g/3oz fresh breadcrumbs*

*1 egg*

TO FINISH:

*15ml/1 tablespoon honey*

FOR THE GRAVY:

*570ml/1 pint white stock (see page 178) or goose*
*    stock made from the giblets without the liver (see*
*    recipe for turkey stock (1) on page 179)*

*30ml/2 tablespoons Calvados*

TO GARNISH:

*bunch of watercress*

1. Wipe the goose all over. Season the inside with salt and pepper and rub with a cut lemon.

2. Set the oven to 190°C/375°F/gas mark 5.

3. Make the stuffing: melt the butter, add the onion and cook for about 10 minutes until soft but not coloured. Beat together the chicken, onion, sage, apple, apricots, pistachio nuts and suet. Add enough of the breadcrumbs to make a firm but not solid stuffing. Season to taste. Add the egg and beat really well. You can make it in a food processor, but leave out the pistachios and stir them in at the end.

4. Fill the goose cavity with the stuffing. Weigh the goose, with stuffing, to establish the cooking time. Allow 15 minutes to 450g/1lb and 15 minutes over.

5. Prick the goose all over and sprinkle with salt. Place on a wire rack over a roasting pan. Roast, basting occasionally, but do not worry if you forget as a goose is very fatty. Every so often you will have to remove fat from the roasting tin with a plastic baster. Do not throw it away as it is wonderful for cooking. If the goose gets too dark, cover it with tin foil.

6. Ten minutes before the bird is cooked, spread the honey evenly over the skin. This will help to make it crisp. When the goose is cooked, place on a serving plate and return to the oven, which you have turned off.

7. Make the gravy: carefully spoon off all the fat in the roasting pan, leaving the cooking juices behind. Scrape off and discard any burnt pieces stuck to the bottom of the pan. Add the stock and, if you can, a little of the stuffing. Bring up to the boil, whisk well and simmer for about 15 minutes. Increase the heat and boil until syrupy, add the Calvados, season to taste and boil for 30 seconds. Taste and strain into a warm gravy boat.

8. Garnish the goose with watercress.

RED BURGUNDY

❄ ❄ ❄ ❄ ❄ ❄ ❄ ❄ ❄ ❄ ❄ ❄ ❄ ❄ ❄ ❄ ❄ ❄ ❄ ❄

# Spicy Grilled Chicken

When we tested this recipe we inadvertently left the chicken breasts marinating for 24 hours. The result was wonderful – the chicken tasted spicy and almost smoked, and the texture was meltingly tender.

SERVES 4

*4 chicken breasts, skinned*
*1 large red pepper*
*8 large shitake mushrooms*
*1 small garlic clove, crushed*
*15ml/1 tablespoon olive oil*
*110g/4oz mange tout*
*45ml/1 1/2 fl oz extra virgin olive oil*

FOR THE MARINADE:

*7.5ml/1 1/2 teaspoons Hoisin sauce*
*85ml/3fl oz soy sauce*
*85ml/3fl oz dry vermouth*
*85ml/3fl oz orange juice, strained*
*4ml/1 scant teaspoon five spice powder*
*2.5ml/1/2 teaspoon ground cumin*
*1 garlic clove, crushed or chopped*
*10ml/2 teaspoons honey*
*2 cardamom pods, hulled and the seeds crushed*
*1 small strip orange peel*

TO GARNISH:
*fresh coriander*

1. Mix together all the ingredients for the marinade. Put the chicken breasts in a bowl, pour over the marinade and leave for at least 4 hours – preferably 24 hours.
2. Heat the grill.
3. Cut the pepper into quarters and grill, skin side up until black and blistered. Peel off the skin and cut the pepper into wide strips.
4. Divide the garlic between the upturned cups of the shitake mushrooms, drizzle with oil and set aside until ready to grill.
5. Top and tail the mange tout and blanch in salted water for 1 minute. Drain.
6. Remove the chicken breasts from their marinade (but reserve the marinade). Grill, brushing regularly with the marinade, until cooked, about 12 minutes. Remove and set aside for 5 minutes until cool enough to handle. Grill the prepared mushrooms for 2 minutes.
7. Meanwhile, strain the reserved marinade into a saucepan and reduce, by boiling rapidly, to a syrupy consistency.
8. While the marinade reduces, slice the chicken flesh into 1.25cm/1/2in strips.
9. Mix together the chicken, peppers, mange tout and grilled mushrooms.
10. When the marinade is syrupy, whisk in the olive oil and pour the sauce over the chicken and vegetables. Garnish with fresh coriander.

NOTE: This recipe has been adapted from a recipe in *Belle Entertaining*.

LIGHT RED

✳ ✳ ✳ ✳ ✳ ✳ ✳ ✳ ✳ ✳ ✳ ✳ ✳ ✳ ✳ ✳ ✳ ✳ ✳ ✳

# Boned Stuffed Chicken

SERVES 6

*1 x 1.8kg/4lb chicken*
*55g/2oz butter, melted*

FOR THE STUFFING:

*170g/6oz ricotta cheese*
*1 egg*
*85g/3oz white breadcrumbs*
*55g/2oz sun-dried tomatoes, cut into slivers*
*30g/1oz black olives, pitted*
*15ml/1 tablespoon coarsely chopped fresh basil*
*salt and freshly ground black pepper*

FOR THE GARNISH:
*extra basil*

1. Bone the chicken completely, including the legs and wings (see page 209).
2. Set the oven to 200°C/400°F/gas mark 6.
3. Make the stuffing: beat the ricotta cheese, add the egg and beat again. Add the breadcrumbs, sun-dried tomatoes, olives and basil. Season to taste.
4. Use this stuffing to fill the boned chicken. Draw up the sides and wrap the chicken up in a piece of muslin or a clean 'J' cloth saturated with the melted butter. Tie the chicken at either end so that it looks rather like a Christmas cracker.
5. Place the chicken on a wire rack over a roasting pan and bake for 1½ hours.
6. Unwrap the chicken and serve hot or cold garnished with fresh basil leaves.

LIGHT RED/ROSE

# Scallops with Red Pepper Butter Sauce

SERVES 4

*1 large red pepper, halved and deseeded*
*12 scallops, cut in half horizontally*
*30ml/2 tablespoons white wine*
*140g/5oz unsalted butter*
*1 shallot, chopped*
*110ml/4fl oz Noilly Prat or other dry Vermouth*
*150ml/¼ pint double cream*

FOR THE GARNISH:
*1 small cucumber cut into julienne strips, blanched*
*15g/½oz butter*

1. Preheat the oven to 190°C/375°F/gas mark 5.
2. Put the red pepper, cut side down, on to a greased baking tray. Bake in the preheated oven for about 20 minutes or until the skin blisters and the flesh is cooked. Allow to cool and then remove the skin. Purée the flesh in a liquidizer. Turn the oven off.
3. Season the scallops with salt and pepper. Put them in a pan with the wine and 15ml/ 1 tablespoon water. Toss them quickly over a medium heat until they are just cooked. Keep warm in the switched-off oven.

4. Melt 30g/1oz of the butter, add the shallot, and cook for 1 minute. Add the Noilly Prat, bring to the boil and reduce, by boiling rapidly, to half its original quantity. Add the cream, bring back up to the boil and simmer for 1 minute. Carefully whisk in the remaining butter, little by little. Add the red pepper purée, reheat and season. Strain the sauce.

5. Pour a little of the sauce on to 4 large plates. Place the cooked scallops in a circle on top of the sauce. Quickly toss the cucumber strips in the butter and arrange in the centre of each circle of scallops.

VERY DRY WHITE

# Polenta and ✔ Aubergine Cakes

SERVES 4

*2 aubergines*
*salt and freshly ground black pepper*
*225g/8oz coarse grained cornmeal*
*110g/4oz Parmesan cheese, grated*
*pinch of cayenne pepper*
*55ml/2fl oz olive oil*
*1 shallot, finely chopped*
*1 garlic clove, finely chopped*
*1 sprig of thyme*
*225g/8oz tomatoes, skinned, deseeded and*
    *roughly chopped*
*15ml/1 tablespoon tomato purée*
*pinch of sugar*
*8 basil leaves, roughly chopped*
*15ml/1 tablespoon oregano, roughly chopped*
*85g/3oz Feta cheese, crumbled*
*55g/2oz Mozzarella, grated*

1. Set the oven to 180°C/350°F/gas mark 4.
2. Slice the aubergine into 1cm/½ inch thick rounds. Place on a wire rack and sprinkle with a little salt. Leave them for 30 minutes.

Rinse the salt off and pat dry.
3. Bring 1 litre/1¾ pints water to the boil and add 7.5ml/1½ teaspoons salt. Add the cornmeal in a steady stream, whisking steadily to prevent the formation of lumps. Cook slowly for 20-25 minutes, stirring all the time. If necessary, add more water. The polenta should be thick enough for a wooden spoon to stand up in it. While it is still very hot, add the cheese, cayenne pepper and freshly ground black pepper. Taste and add more seasoning if necessary.

Pour the mixture on to a greased tray in a layer 5mm/¼ inch thick. Set aside to cool.
4. Heal 15ml/1 tablespoon of oil in a saucepan and in it gently cook the shallot and garlic until soft. Add the thyme, tomatoes, tomato purée, sugar, salt and pepper. Cook for 6-7 minutes until it is almost a purée. Taste and add more seasoning if necessary.
5. Heat the remaining olive oil in a frying pan and fry the aubergine slices on both sides until golden brown, adding more oil if necessary. Drain well on kitchen paper.
6. Cut the polenta into 12 x 7.5cm/3 inch diameter rounds.
7. To assemble: put 4 rings of polenta into a greased ovenproof gratin dish. Spread each one

with a spoonful of the tomato sauce and lay a slice of aubergine on top. Sprinkle with basil, oregano and black pepper. Continue to layer up in the same order but finish with a layer of polenta.
8. Mix the cheeses together and sprinkle over the polenta cakes.

9. Bake in the preheated oven for 20-25 minutes.

NOTE: This recipe has been adapted from a recipe in *Naturally* by Anton Mosimann.

LIGHT RED/ROSE

❋❋❋❋❋❋❋❋❋❋❋❋❋❋❋❋❋❋❋❋

# Chicken Curry with Almonds

SERVES 8

*8 chicken breasts*
*60ml/4 tablespoons sunflower oil*
*85g/3oz blanched almonds*
*10ml/2 teaspoons ground cardamom*
*5ml/1 teaspoon ground cloves*
*5ml/1 teaspoon ground chilli*
*20ml/4 teaspoons ground cumin*
*20ml/4 teaspoons ground coriander*
*10ml/2 teaspoons ground turmeric*
*2 onions, finely chopped*
*2 garlic cloves, crushed*
*2.5cm/1inch piece root ginger, finely chopped*
*400g//14oz tinned tomatoes, chopped*
*150ml/¼ pint water*
*salt and freshly ground black pepper*
*30ml/2 tablespoons Greek yoghurt*
*few leaves coriander to garnish*

1. Set the oven to 190°C/375°F/gas mark 5.
2. Pick over the chicken breasts, removing any fat or gristle. Set aside.
3. Put 15ml/1 tablespoon oil into a saucepan and fry the almonds until golden brown but not burnt. Set aside. Add a further tablespoon of oil and in it slowly cook the spices for 1 minute.
4. Liquidize together the almonds and cooked spices with enough water to make a smooth paste.
5. Rinse out the saucepan, add 30ml/2 more tablespoons of oil and in it fry the onions, garlic and ginger until the onions are golden brown.
6. Reduce the heat and add the tomatoes, spice and almond paste, seasoning and 150ml/¼ pint water. Stir well and simmer for 2 or 3 minutes.
7. Tip the sauce into an ovenproof dish. Add the chicken breasts and spoon over some of the sauce. Cover with tin foil and bake for 40 minutes or until the chicken is cooked.
8. Transfer the chicken to a warm serving dish. Swirl the yoghurt into the sauce. Pour over the chicken breasts and garnish with fresh coriander.

RED RHONE

❋❋❋❋❋❋❋❋❋❋❋❋❋❋❋❋❋❋❋❋

# Leek, Mushroom and Chestnut Filo Pie ✔

SERVES 8–10

2 red peppers
900g/2lb leeks
30ml/2 tablespoons oil
1 cooking apple, peeled, cored and quartered
2 garlic cloves, crushed
450g/1lb mushrooms, sliced
55g/2oz butter
55g/2oz flour
100ml/3½ fl oz white wine
570ml/1 pint milk
pinch of freshly grated nutmeg
salt and freshly ground black pepper
110g/4oz Cheddar cheese, grated
225g/8oz peeled chestnuts
10 sheets of filo pastry
45ml/3 tablespoons oil
15ml/1 tablespoon sesame seeds

1. Preheat the oven to 200°C/400°F/gas mark 6.
2. Cut the red peppers in half, remove the seeds and grill until the skin is charred and blackened. Remove the skin and cut the flesh into dice.
3. Cut the leeks into 2.5cm/1 inch lengths, wash them well and place in a pan of boiling salted water for 3 minutes. Drain and refresh under cold running water.
4. Heat the oil in a large saucepan, add the apple and garlic and fry gently for 2 minutes, or until the apple begins to break up. Add the mushrooms and cook for 5 minutes, stirring all the time. Add the red peppers and then transfer to a large bowl. Add the leeks and leave to cool.
5. Melt the butter in a large pan, add the flour and cook for 2 minutes. Take the pan off the heat and add the white wine. Stir well and add half of the milk. Bring to the boil, stirring all the time, and add the rest of the milk. Allow the sauce to boil for at least 2 minutes. Season with nutmeg, salt and pepper. Remove from the heat and stir in the cheese. Pour over the vegetables, and mix well. Allow to cool, then stir in the chestnuts.
6. When the sauce is cold, line a large ovenproof dish, 25x20cm/10x8 inches with 3 sheets of filo pastry, brushing each sheet with oil. Pour in the vegetable mixture and cover with 7 more layers of filo pastry, again brushing each layer with oil. Brush the top with oil and sprinkle with sesame seeds.
7. Bake in the preheated oven for 45 minutes until the top is golden brown.

RED BURGUNDY

❈❈❈❈❈❈❈❈❈❈❈❈❈❈❈❈❈❈❈❈❈❈

\*\*\*\*\*\*\*\*\*\*\*\*\*\*\*\*\*\*\*\*\*\*\*\*\*\*\*

# VEGETABLES

\*\*\*\*\*\*\*\*\*\*\*\*\*\*\*\*\*\*\*\*\*\*\*\*\*\*\*

*Mashed potatoes*
*Pommes Anna*
*Rösti potatoes*
*Boulangère potatoes*
*Leith's Good Food's Dauphinoise potatoes*
*Celeriac purée*
*Parsnip purée*
*Glazed vegetables*
*Red cabbage*
*Roast parsnips*

\*\*\*\*\*\*\*\*\*\*\*\*\*\*\*\*\*\*\*\*\*\*\*\*\*\*\*

# Mashed Potatoes

SERVES 4

*675g/1¹/2lb potatoes, peeled*
*about 290ml/¹/2 pint milk*
*55g/2oz butter*
*salt and pepper*
*a little grated nutmeg*

1. Boil the potatoes in salted water until tender. Drain thoroughly.
2. Push the potatoes through a sieve or mouli. Return them to the dry saucepan. Heat carefully, stirring to allow the potato to steam dry.
3. Push the mass of potato to one side of the pan. Put the exposed part of the pan over direct heat and pour in the milk. Tilt the pan to allow the milk to boil without burning the potato.
4. When the milk is boiling, or near it, beat it into the potato. Add the butter. Season with salt, pepper and nutmeg.

NOTE I: This recipe is for very soft mashed potatoes. If you want a stiffer consistency add less milk.

NOTE II: For mashed potatoes with olive oil, add half the quantity of milk, as above, then beat in 150ml/¹/4 pint olive oil instead of the butter and season to taste.

# Pommes Anna

SERVES 4

*675g/1¹/2lb potatoes, peeled and finely sliced*
*55g/2oz butter, clarified (see note below)*
*salt and pepper*
*grated nutmeg*

1. Heat the oven to 190°C/375°F/gas mark 5. Brush a heavy ovenproof pan with the butter.
2. Arrange a neat layer of overlapping potato slices on the bottom of the pan. Brush the potatoes with the melted butter and season well with salt, pepper and nutmeg.
3. Continue to layer the potatoes, butter and seasoning until all the potatoes have been used. Finish with butter and seasoning.
4. Hold the pan over direct medium heat for 2 minutes to brown the bottom layer of potatoes.
5. Take off and cover with greased paper and a lid or foil. Bake in the oven for about 45 minutes.
6. When the potatoes are tender, invert a serving plate over the pan and turn the potatoes out so that the neat first layer is now on top.

NOTE: To make clarified butter, heat the butter until foaming without allowing it to burn. Pour it through fine muslin or a double layer of 'J' cloth.

# Rösti Potatoes

SERVES 4

*1 Spanish onion, finely chopped*
*55g/2oz streaky bacon, finely chopped*
*oil*
*675g/1 1/2lb large potatoes, peeled*
*salt and freshly ground black pepper*
*butter*

1. Take a 23cm/9 inch frying pan and put into it the onion and bacon and 15ml/1 tablespoon oil.
2. Cook slowly over gentle heat until the onion is transparent and soft but not coloured. Remove from the heat.
3. Coarsely grate the potatoes. Season with salt and pepper. Fork in the onion and bacon.
4. Heat 15ml/1 tablespoon mixed butter and oil in the frying pan. Add the potato mixture. Pat it lightly into a flat cake with straight sides.
5. Fry gently until the underside is crusty and golden brown (about 15 minutes). Shake the pan every so often to ensure that the cake does not stick.
6. Place a plate larger than the frying pan over the pan and turn both plate and pan over to tip the rösti out on to the plate. Slip it immediately back into the pan to cook the other side for 5 minutes. Place in a warm oven for 15 minutes, if necessary. Serve on a large flat dish, cut into wedges like a cake.

NOTE: Finely grated raw carrots are sometimes added to the mixture. The potato cake can be baked in the oven at 190°C/375°F/gas mark 5 for about 30 minutes rather than fried.

# Boulangère Potatoes

SERVES 4

*675g/1 1/2lb potatoes, very thinly sliced*
*30g/1oz butter*
*1 small onion, very thinly sliced*
*salt and freshly ground black pepper*
*290ml/1/2 pint chicken stock*

1. Heat the oven to 170°C/325°F/gas mark 3.
2. Butter a pie dish and arrange the potatoes in layers with the onion, adding a little salt and pepper as you go.
3. Arrange the top layer of potatoes in overlapping slices.
4. Dot with the rest of the butter and pour in the stock. Press the potatoes down firmly – they should be completely submerged in the stock.
5. Bake in the oven for about 1 1/2 hours or until the potatoes are tender and the top browned.

# Leith's Good Food's Dauphinoise Potatoes

900g/2lb old floury potatoes, peeled and finely sliced
1 onion, finely sliced
1 garlic clove, crushed (optional)
15g/½oz butter

425ml/¾ pint mixed single and double cream
150ml/¼ pint soured cream, let down to double cream consistency with milk
salt and freshly ground black pepper

1. Preheat the oven to 170°C/325°F/gas mark 3.
2. Cook the onions and garlic in the butter until soft but not brown.
3. Layer up the potatoes and creams with the onions and seasoning in a lightly buttered dish, and bake in the oven for 1½ hours.

# Celeriac Purée

SERVES 4
2 medium potatoes
225/8oz celeriac
290ml/½ pint milk
55g/2oz butter
salt and white pepper

1. Wash and peel the potatoes and place them in a pan of cold salted water. Bring to the boil, cover and simmer for 25 minutes until tender.
2. Meanwhile, wash the celeriac, peel it and cut into chunks. Simmer slowly in the milk for about 20-30 minutes until tender.
3. Mash the celeriac with its milk, which should by now be much reduced.
4. Drain the potatoes and mash or sieve them. Place the potatoes and celeriac together in a pan. Beat over a gentle heat, adding the butter as you mix. Add salt and pepper to taste.
5. Pile into a serving dish and serve at once.

# Parsnip Purée

SERVES 6

*675g/1 1/2lb parsnips*
*55ml/2 fl oz double cream*
*30g/1oz butter*
*salt and pepper*

1. Peel the parsnips and cut them into large chunks.

2. Tip into a pan of lightly salted boiling water and simmer until very tender.

3. Drain the parsnips and either put into a food processor and process with the cream and butter, or mash with a fork or potato masher, adding the cream and butter. Season to taste with salt and pepper.

NOTE: This can be made in advance and reheated in the oven in a covered dish.

✳ ✳ ✳ ✳ ✳ ✳ ✳ ✳ ✳ ✳ ✳ ✳ ✳ ✳ ✳ ✳ ✳ ✳ ✳ ✳

# Glazed Vegetables

SERVES 6-8

*450g/1lb large potatoes*
*450g/1lb carrots*
*450g/1lb turnips*
*12 button onions*
*15ml/1 tablespoon bacon or pork dripping*
*2.5ml/1/2 teaspoon sugar*
*salt and freshly ground black pepper*
*55g/2oz butter*
*110g/4oz button mushrooms*
*juice of 1/2 lemon*
*15ml/1 tablespoon chopped fresh parsley*

1. Wash and peel the potatoes, carrots and turnips. Using a melon scoop, scoop the flesh of the potato into balls. Dry them in a clean cloth. Trim the carrots and turnips into small barrel shapes.

2. Peel the onions. Dipping them into boiling water for 10 seconds makes this easier.

3. Heat the oven to 200°C/400°F/gas mark 6.

4. Put the prepared vegetables in a roasting pan and baste with the dripping. Roast, shaking the pan occasionally and turning the vegetables over, for 45 minutes.

5. When the vegetables are tender, put the roasting pan over direct heat, add the sugar and shake the pan until browned to a good even colour. Season with salt and pepper. Keep warm.

6. Melt the butter over a good heat and toss the mushrooms in it. Shake the pan to make sure that every mushroom is coated with butter. When they are beginning to brown, add the lemon juice and allow this to sizzle and evaporate a little. Add salt and pepper and the chopped parsley.

7. Serve the vegetables mixed together on a heated dish.

NOTE I: If these vegetables are to accompany a roast meat, the root vegetables can be cooked in the meat roasting tin. Add them about 30 minutes before the meat is due to come out.

NOTE II: The root vegetables can be 'pot roasted' instead of cooked in the oven. This is a good idea if nothing else is being baked or roasted at the time, when it would be wasteful to heat the oven just for this dish. In a heavy casserole or pan toss the vegetables in the fat. Cover with a lid, and turn the heat down low. Cook like this for 20 minutes or until the vegetables are tender, giving the pan a

shake every now and then to prevent sticking. When they are cooked, brown them with the sugar, and fry the mushrooms etc. as described above.

# Red Cabbage

SERVES 6
*1 small red cabbage*
*1 onion, sliced*
*30g/1oz butter*
*1 small cooking apple, peeled, cored and sliced*
*1 small dessert apple, peeled, cored and sliced*
*10ml/2 teaspoons brown sugar*
*10ml/2 teaspoons vinegar*
*pinch of ground cloves*
*salt and freshly ground black pepper*

1. Shred the cabbage and discard the hard stalks. Rinse well.
2. In a large saucepan, fry the onion in the butter until it begins to soften.
3. Add the drained but still wet cabbage, the apples, sugar, vinegar and cloves, and season with salt and pepper.
4. Cover tightly and cook very slowly, mixing well and stirring every 15 minutes or so. Cook for 2 hours, or until the whole mass is soft and reduced in bulk. (During the cooking it may be necessary to add a little water.)
5. Taste and add more salt, pepper or sugar if necessary.

# Roast Parsnips

SERVES 4
*75g/1 1/2lb parsnips*
*oil*
*salt and freshly ground black pepper*

1. Heat the oven to 200°C/400°F/gas mark 6.
2. Wash and peel the parsnips. Cut in half lengthways.
3. Boil in salted water for 5 minutes. Drain well.
4. Heat 1cm/1/2 inch of oil in a roasting tin in the oven. When the oil is hot, add the parsnips. Season with salt and pepper.
5. Roast the parsnips, basting and turning during cooking until they are crisp and golden brown – this will take about 30 minutes.

❄❄❄❄❄❄❄❄❄❄❄❄❄❄❄❄❄❄❄❄❄❄❄

# PUDDINGS

❄❄❄❄❄❄❄❄❄❄❄❄❄❄❄❄❄❄❄❄❄❄❄

*Apple and orange crumble*
*Orange mousse*
*Bread and butter pudding*
*Melon and champagne sorbet*
*Lemon curd ice cream*
*Rich vanilla ice cream*
*Vanilla and prune ice cream*
*Ginger ice cream*
*Warm winter fruit salad*
*Mincemeat flan (1)*
*Mincemeat flan (2)*
*Banana pudding with toffee sauce*
*Apple Charlottes*
*Light Christmas pudding*
*Chocolate layer pudding*
*St Clements flan*
*Oranges in caramel*
*Caramel sauce*
*Atholl Brose*
*Trifle*
*Meringues (Swiss meringues)*

❄❄❄❄❄❄❄❄❄❄❄❄❄❄❄❄❄❄❄❄❄❄❄

# Apple and Orange Crumble

SERVES 4

*3 oranges*
*900g/2lb cooking apples*
*45ml/3 tablespoons demerara sugar*
*pinch of cinnamon*

FOR THE CRUMBLE:
*170g/6oz plain flour*
*pinch of salt*
*110g/4oz butter*
*55g/2oz sugar*

1. Peel the oranges as you would an apple, with a sharp knife, removing all the pith. Cut out the orange segments leaving behind the membranes.
2. Peel and core the apples. Cut into thick slices. Mix with the orange segments and their juice. Add the sugar and cinnamon. Tip into an ovenproof dish.
3. Set the oven to 200°C/400°F/gas mark 6.
4. Sift the flour and salt into a bowl. Rub in the fat and when the mixture resembles coarse breadcrumbs mix in the sugar. Sprinkle it over the apples and oranges.
5. Bake on a hot baking sheet for 45 minutes or until hot and slightly browned on top.

NOTE: If using wholemeal flour for the crumble topping, use 140g/5oz of melted butter. Instead of rubbing it into the flour, mix briskly with a knife.

SWEET WHITE

# Orange Mousse

This is a very low-fat, sugar-free mousse.

SERVES 4-6
*150ml/¹/4 pint water*
*15g/¹/2oz or 1 envelope of gelatine*
*200ml/7 fl oz carton frozen concentrated orange juice, defrosted*
*15ml/1 tablespoon brandy*
*290ml/¹/2 pint low-fat natural yoghurt*
*2 egg whites*

1. Put 3 tablespoons of the water into a small saucepan. Sprinkle on the gelatine and leave it to become spongy. Dissolve the gelatine over a gentle heat; do not allow it to boil. When it is clear and warm, add it to the orange juice with the remaining water and the brandy. Stir this into the yoghurt.
2. Refrigerate the mixture until it is just beginning to set.
3. Whisk the egg whites until they are stiff but not dry. Fold them into the setting orange base and pour the mixture into a glass bowl. Leave it to set in the refrigerator for a few hours.

NOTE: To make orange ice cream, make the mousse as above and freeze until solid. Remove from the freezer 20 minutes before serving.

MEDIUM SWEET WHITE

# Bread and Butter Pudding

SERVES 4

*2 slices of plain bread*
*30g/1oz butter*
*30ml/2 tablespoons currants and sultanas, mixed*
*10ml/2 teaspoons candied peel*
*2 eggs and 1 yolk*
*15ml/1 rounded tablespoon sugar*
*290ml/¹/2 pint creamy milk*
*vanilla essence*
*ground cinnamon*
*demerara sugar*

1. Cut the crusts off the bread and spread with butter. Cut into quarters. Arrange in a shallow ovenproof dish, buttered side up, and sprinkle with currants, sultanas and candied peel.
2. Make the custard: mix the eggs and yolk with the sugar and stir in the milk and vanilla essence.
3. Pour the custard carefully over the bread and leave to soak for 30 minutes. Sprinkle with ground cinnamon and demerara sugar.
4. Heat the oven to 180°C/350°F/gas mark 4.
5. Place the pudding in a roasting pan of hot water and cook in the middle of the oven for about 45 minutes or until the custard is set and the top is brown and crusty.

NOTE: The pudding may be baked without the bain-marie (hot-water bath) quite successfully, but if used it will ensure a smooth, not bubbly, custard.

SWEET WHITE

❋ ❋ ❋ ❋ ❋ ❋ ❋ ❋ ❋ ❋ ❋ ❋ ❋ ❋ ❋ ❋ ❋ ❋ ❋ ❋ ❋

# Melon and Champagne Sorbet

SERVES 4-6

*1 large Ogen melon*
*340g/12oz granulated sugar*
*75ml/5 tablespoons water*
*juice of 1 lemon*
*425 ml/³/4 pint champagne*

1. Cut the melon into quarters. Remove the skin and seeds and liquidize or process until smooth.
2. Put the sugar and water into a heavy saucepan. Dissolve slowly on a gentle heat.
3. When the sugar has completely dissolved, boil rapidly until the syrup is tacky and a short thread can be formed if the syrup is pulled between finger and thumb.
4. Mix together the melon purée, lemon juice, champagne and warm syrup. Allow to cool.
5. Freeze overnight or until icy, then whisk until smooth and return to the freezer. Serve in well-chilled goblets.

NOTE: If you have an ice-cream machine, it makes short work of this sorbet. It is a soft sorbet because of the high alcoholic content.

SWEET CHAMPAGNE OR
SPARKLING WINE

# Lemon Curd Ice Cream

SERVES 6

*4 egg yolks*

*grated rind and juice of 2 lemons*

*125g/4¹/₂oz caster sugar*

*110g/4oz unsalted butter, at room temperature,*
*    cut into small pieces*

*570ml/1 pint natural yoghurt*

1. Put the egg yolks, lemon rind and juice, sugar and butter into a small saucepan. Put over a gentle heat and stir until the butter has melted and the curd coats the back of the spoon.
2. Allow the curd to cool and then stir the yoghurt into it. Cover closely and freeze.
3. Take the ice cream out of the freezer and put it into the refrigerator about an hour before serving.

MEDIUM SWEET WHITE

❄ ❄ ❄ ❄ ❄ ❄ ❄ ❄ ❄ ❄ ❄ ❄ ❄ ❄ ❄ ❄ ❄ ❄ ❄ ❄

# Rich Vanilla Ice Cream

This ice cream is made with a mousse base.

SERVES 6-8

*70g/2¹/₂oz granulated sugar*

*120ml/8 tablespoons water*

*1 vanilla pod*

*3 egg yolks*

*425ml/³/₄ pint double or single cream*

1. Put the sugar, water and vanilla pod into a saucepan and dissolve the sugar over a gentle heat, stirring.
2. Beat the egg yolks well. Half whip the cream.
3. When the sugar has dissolved, bring the syrup up to boiling point and boil 'to the thread'. Allow to cool for 1 minute. Remove the vanilla pod.
4. Whisk the egg yolks and gradually pour in the sugar syrup. Whisk until the mixture is very thick and will leave a trail.
5. Cool, whisking occasionally. Fold in the cream and freeze.
6. When the ice cream is half frozen, whisk again and return to the freezer.

NOTE: To boil to the thread: to test, dip your finger into cold water, then into a teaspoon of the hot syrup, which should form threads between your thumb and forefinger when they are drawn apart.

MEDIUM SWEET WHITE

❄ ❄ ❄ ❄ ❄ ❄ ❄ ❄ ❄ ❄ ❄ ❄ ❄ ❄ ❄ ❄ ❄ ❄ ❄ ❄

# Vanilla and Prune Ice Cream

SERVES 4

290ml/½ pint milk
290ml/½ pint double cream
2 vanilla pods, split lengthways
6 egg yolks
100g/3½oz sugar
8 prunes, stoned, cut in half and marinated in
    brandy for 24 hours

TO SERVE:
2 ripe peaches, halved

1. Scald the milk and cream with the vanilla pods.
2. Beat the egg yolks and sugar until creamy, add the milk mixture gradually and whisk together.
3. Return it to the saucepan and cook over a low heat, stirring constantly, until the custard coats the back of the spoon. Strain through a sieve into a bowl and allow to cool.
4. Freeze the mixture in a shallow tray.
5. Once frozen, take the ice cream out of the freezer and allow to soften at room temperature. Either place in a food processor and whizz to remove the ice crystals or use an electric beater. Fold in the prunes and brandy.
6. Place the ice cream back in the container and refreeze.
7. Serve with the peaches.

SWEET WHITE

# Ginger Ice Cream

SERVES 6

85g/3oz granulated sugar
150ml/¼ pint water
4 egg yolks
10ml/2 teaspoons ground ginger
570ml/1 pint double cream, lightly whipped
4 pieces stem ginger, cut into fine strips

1. Put the sugar and water into a small heavy pan. Dissolve over a gentle heat. Boil for 3 minutes. Remove from the heat and cool for 1 minute.
2. Put the egg yolks into a large bowl with the ground ginger, whisk lightly and pour on the warm sugar syrup (do not allow the syrup to touch the whisk if doing this in a machine). Fold in the cream. Freeze.
3. When the ice cream is half-frozen, whisk again and add the stem ginger. Freeze again.
4. Remove from the freezer half an hour before it is to be eaten and scoop into a glass bowl.

SWEET WHITE

# Warm Winter Fruit Salad

SERVES 4

450g/1lb mixed dried fruits, such as prunes,
    apricots, figs and apples
15ml/1 tablespoon Calvados or brandy
1.1 litres/2 pints cold Earl Grey tea
water to cover
60ml/4 tablespoons orange juice
3-4 cloves
5ml/1 teaspoon concentrated apple juice
5cm/2 inch cinnamon stick
1.25ml/¼ teaspoon mixed spice

pared rind of 1 lemon
1 star anise

1. Soak the mixed fruits in the Calvados or brandy and the tea and water. Leave overnight.
2. Pour the fruit into a saucepan, add the orange juice, cloves, apple juice, cinnamon, mixed spice, lemon rind and star anise. Bring the liquid to the boil and let it simmer slowly until the fruit is soft – this will take about 20 minutes. Remove the cloves, cinnamon, lemon rind and star anise. Serve hot, although the salad tastes equally good cold.

SWEET WHITE

✳ ✳ ✳ ✳ ✳ ✳ ✳ ✳ ✳ ✳ ✳ ✳ ✳ ✳ ✳ ✳ ✳ ✳ ✳ ✳ ✳ ✳

# Mincemeat Flan (1)

SERVES 8

rich shortcrust pastry made with 225g/8oz flour
    (see page 200) or pâte sucrée (see page 204)
caster sugar

FOR THE FILLING:
1 small cooking apple
55g/2oz butter
85g/3oz sultanas
85g/3oz raisins
85g/3oz currants
45g/1½oz mixed peel, chopped
45g/1½oz chopped almonds
grated rind of large lemon
2.5ml/½ teaspoon mixed spice
15ml/1 tablespoon brandy

85g/3oz brown sugar
1 banana, chopped

1. Heat the oven to 190°C/375°F/gas mark 5.
2. Roll the pastry out to 5mm/¼ inch thick, and line a 25cm/10 inch flan ring, keeping the pastry trimmings for the lattice decoration.
3. Bake blind for 20 minutes (see page 60).
4. For the mincemeat: grate the apple, skin and all. Melt the butter and add it, with all the other filling ingredients, to the apple. Mix well.
5. Fill the flan with the mincemeat. Cut the pastry trimmings into thin strips and lattice the top of the flan with them, sticking the ends down with a little water. Brush the lattice with water and sprinkle with caster sugar. Return to the oven for 10-12 minutes, removing the flan ring after 5 minutes to allow the sides of the pastry to cook to a pale brown.

# Mincemeat Flan (2)

SERVES 6-8

*340g/12oz quantity almond pastry (see page 200)*
*675g/1 ½lb mincemeat (see page 65)*
*icing sugar*

1. Preheat the oven to 180°C/350°F/gas mark 4.
2. Divide the pastry in half, and roll out one half to line the base and sides of a 22cm/9inch flan ring. Fill with the mincemeat and spread flat.
3. Roll out the remaining pastry to 5mm/¼inch thickness. Using a star cutter, if you have one, or a fluted biscuit cutter if not, cut out as many shapes as possible from the pastry. Arrange them on top of the mincemeat, starting at the outside and overlapping the shapes. Continue in this way until the top is completely covered.
4. Chill the flan in the refrigerator for 20 minutes and then bake in the preheated oven for 40 minutes, lowering the temperature if the pastry gets too brown.
5. Allow to cool slightly and then dust with sifted icing sugar.

FORTIFIED SWEET WINE

# Banana Pudding with Toffee Sauce

SERVES 6

*4 large ripe bananas*
*30ml/2 tablespoons water*
*225g/8oz butter*
*225g/8oz sugar*
*4 eggs, beaten*
*125g/4oz self-raising flour*
*5ml/1 teaspoon baking powder*
*5ml/1 teaspoon vanilla essence*

FOR THE TOFFEE SAUCE:
*140g/5oz butter*
*140g/5oz light soft brown sugar*
*290ml/½ pint double cream*

1. Set the oven to 180°C/350°F/gas mark 4.
2. To make the banana pudding: mash the bananas with a little water and cook for a few minutes over a low heat, then allow to cool.
3. Cream the butter and sugar together until pale and creamy and add the beaten eggs little by little beating well between each addition.
4. Sift the flour and baking powder together and fold them into the egg mixture. Add the banana and vanilla essence and mix well.
5. Pour the mixture into a greased and floured 18cm/7inch cake tin and bake in the preheated oven for 40 minutes or until the pudding is firm.
6. To make the toffee sauce: melt the butter, add the sugar and cook for 10 minutes, stirring constantly to prevent the sugar from burning. Take the mixture off the heat and slowly pour in the cream. It will hiss and splutter so take care. Bring the mixture to the boil again and cook until all the sugar lumps are dissolved.
7. Serve warm with the toffee sauce.

AUSTRALIAN LIQUEUR MUSCAT

# Apple Charlottes

SERVES 4

*55g/2oz granulated sugar*

*5 dessert apples, e.g. Discovery or Cox, peeled,
    cored and sliced*

*30ml/2 tablespoons Calvados*

*juice of 1 orange*

*pinch of ground cinnamon*

*70g/2¹/₂oz butter*

*8 slices white bread, crustless*

FOR THE SAUCE:

*55g/2oz granulated sugar*

*grated rind of 1 orange*

*15ml/1 tablespoon Calvados*

*55g/2oz butter, cut into small pieces*

1. Put the sugar into a heavy saucepan with 2 tablespoons of water and place over a low heat. The sugar should dissolve slowly and become lightly caramelized.

2. Add the apples to the caramel, stir and then add the Calvados, the orange juice, cinnamon and all but 15g/¹/₂oz of the butter. Simmer together for 2 minutes.

3. Set the oven to 200°C/400°F/gas mark 6.

4. Butter 4 ramekin dishes using most of the reserved butter.

5. Flatten the bread slightly with a rolling pin. Cut out 8 rounds and use 4 of the rounds to line the base of the ramekins. Use the rest of the bread to line the sides.

6. Drain the apple filling (but reserve the strained liquor) and pile the apple slices into the lined ramekins. Cover with the remaining rounds of bread, buttered on both sides.

7. Put the ramekins on to a baking tray and bake for 15-20 minutes.

8. Meanwhile, prepare the sauce: reduce the apple liquor, by boiling rapidly, to 150ml/¹/₄ pint. Set aside.

9. Put the sugar with 2 tablespoons of water into a heavy saucepan, and place over a low heat. Allow the sugar to dissolve and then caramelize. When lightly browned add the reduced apple juice, the orange rind and Calvados. Simmer for 1 minute and gradually whisk in the butter pieces.

10. To serve, turn the Apple Charlottes out on to individual plates and serve with the caramel sauce.

SWEET WHITE

❋ ❋ ❋ ❋ ❋ ❋ ❋ ❋ ❋ ❋ ❋ ❋ ❋ ❋ ❋ ❋ ❋ ❋

# Light Christmas Pudding

This pudding is made with no added fat or sugar and therefore is less rich and more moist and tangy than the traditional Christmas pudding (see page 26). The fruit should be soaked for 1-7 days in advance.

MAKES 2 PUDDINGS

*110g/4oz dried apple, chopped*
*110g/4oz dried apricots, chopped*
*110g/4oz dried figs, chopped*
*110g/4oz dried pitted prunes, chopped*
*225g/8oz raisins*
*225g/8oz sultanas*
*110g/4oz currants*
*55g/2oz candied orange peel*
*290ml/$^1$/2 pint cold tea*
*60ml/4 tablespoons brandy or rum*
*60ml/4 tablespoons medium sherry*
*1 large banana, mashed*
*225g/8oz grated carrot*
*30g/1oz chopped hazelnuts*
*30g/1oz ground almonds*
*3 eggs*
*15ml/1 tablespoon honey*
*5ml/1 teaspoon cinnamon*
*5ml/1 teaspoon mixed spice*
*5ml/1 teaspoon ginger*
*pinch of grated nutmeg*
*85g/3oz plain flour*
*170g/6oz fresh brown breadcrumbs*

1. Put all the dried fruit and candied peel in a bowl, and pour in the tea, brandy and sherry. Mix well and leave to soak in a cool place for at least 1 day or up to 7 days.
2. When the fruit has soaked, add the banana, carrot, hazelnuts and ground almonds to the mixture.
3. Beat the eggs with the honey and stir into the fruit mixture.
4. Sift the spices with the flour and add with the breadcrumbs to the pudding mixture. Stir well.
5. Place in 2x1.1litre/2 pint greased pudding basins and cover with two layers of greaseproof paper and one piece of foil. Tie with string and steam for 6 hours in the usual way.

NOTE: Christmas puddings can be kept for up to 1 year – after this period they begin to dry out. They can be frozen very successfully. Ideally a pudding should be made about 3-4 months before Christmas. To store a pudding recover it and keep in a cool dark place. To reheat steam for about 2 hours.

FORTIFIED DESSERT WINE

❄ ❄ ❄ ❄ ❄ ❄ ❄ ❄ ❄ ❄ ❄ ❄ ❄ ❄ ❄ ❄ ❄ ❄ ❄

# Chocolate Layer Pudding

A very easy pudding which needs to be made at least 3 hours in advance but no more than 24 hours in advance.

*35g/1¼oz cocoa powder*
*15g/½oz icing sugar*
*110g/4oz fresh brown breadcrumbs*
*85g/3oz demerara sugar*
*10g/⅓oz instant coffee powder*
*425ml/¾ pint whipping or double cream*
*55g/2oz dark chocolate, grated*

1. Mix together the cocoa powder and icing sugar, and add to the breadcrumbs, demerara sugar and coffee and stir well.
2. Whip the cream until it holds its shape.
3. Put a layer of cream in a glass bowl. Scatter over some of the chocolate crumb mixture and cover carefully with another layer of cream. Continue to layer up until you have 2 or 3 layers finishing with a chocolate layer.
4. Sprinkle the grated chocolate over the top, cover the bowl and place in the refrigerator for at least 3 hours before serving.

NOTE: Greek yoghurt can be used in place of one-third of the cream and stirred into the whipped cream before layering.

FORTIFIED SWEET WHITE

✳ ✳ ✳ ✳ ✳ ✳ ✳ ✳ ✳ ✳ ✳ ✳ ✳ ✳ ✳ ✳ ✳ ✳ ✳

# St Clements Flan

SERVES 8-10

FOR THE PASTRY:
*255g/9oz flour*
*170g/6oz butter*
*85g/3oz caster sugar*
*100g/3½oz toasted hazelnuts, finely chopped*
*1 egg, beaten*

FOR THE FILLING:
*6 eggs*
*juice and finely grated rind of 3 oranges*
*juice and finely grated rind of 1 lemon*
*110g/4oz caster sugar*
*290ml/½ pint Greek yoghurt*

1. Preheat the oven to 190°C/375°F/gas mark 5.
2. First make the pastry: sift the flour and rub in the butter until the mixture resembles coarse breadcrumbs. Add the sugar, hazelnuts and beaten egg. Bind it together with your hands.
3. Roll out the pastry and line a deep 27cm/ 11 inch flan tin (if the pastry is too soft, press it into the tin).
4. Bake the pastry blind, removing the paper and beans after 10 minutes. Bake for a further 10 minutes or until the pastry looks dry and pale brown. Reduce the oven temperature to 150°C/300°F/gas mark 2.
5. Meanwhile, make the filling: gently beat the eggs, but do not make them too frothy. Add the orange juice and rind, lemon juice and

rind, sugar and yoghurt. Taste, and add more sugar if necessary (depending on the sweetness of the oranges).

6. Pour the filling into the baked flan case and place in the centre of the oven. Bake for 50 minutes or until the filling is set. Serve cold.

SWEET WHITE

# Oranges in Caramel

*1 large orange per person*
*caramel sauce (see below)*

1. With a potato peeler, pare the rind of 1 or 2 oranges very finely, making sure that there is no pith on the back of the strips. Cut into fine shreds.
2. Simmer these needleshreds in caramel sauce or sugar syrup until soft and almost candied. They should be very sticky and quite dark.
3. Peel the oranges with a knife as you would an apple, making sure that all the pith is removed.

4. Slice each orange horiziontally. Remove any pips.
5. Place the oranges in a glass bowl and pour over the cold caramel sauce. Chill well.
6. Scatter with needleshreds of orange rind before serving.

NOTE: Tangerines or satsumas make a very good alternative to the oranges. Peel them carefully and serve them whole in the caramel sauce.

SWEET MUSCAT, SUCH AS
BEAUMES DE VENISE

# Caramel Sauce

*225g/8oz granulated sugar*
*290ml/¹/₂ pint water*

1. Place the sugar in a heavy-bottomed saucepan with half the quantity of water.
2. Dissolve the sugar slowly without stirring

it or allowing the water to boil.
3. Once all the sugar has dissolved turn up the heat and boil until it is a good caramel colour.
4. Immediately, tip in the remaining water (it will fizz dangerously, so stand back).
5. Stir until any lumps have dissolved, then remove from the heat and allow to cool.

# Atholl Brose

The Duke of Atholl's original recipe for Atholl Brose involved steeping oatmeal in boiling water and then draining off the milky liquid and mixing it with whisky and heather honey to make a warming drink. This recipe for a pudding has been adapted from the original.

SERVES 4-6

*55g/2oz medium oatmeal*
*290ml/1/2 pint double cream*
*30ml/2 level tablespoons runny honey or more
    to taste*
*85ml/3 fl oz whisky*

1. Toast the oatmeal under the grill and allow to cool.
2. Whip the cream until it just holds its shape and stir in the cooked oatmeal and honey. Add the whisky and transfer to a glass serving dish.
3. Cover and place in the refrigerator. Leave to stand for at least 1 hour before serving.

NOTE: This also freezes well. Because of the amount of alcohol it remains soft but it is very powerful and goes well with mince pies or Christmas pudding instead of brandy butter.

# Trifle

Most people have a firm idea of their ideal trifle and there are many different ways of making it. This version is particularly suitable for Christmas as it is both rich and alcoholic. It is best made a few hours in advance so that the flavours can mingle.

SERVES 8

*450g/1lb sponge cake*
*raspberry jam*
*20 Ratafia biscuits*
*120ml/4 fl oz medium sweet sherry*
*20 marachino cherries*
*570ml/1 pint milk (or single cream for extra
    richness)*
*6 egg yolks*
*30g/1oz caster sugar*
*vanilla essence*

FOR THE SYLLABUB TOPPING:
*120ml/4 fl oz white wine*
*15ml/1 tablespoon brandy*
*pared rind and juice of 1 lemon*
*55g/2oz caster sugar*
*340ml/3/4 pint double cream*

FOR THE DECORATION:
*A few toasted almonds or silvered almonds*

1. Cut the sponge cake into large pieces approximately 7.5cm x 5cm/3 inches x 2 inches and spread with raspberry jam. Place in the bottom of a large glass bowl (about 13/4-21/4 litres/3-4 pints in capacity). Scatter over the Ratafia biscuits and soak the sponge carefully with the sherry.
2. Cut the cherries in half and distribute over the top of the sponge and biscuits.
3. Heat the milk or single cream in a saucepan

and bring to just below boiling point.

4. Meanwhile beat the egg yolks and sugar in a bowl with a wooden spoon. Pour over the hot milk or cream, mix well and return to the saucepan. Cook over a gentle heat, stirring all the time until the custard coats the back of the spoon. Do not allow to boil or it will curdle. Add a few drops of vanilla essence, taste and add more sugar if necessary. Pour through a sieve over the sponge cake in the glass dish. Allow to cool completely.

5. Meanwhile mix together the wine, brandy, sugar, lemon rind and juice and allow to stand for 1 hour (or overnight if you have time).

6. Remove the lemon rind, whip the double cream until it just holds its shape and add the wine and sugar mixture – it can easily separate but it should be whipped again until it has the consistency of lightly whipped double cream.

7. Spoon the syllabub over the cooled custard and decorate with the toasted or silvered almonds. Refrigerate until half an hour before serving.

NOTE: If preferred, the trifle can be topped with 340ml/³⁄4 pint whipped double cream instead of syllabub.

SWEET WHITE

# Meringues (Swiss Meringues)

This quantity makes 50 miniature or 12 large meringues.

*4 egg whites*
*pinch of salt*
*225g/8oz caster sugar*

FOR THE FILLING:
*whipped cream*

1. Set the oven to 110°C/225°F/gas mark ¹⁄2.
2. Place silicone paper on 2 baking sheets.
3. Whisk the egg whites with a pinch of salt until stiff but not dry.

4. Add 30ml/2 tablespoons of the sugar and whisk again until very stiff and shiny.
5. Fold in the rest of the sugar.
6. Drop the meringue mixture on to the paper-covered baking sheets in spoonfuls set fairly apart. Use a teaspoon for tiny meringues; a dessertspoon for larger ones.
7. Bake in the oven for about 2 hours until the meringues are dry right through and will lift easily off the paper.
8. When cold, sandwich the meringues together in pairs with whipped cream.

NOTE : If making a meringue mixture with a powerful electric mixer, when the whites are stiff gradually add half the sugar. Whisk again until very shiny, then add the remaining sugar and whisk lightly until just incorporated.

✳✳✳✳✳✳✳✳✳✳✳✳✳✳✳✳✳✳✳✳✳

# CANAPÉS

✳✳✳✳✳✳✳✳✳✳✳✳✳✳✳✳✳✳✳✳✳

*We have only included a few simple canapés here – just bites for your guests to nibble at whilst you wonder if your other guests have broken down or simply forgotten to turn up.*

### CANAPÉS
*Sun-dried tomato, mozzarella, avocado and basil tartlets*
*Smoked salmon triangles*
*Smoked salmon on rye with horseradish*
*Salami wedges*
*Mascarpone tartlets with salmon roe*
*Cheese sablés*
*Crudités*

### DIPS
*Carrot and cardamom*
*Taramasalata*
*Hummus*
*Tzatziki*

✳✳✳✳✳✳✳✳✳✳✳✳✳✳✳✳✳✳✳✳✳

# Sun-Dried Tomato, Mozzarella, Avocado and Basil Tartlets

MAKES 60 TARTLETS
*85g/3oz good quality sun-dried tomatoes*
*1 ripe avocado pear*
*110g/4oz buffalo mozzarella cheese*
*30ml/2 tablespoons French dressing made with*
*virgin olive oil (see page 195)*
*4 basil leaves, roughly chopped*
*60 tartlet cases (see page 201)*

1. Cut the sun-dried tomatoes into smallish pieces.
2. Peel the avocado, remove the stone and cut the flesh into small dice.
3. Chop the mozzarella into dice – the same size as the avocado.
4. Mix the tomatoes, avocado and mozzarella with the French dressing and chopped basil.
5. Pile into the tartlet cases and serve pretty quickly.

# Smoked Salmon Triangles

MAKES 40 SMALL TRIANGLES
*5 slices brown bread*
*butter for spreading*
*freshly ground black pepper*
*110g/4oz smoked salmon*
*lemon juice*

1. Butter the bread, sprinkle with black pepper and lay the smoked salmon slices carefully on top.
2. Sprinkle with lemon juice, then cut off the crusts and cut each slice into 8 triangles.

CANAPÉS

LAMB EN BALLON

ROAST GOOSE WITH APPLE SAUCE

Christmas Cake

OLD-FASHIONED BOILED CHRISTMAS CAKE

APPLE CHARLOTTES

BLACK BUN

BREADS

# Smoked Salmon on Rye with Horseradish

MAKES 50

*12-14 slices rye bread*
*225g/8oz cream cheese*
*creamed horseradish*
*salt and pepper*
*225g/8oz smoked salmon*
*sprigs of fresh dill*

1. Remove the crusts from the bread. Cut out 4 even-sized rectangles approximately 3 x 4cm/ $1^1/4$ x $1^1/2$ inches from each slice.
2. Season the cream cheese with the horseradish, salt and pepper. Spread it on to the bread rectangles, mounding it neatly.
3. Cut the smoked salmon into long thin strips and coil it neatly on top of the cream cheese mixture.
4. Decorate each rectangle with a sprig of dill.

❈ ❈ ❈ ❈ ❈ ❈ ❈ ❈ ❈ ❈ ❈ ❈ ❈ ❈ ❈ ❈ ❈ ❈ ❈ ❈ ❈

# Salami Wedges

MAKES 24

*225g/8oz cream cheese*
*4 spring onions, chopped*
*4 gherkins, chopped*
*15ml/1 tablespoon finely chopped fresh parsley*
*salt and freshly ground black pepper*
*15 slices round pepper salami*

1. Mix the cream cheese with the spring onions, gherkins and herbs and season to taste.
2. Spread a little of the mixture evenly over a slice of salami. Place another slice of salami on top, then spread with some more cream cheese mixture.
3. Continue to layer up the cream cheese and salami until you have used 5 slices of salami. The quantity will make 3 'cakes'.
4. Wrap in cling film and chill.
5. Cut each cake into 8 wedges.

❈ ❈ ❈ ❈ ❈ ❈ ❈ ❈ ❈ ❈ ❈ ❈ ❈ ❈ ❈ ❈ ❈ ❈ ❈ ❈ ❈

# Mascarpone Tartlets with Salmon Roe

MAKES 30 TARTLETS
*225g/8oz Mascarpone cream cheese*
*30 tartlet cases*
*1 small jar salmon roe*
*sprigs of fresh dill*

1. Beat the Mascarpone cheese lightly and use to fill a piping bag fitted with a fluted nozzle.
2. Pipe the cheese into the tartlet cases and top with a little salmon roe.
3. Garnish each tartlet with a small piece of dill.

# Cheese Sablés

MAKES 24
*225g/8oz plain flour*
*salt and freshly ground black pepper*
*225g/8oz butter*
*225g/8oz Gruyère or strong Cheddar cheese, grated*
*pinch of dry mustard*
*pinch of cayenne pepper*
*beaten egg*

1. Set the oven to 190°C/375°F/gas mark 5. Line 2 baking sheets with greaseproof paper.
This will prevent the sablés burning at the edges.
2. Sift the flour with a pinch of salt into a bowl. Rub in the butter until the mixture resembles breadcrumbs.
3. Add the cheese, salt, pepper, mustard and cayenne. Work into a paste but do not over-handle or the pastry will become greasy and be tough.
4. Roll out on a floured board until 5mm/$^1$/4 inch thick. Cut into rounds or triangles and brush with beaten egg.
5. Bake until golden brown (about 10 minutes). Leave to cool on a wire rack.

# Crudités

A SELECTION OF:

*celery*

*green pepper*

*cauliflower*

*radishes*

*button mushrooms*

*spring onions*

*carrots*

*asparagus*

*cherry tomatoes*

*tiny mangetout*

*baby sweetcorns*

*young turnips*

*black olives*

FOR THE DIP:

*1 garlic clove, crushed (optional)*

*150ml/¹/4 pint mayonnaise (see page 184)*

1. Prepare the vegetables, making sure they are perfectly clean, and as far as possible evenly sized. Celery: wash and cut into sticks. Pepper: wipe and cut into strips, discarding the seeds.

Cauliflower: wash and break into florets. Peel the stalks if tough.

Radishes: wash and trim off the root and long leaves, but leave a little of the green stalk.

Mushrooms: wash. Peel only if the skins are tough. Quarter if large.

Spring onions: wash. Cut off most of the green part, and the beard (roots). Leave whole, or cut in half lengthways if large.

Carrots: peel and cut into sticks the same shape and size as the celery.

Asparagus: peel the tough outer stalk and trim away the hard root ends.

Turnip: peel and cut into strips. (Use young turnips only.)

Black olives: stone with a cherry stoner if desired.

2. Mix the garlic (if using) with the mayonnaise. Spoon it into a small serving bowl.

3. Arrange the raw prepared vegetables and the olives in neat clumps on a tray or flat platter with the bowl of mayonnaise dip in the centre.

NOTE: See pages 140-1 for alternative dips.

# DIPS FOR CRUDITÉS

## Carrot and Cardamom Dip

SERVES 4

450g/1lb carrots
570ml/1 pint stock
2 cardamom pods, crushed
1 bay leaf
30ml/2 tablespoons fromage blanc
15ml/1 tablespoon chopped chervil
salt and freshly ground pepper

1. Peel and slice the carrots. Cook in the stock with the cardamom and bay leaf for 20 minutes, or until really soft.
2. Allow to cool slightly, and remove the cardamom pods and bay leaf. Drain well but reserve a little of the liquor.
3. Liquidize the carrots with the fromage blanc to make a firm but soft purée. If too firm, add a little of the reserved cooking liquor. Add the chervil and season to taste.

❊ ❊ ❊ ❊ ❊ ❊ ❊ ❊ ❊ ❊ ❊ ❊ ❊ ❊ ❊ ❊ ❊ ❊ ❊ ❊

## Taramasalata

SERVES 6

1 slice of white bread, crusts removed
225g/8oz fresh smoked soft roe, skinned, or
    110g/4oz bottled smoked cod roe
1 large garlic clove, crushed
about 150ml/¼ pint each salad oil and olive oil
freshly ground black pepper
juice of ½ lemon

1. Hold the bread slice under the tap to wet it. Squeeze dry and put it in a bowl with the cod roe and the garlic. With a wooden spoon or electric whisk, beat very well.
2. Now add the oils very slowly, almost drop by drop (as with mayonnaise), beating all the time. The idea is to form a smooth emulsion, and adding the oil too fast will result in a rather oily, curdled mixture.
3. The amount of oil added is a matter of personal taste: the more you add, the paler and creamier the mixture becomes and the more delicate the flavour. Stop when you think the right balance is achieved.
4. Add black pepper and lemon juice to taste. If it seems too thick or bitter add a little hot water.

NOTE: If it begins to separate, add a little boiling water.

# Hummus

This is a spicy hummus and has been adapted from a recipe by one of Leith's most popular guest lecturers, Claudia Roden.

SERVES 4
*225g/8oz chickpeas*
*salt and freshly ground black pepper*
*10ml/2 teaspoons ground cumin*
*2 garlic cloves, crushed*
*juice of 1 lemon*
*60ml/4 tablespoons olive oil*
*pinch of cayenne pepper*
*Greek parsley to garnish*

1. Soak the chickpeas overnight in cold water.
2. Drain and cook slowly in clean water for 1-1½ hours. Add the salt towards the end of cooking. Drain and reserve the cooking liquor.
3. Cool for a few minutes and tip into a food processor. Whizz and add the remaining ingredients. Add enough of the cooking liquor to produce a soft cream.
4. Serve on a flat plate garnished with the Greek parsley. Hand hot pitta bread separately.

# Tzatziki

Recipes for this are legion: some have mint; some do not call for garlic.

SERVES 6
*1 medium cucumber*
*570ml/1 pint low-fat plain yoghurt*
*1 garlic clove, crushed*
*freshly ground black pepper*

1. Cut the cucumber into very fine dice. Place in a sieve, sprinkle liberally with salt and leave to 'degorge' for 30 minutes. Rinse very well, drain and pat dry.
2. Mix the cucumber with the yoghurt, garlic and plenty of black pepper.

NOTE: The yoghurt can be thickened by draining it in a muslin-lined sieve; this will make for a creamier finish.

✳✳✳✳✳✳✳✳✳✳✳✳✳✳✳✳✳✳✳✳✳✳✳

# CAKES

✳✳✳✳✳✳✳✳✳✳✳✳✳✳✳✳✳✳✳✳✳✳✳

*Stollen*
*Black bun*
*Pear and ginger muffins*
*Apple sauce cake*
*Old-fashioned boiled Christmas cake*
*Christmas cake*

✳✳✳✳✳✳✳✳✳✳✳✳✳✳✳✳✳✳✳✳✳✳✳

# Stollen

*450g/1lb strong white flour*
*5ml/1 teaspoon caster sugar*
*15g/¹/2 oz fresh yeast, or 1¹/2 teaspoons dried yeast*
*250ml/8 fl oz warm milk*
*5ml/1 teaspoon salt*
*85g/3oz butter*
*110g/4oz currants*
*110g/4oz sultanas*
*30g/1oz chopped mixed peel*
*30g/1oz walnuts or almonds, chopped*
*10ml/2 teaspoons grated orange or lemon rind*
*1 egg*
*55g/2oz glacé cherries*
*icing sugar for dusting*

1. Prepare a yeast batter: mix together 110g/4oz flour, the sugar, yeast and warm milk. Set aside until bubbly. This will take about 20 minutes in a warm place.

2. Mix the remaining flour with the salt. Rub in 55g/2oz of the butter. Add the currants, sultanas, mixed peel, nuts and citrus rind.

3. Beat the egg, add it to the yeast batter with the flour, fruit and nuts. Mix well to a soft but not too sticky dough.

4. Knead until smooth and elastic. This will take about 10 minutes. Shape into a ball and leave in a warm place in a clean bowl covered with cling wrap or in a polythene bag, until doubled in bulk. This will take at least 1 hour. The dried fruits and nuts slow down the rising and proving of a bread dough.

5. Knead again (knock down) for 2 minutes and shape into an oval 30 x 20cm/12 x 8 inches. Place on a baking sheet.

6. Melt the remaining butter and brush half of it over the bread dough. Spread the glacé cherries over half the dough. Fold the other half over the dough and press down lightly. Cover with greased polythene and leave to prove until 1¹/2 times its original size – this may take between 15 minutes and half an hour.

7. Set the oven to 190°C/375°F/gas mark 5.

8. Brush the remaining butter over the proved loaf and bake for 20-25 minutes. Leave to cool on a wire rack. Dust with icing sugar.

NOTE: An alternative version is to use 225g/8oz made-up marzipan to stuff the Stollen in place of the cherries and butter. Roll the marzipan into a sausage and place in the middle of the dough. Roll up and seal the ends by pinching them together. Bake as before.

# Black Bun

A rich, dense, fruity cake which is served in
Scotland over the Christmas holiday,
but particularly at Hogmanay. Serve in very
small pieces.

FOR THE PASTRY:
340g/12oz plain flour
1/2 level teaspoon baking powder
pinch of salt
55g/2oz lard
110g/4oz butter
egg glaze

FOR THE FILLING:
450g/1lb currants
340g/12oz raisins
45ml/3 tablespoons whisky
55g/2oz mixed peel
55g/2oz chopped almonds
85g/3oz soft dark brown sugar
170g/6oz plain flour
2.5ml/1/2 level teaspoon baking powder
2.5ml/1/2 level teaspoon cream of tartar
5 ml/1 teaspoon ground allspice
2.5ml/1/2 teaspoon ground ginger
2.5ml/1/2 teaspoon ground cinnamon
2.5ml/1/2 teaspoon grated nutmeg
2.5ml/1/2 teaspoon ground black pepper
pinch of salt
290ml/1/2 pint milk

1. Grease a 900g/2lb loaf tin. Preheat the oven
to 160°C/325°F/gas mark 3.
2. Make the pastry: sift the flour with the baking
powder and salt. Chop the lard and butter into
small pieces and rub into the flour until the
mixture looks like coarse breadcrumbs. Add
enough cold water to bind the pastry together.
3. Roll out three-quarters of the pastry and use to
line the loaf tin. If it cracks, push it into the tin to
seal. Chill in the refrigerator for 30 minutes.
4. Soak the currants and raisins in the whisky for
30 minutes. Add the mixed peel, almonds and
sugar, and mix thoroughly.
5. Sift the flour with all the other dry
ingredients and stir into the fruit mixture.
6. Add the milk to bind the fruit together.
7. Pack tightly into the prepared pastry case.
8. Roll out the remaining pastry and place on
top of the fruit. Crimp the edges and glaze with
egg glaze. Push a skewer right through the bun,
making a hole to the base. Make 4 holes along
the length of the bun, and prick the top surface
all over with a fork.
9. Place in the middle of the preheated oven and
bake for 3 hours.
10. Allow to cool before removing from the tin.

NOTE I: It is best if kept for 2 weeks before eating.
NOTE II: If this is made in a deep loaf tin,
line the tin with a strip of greaseproof paper
which can later be used as a handle to help lift
the bun out of the tin.

❋ ❋ ❋ ❋ ❋ ❋ ❋ ❋ ❋ ❋ ❋ ❋ ❋ ❋ ❋ ❋ ❋ ❋ ❋ ❋ ❋ ❋

# Pear and Ginger Muffins

You will need 10 muffin paper cases and a muffin tin to hold the cases.

*110g/4oz butter*

*55g/2oz honey*

*140g/5oz soft light brown sugar*

*2 medium pears, peeled, cored and roughly chopped*

*70g/2¹/₂oz pecan nuts, roughly chopped*

*225g/8oz plain flour*

*5ml/1 teaspoon bicarbonate of soda*

*5ml/1 teaspoon ground cinnamon*

*2.5ml/¹/₂ teaspoon grated nutmeg*

*2.5ml/¹/₂ teaspoon ground cloves*

*pinch of salt*

*2 small eggs*

1. Preheat the oven to 180°C/350°F/gas mark 4.
2. Melt the butter, honey and sugar together. Do not allow to boil.
3. Toss the pears and nuts in the butter and honey mixture.
4. Sift the flour, bicarbonate of soda, spices and salt together.
5. Beat the eggs and add to the butter and pear mixture.
6. Fold in the dry ingredients.
7. Fill the muffin cases to the top and place in the top of the preheated oven for 35-40 minutes, or until they spring back when touched.

❊ ❊ ❊ ❊ ❊ ❊ ❊ ❊ ❊ ❊ ❊ ❊ ❊ ❊ ❊ ❊ ❊ ❊ ❊ ❊

# Apple Sauce Cake

*340g/12oz cooking apples*

*110g/4oz butter*

*225g/8oz caster sugar*

*225g/8oz plain flour*

*5ml/1 teaspoon mixed spice*

*5ml/1 teaspoon bicarbonate of soda*

*170g/6oz chopped dried apricots*

*15ml/1 tablespoon demerara sugar*

1. Set the oven to 180°C/350°F/gas mark 4. Grease an 18cm/7 inch cake tin and line the base with a disc of greaseproof paper.
2. Wash the apples and cut into chunks, skin and all. Put in a saucepan with 15ml/ 1 tablespoon of water. Cover with a lid and place over a low heat, stirring occasionally. When the apples have become pulpy, push them through a sieve and set aside to cool.
3. Meanwhile, cream the butter and add the sugar. Beat together until soft and creamy.
4. Add the cooled apple purée, sifted flour, mixed spice, bicarbonate of soda and dried apricots. Mix well.
5. Pour into the prepared cake tin, place in the preheated oven and bake for approximately 1¹/₂ hours. Ten minutes before the end of cooking sprinkle the top with demerara sugar.

NOTE: This can also be cooked in a 900g/2lb loaf tin.

❊ ❊ ❊ ❊ ❊ ❊ ❊ ❊ ❊ ❊ ❊ ❊ ❊ ❊ ❊ ❊ ❊ ❊ ❊ ❊

# Old-Fashioned Boiled Christmas Cake

This cake is not, as the name suggests, boiled instead of baked, but the fruit is boiled in water and orange juice and allowed to stand for 3 days before completing. This gives the fruit a wonderful plumpness. Instead of being decorated with marzipan and icing it is finished with a glazed fruit and nut topping and a pretty ribbon.

225g/8oz sultanas
225g/8oz raisins
110g/4oz currants
55g/2oz mixed peel
55g/2oz glacé cherries, halved
170g/6oz dried apricots, chopped
55g/2oz dried apples, chopped
110g/4oz dried dates, chopped
110g/4oz dried peaches, chopped
110g/4oz dried pears, chopped
225g/8oz butter
225g/8oz brown sugar
grated rind and juice of 1 lemon
grated rind and juice of 1 orange
110ml/4 fl oz water
110ml/4 fl oz orange juice
110ml/4 fl oz brandy
2.5ml/$\frac{1}{2}$ teaspoon grated nutmeg
5ml/1 teaspoon ground cinnamon
5ml/1 teaspoon allspice
2.5ml/$\frac{1}{2}$ teaspoon ground ginger
1.25ml/$\frac{1}{4}$ teaspoon ground cardamom
15ml/1 tablespoon black treacle
5 eggs, beaten
310g/11oz plain flour
5ml/1 teaspoon baking powder

FOR THE FRUIT TOPPING:
340g/12oz mixed dried fruit and nuts, e.g. pecans, brazils, almonds, apricots, red and green cherries, prunes, peaches, pears etc.
340g/12oz apricot jam

1. Put the sultanas, raisins, currants, mixed peel, cherries, apricots, apples, dates, peaches, pears, butter, sugar, lemon and orange rind and juice, water and orange juice into a large pan. Bring slowly up to the boil. Stir with a wooden spoon, cover with a lid, and simmer for 10 minutes.

2. Remove from the heat and allow to cool slightly. Add the brandy and spices and transfer to a large bowl. When it is completely cold, cover and put in a cool place (not the refrigerator) for 3 days, stirring daily.

3. Prepare a 25cm/10 inch round cake tin by lining with double sheets of greaseproof paper as described on page 153. Preheat the oven to 170°C/325°F/gas mark 3.

4. Stir the treacle into the boiled fruit mixture and beat in the eggs. Sift together the flour and baking powder and stir into the cake mixture, which will be slightly sloppy. Turn it into the prepared cake tin and bake for approximately 4$\frac{1}{2}$ hours, or until a skewer inserted into the centre of the cake comes out clean.

5. Leave to cool in the tin.

6. When completely cold, wrap up carefully in aluminium foil until ready to decorate. It will mature well for 2-3 months.

7. To decorate the cake: put the apricot jam in a pan with 15ml/1 tablespoon of water. Heat until boiling and then push through a sieve. Allow to cool slightly and then brush the top of the cake with the apricot glaze. Arrange the fruit and nuts all over the top of the cake in a haphazard fashion and then, using a pastry brush, glaze carefully with the apricot glaze.

NOTE I: The glaze will remain shiny on the cake for a few days but after a week it will begin to lose its gloss so it is better not to decorate the cake too early.

NOTE II: If the cake top becomes very dark whilst cooking cover it with a double layer of damp greaseproof paper.

# Christmas Cake

*110g/4oz glacé cherries*
*55g/2oz mixed peel*
*450g/1lb raisins*
*285g/10oz sultanas*
*110g/4oz currants*
*225g/8oz butter*
*225g/8oz soft brown sugar*
*5 eggs, beaten*
*285g/10oz flour*
*10ml/2 teaspoons mixed spice*
*30ml/2 tablespoons black treacle*
*grated lemon rind*
*2 wine glasses of beer or sherry (200ml/7 fl oz)*
*110g/4oz ground almonds*

1. Set the oven to 170°C/325°F/gas mark 3 and prepare a 22cm/9 inch round cake tin or a 20cm/8inch square cake tin (see page 153).
2. Cut up the cherries and mix with the rest of the fruit.

3. Cream the butter until soft. Add the sugar and beat together until light and fluffy.
4. Add the beaten eggs slowly, beating well between each addition. If the mixture curdles, beat in 5ml/1 teaspoon of flour.
5. Fold in the flour, mixed spice, lemon rind, black treacle and beer or sherry.
6. Stir in the ground almonds and fruit.
7. Place the mixture in the prepared tin and make a deep hollow in the middle.
8. Bake for $2\frac{1}{2}$ hours or until a skewer emerges clean from being stuck in the middle of the cake.
9. Allow to cool on a wire rack.

NOTE: This cake must now be covered with marzipan (see page 151) before being generously iced with royal icing (see page 148). If your family does not like icing, cover the top with marzipan, rough it lightly with a fork and toast it under the grill until golden brown.

❋ ❋ ❋ ❋ ❋ ❋ ❋ ❋ ❋ ❋ ❋ ❋ ❋ ❋ ❋ ❋ ❋ ❋ ❋ ❋ ❋

# ROYAL ICING

❋ ❋ ❋ ❋ ❋ ❋ ❋ ❋ ❋ ❋ ❋ ❋ ❋ ❋ ❋ ❋ ❋ ❋ ❋ ❋ ❋

*Icing a cake with royal icing is an advanced skill, and these notes are intended as a reminder for those who have already iced a cake or two. Royal icing is traditionally used (over a layer of marzipan) for the coating and decoration of special-occasion fruit cakes. It keeps very well.*

1. More than with any other cooking, it is vital to clean up as you go along. It is almost impossible to produce delicate and neat work from a cluttered work surface. Get all the nozzles and piping bags lined up before you begin icing.

2. Never overfill the piping bag. This leads to the sticky icing squeezing out of the top.

3. Keep all full piping bags under a damp cloth or in a plastic bag to prevent the icing in the nozzle drying out.

4. Always keep the icing covered with a damp cloth when not in use to prevent it drying out.

5. Always clean the nozzles immediately after use, using a pin to ensure that no icing is left in the tip.

6. Practise the required pattern on the work surface before tackling the cake. Don't try complicated things like roses and scrolls before you have mastered thoroughly the easier decorations like trellis, shells, stars and dots.

7. Follow the instructions slavishly.

8. Never lick your fingers or equipment. Even a little wet icing can make you feel sick.

FOR 1 COAT OF ICING FOR A 22CM/9INCH ROUND OR A 20CM/8 INCH SQUARE CAKE:

*1 1/2 egg whites*
*675/1 1/2lb icing sugar*

Mix the egg white with 45ml/3 tablespoons of the sugar, and add lemon juice or glycerine if required (see below). Gradually add the remaining sugar and mix very well until the icing is soft, very white, fluffy and will hold its shape. More sugar can be added if the mixture is too sloppy. Blue colouring, if used (see below), is added last.

## FLAVOURINGS AND COLOURINGS

1. 1 drop blue food colouring makes white icing very bright white.

2. 5ml/1 teaspoon lemon juice to each 225g/8oz sugar makes the icing sharper and less sickly.

3. 2.5ml/1/2 teaspoon glycerine to each 225g/8oz sugar produces a softer icing which will not splinter when cut. Without glycerine, royal icing eventually hardens to an unbreakable cement.

More glycerine can be added, but this will give a softer icing. None need be used if the cake is to be eaten within 24 hours of icing.

## CONSISTENCY

A cake is normally covered with 2-3 coats of icing and decorated with either piping or 'run-in' work. The consistency varies for each coat. First coating: very thick – the icing should stand up in points if the beating spoon is lifted from the bowl.

Second coating: a little thinner (the points should flop over at the tips, like rabbit ears).

Third coating: the icing should be of thick pouring consistency.

For piping: consistency as for the first coating.

For run-in work: as for the third coating.

## BUBBLES

Royal icing should be beaten as little as possible: if making it by hand or in an electric machine, stop as soon as it is smooth and glossy. If there are any bubbles, leave the icing, covered with a damp cloth, in the refrigerator overnight.

## APPLYING THE FIRST COAT

It is easier to apply the first layer of royal icing in two (for a round cake) or three (for a square cake) stages rather than all at once. The top is iced first and allowed to dry for 24 hours before icing the sides. On a square cake two of the opposite sides are iced and allowed to dry before the second two sides are iced.

Place a small spoonful of icing on a cake board about 5cm/2 inches larger in diameter than the cake, and put the cake on top. It will now stick to the board. Spoon half the icing on to the top of the cake with a palette knife and spread to the edge, using a paddling action to remove any air bubbles. Then, using a clean metal ruler, a 'straight edge' or large palette knife placed in the centre of the cake, draw the icing forwards and backwards across the cake until it is completely smooth and level and can be drawn off the cake.

Carefully remove any icing that has fallen down the sides of the cake. Leave to dry for 24 hours. Put the cake and board on an icing turntable or upturned bowl and spread the icing evenly around the sides, using a special icing scraper or a palette knife held at an angle of 45 degrees to the cake. Try to turn the cake around in one movement as you ice in order to ensure a smooth finish. For a square cake, ice two of the opposite sides.

Store the cake for at least 24 hours in a clean, cool, dry place to dry before you ice the other two sides. If the storage place is damp, it will prevent the icing from drying and it will slowly slip down the sides of the cake. If it is too warm, the cake will 'sweat' and oil from the marzipan will be drawn into the icing.

## APPLYING THE SECOND COAT

This may not be necessary if the first layer is very smooth. If it is not perfect, smooth it down with fine sandpaper. Brush the surface well with a grease-free brush to remove any loose icing. Ice the cake as for the first coating, but use a slightly thinner icing.

## APPLYING THE THIRD COAT OR FLOAT

A less than perfectly iced cake may need a third layer of icing. If this is necessary, proceed when the second coating is dry. Prepare the surface as previously instructed.

Before converting the icing into the desired pouring consistency, pile a little thick icing into an icing bag fitted with a no. 1 or 2 writing nozzle and cover it with a damp cloth.

Add a little egg white to the remaining icing and beat until smooth and of a pouring consistency. Leave in a tightly covered container for 30 minutes. (Stretching a piece of polythene wrap over the bowl will do. ) This is to make the air bubbles rise to the surface. If you do not do this, air bubbles will break all over the surface of the cake, making little holes in the icing.

With the writing tube, pipe an unbroken line of icing around the top edge of the cake. Now pour the runny icing into a piping bag, remove the nozzle and guide it over the top of the cake, flooding the surface and carefully avoiding the piped line. With the handle of a teaspoon, work the flooding to the edge of the cake. The piped line will prevent the icing running off.

## DECORATING WITH ICING

You must have a clear idea of the design before you begin. If it is a geometric pattern, draw it on a piece of tracing paper and place this on the cake. Using a large pin, prick where the lines meet. Remove the paper and you will be left with guidelines made by the pinpoints. Join these up with more pricked holes so that the design is visible. Half-fill the piping bags, fitted with the chosen nozzles, with the icing

mixed to the correct consistency. Put them under a wet cloth until needed. Get everything you will need ready on or near your work surface (e.g. more bags and extra nozzles, a large spoon, a palette knife, a small basin of hot water for washing the nozzles).

## DIRECT PIPING

**Star piping:** use a star nozzle. Hold the pipe upright, immediately above and almost touching the top of the cake, and squeeze gently from the top of the bag. Stop pressing and then lift the bag away.

**Dot or pearl piping:** use a plain nozzle, and pipe as for stars. If the dots are too small, do not try to increase their size by squeezing out more icing; use a larger nozzle.

**Straight lines:** with a plain nozzle, press the bag as for making a dot but leave the icing attached to the cake surface – do not draw away by lifting the bag. Hold the point of the nozzle about 4cm/1$\frac{1}{2}$ inches above the surface of the cake and, pressing gently as you go, guide rather than drag the icing into place. The icing can be directed more easily into place if it is allowed to hang from the tube.

**Trellis work:** with a plain nozzle, pipe parallel lines 5mm/$\frac{1}{4}$ inch apart. Pipe a second layer over the top at right angles or at an angle of 45 degrees to the first. Then pipe another layer as closely as possible over the first set of lines, then another set over the second layer, and so on until you have the desired height of trellis. Six layers (three in each direction) is usual for an elaborate cake.

**Shells:** use a star nozzle. Hold the bag at an angle of about 45 degrees. Pipe a shell, release the pressure on the bag and begin a new shell one-eighth of the way up the first shell, so that each new shell overlaps its predecessor.

**Scrolls:** use a star nozzle. Hold the bag at an angle of about 45 degrees. Pipe a scroll first from left to right and then from right to left.

**Run-in work:** using a writing nozzle, pipe the outline of a design (e.g. leaf, Father Christmas, etc.) on to oiled foil, oiled greaseproof, waxed or bakewell paper. 'Float' runny icing in the centre, and leave to set. Lift off and stick on to the cake with wet icing.

NOTE: Variations of pressure when piping both shells and scrolls make the icing emerge in the required thicknesses. Shells and scrolls can be made into very attractive borders when combined with trellis work and edged with pearls.

## CAUSES OF FAILURE

BROKEN LINES
> Icing too stiff.
> Pulling rather than easing into place.
> Making the icing with a mixer set at too high a speed, causing air bubbles.

WOBBLY LINES
> Squeezing the icing out too quickly.
> Icing too liquid.

FLATTENED LINES
> Icing too liquid.
> Bag held too near the surface

❋ ❋ ❋ ❋ ❋ ❋ ❋ ❋ ❋ ❋ ❋ ❋ ❋ ❋ ❋ ❋ ❋ ❋ ❋ ❋ ❋

# Marzipan or Almond Paste (Uncooked)

*225g/8oz caster sugar*
*225g/8oz icing sugar*
*450g/1lb ground almonds*
*2 egg yolks*
*2 whole eggs*
*10ml/2 teaspoons lemon juice*
*6 drops vanilla essence*

1. Sift the sugars together into a bowl and mix with the ground almonds.
2. Mix together the egg yolks, whole eggs, lemon juice and vanilla essence. Add this to the sugar mixture and beat briefly with a wooden spoon.

3. Lightly dust the working surface with icing sugar. Knead the paste until just smooth (overworking will draw the oil out of the almonds, giving a too greasy paste).
4. Wrap well and store in a cool place.

## TO COVER A ROUND CAKE WITH UNCOOKED MARZIPAN

FOR A 22CM/9 INCH DIAMETER CAKE:
*uncooked marzipan made with 450g/1lb ground almonds*
*apricot glaze (see page 146)*
*icing sugar*

1. If the cake is not level, carefully shave off some of the top and turn it upside down.
2. Measure around the side with a piece of string.
3. Lightly dust a very clean work surface with

icing sugar and roll out two-thirds of the marzipan to a strip the length of the piece of string and the depth of the cake. Trim it neatly.

4. Roll out the remaining marzipan to a circle the size of the cake top.

5. Brush the sides of the cake with apricot glaze and, holding the cake firmly between both hands, turn it on to its side and roll it along the prepared strip of marzipan. Turn the cake right side up again. Use a round-bladed knife to smooth the join. Take a jam jar or straight-sided tin and roll it around the side of the cake.

6. Brush the top with apricot glaze and, using a rolling pin, lift the circle of marzipan on to the cake. Seal the edges with the knife and smooth the top with a rolling pin.

7. Leave to dry on a cake board 5cm/2 inches larger in diameter than the cake.

## TO COVER A SQUARE CAKE WITH UNCOOKED MARZIPAN

FOR A 20CM/8 INCH SQUARE CAKE:
*uncooked marzipan made with 450g/1lb ground*
*almonds*
*apricot glaze (see page 146)*
*icing sugar*

1. If the cake is not level, shave off a little of the top. Turn it upside down.

2. Measure one side of the cake with a piece of string.

3. Lightly dust a very clean work surface with icing sugar and roll out two-thirds of the marzipan into 4 strips the length of the piece of string and the depth of the cake. Trim neatly.

4. Roll the remaining marzipan, with any trimmings, to a square to fit the top of the cake.

5. Brush one side of the cake with apricot glaze. Turn the cake on to its side and, holding it firmly between both hands, place the glazed edge on one strip of marzipan. Trim the edges and repeat with the other three sides. Smooth the joins with a round-bladed knife. Take a jam jar or straight-sided tin and roll it around the sides of the cake, keeping the corners square.

6. Brush the top of the cake with apricot glaze and, using a rolling pin, lift the square of marzipan on to the cake. Seal the edges with the knife and smooth the top with a rolling pin. Leave to dry on a cake board about 5cm/ 2 inches wider, all round, than the cake.

NOTE: Square cakes are normally covered with uncooked marzipan. The cooked paste is too pliable and it is therefore difficult to get square corners.

❄ ❄ ❄ ❄ ❄ ❄ ❄ ❄ ❄ ❄ ❄ ❄ ❄ ❄ ❄ ❄ ❄ ❄ ❄ ❄ ❄

# Cooked Marzipan

This recipe gives a softer, easier-to-handle paste than the more usual uncooked marzipan.

*3 small eggs*
*225g/8oz caster sugar*
*225g/8oz icing sugar*
*450g/1lb ground almonds*
*4 drops vanilla essence*
*7.5ml/1½ teaspoons lemon juice*
*icing sugar for kneading*

1. Lightly beat the eggs.
2. Sift the sugars together and mix with the eggs.
3. Place the bowl over a pan of boiling water and whisk until light and creamy. Remove from the heat and allow to cool.
4. Add the almonds, vanilla and lemon juice.
5. Lightly dust the working surface with icing sugar. Carefully knead the paste until just smooth. (Overworking will draw out the oil from the almonds giving a too greasy paste.) Wrap well and store in a cool place.

## TO COVER A ROUND CAKE WITH COOKED MARZIPAN

FOR A 22CM/9 INCH DIAMETER CAKE:
*cooked marzipan made with 450g/1lb ground almonds*
*apricot glaze (see page 146)*
*icing sugar*

1. If the cake is not very level shave off the top carefully. Turn it upside down, so that the level bottom becomes the top of the cake. Brush lightly with apricot glaze.
2. Lightly dust a very clean worktop with icing sugar and roll out the marzipan to a circle 20cm/8 inches larger in diameter than the cake.
3. Place the glazed cake upside down in the centre of the marzipan and, using your hands, carefully work the marzipan up the sides of the cake.
4. Take a jam jar or straight-sided tin and roll it around the sides of the cake to make sure that the sides are quite straight, and the edges square.
5. Turn it the right way up and place on a cake board 5cm/2 inches larger in diameter than the cake.

NOTE: Once a cake has been covered with marzipan, it should be left for a minimum of 2 days, but ideally a week, before icing, otherwise the marzipan colour can leak into the icing.

## TO PREPARE A CAKE TIN

1. Cut 2 pieces of greaseproof paper to fit the base of the cake tin.
2. Cut another piece long enough to go round the sides of the tin and to overlap slightly. It should be 2.5cm/1inch deeper than the cake tin.
3. Fold one long edge of this strip over 2.5cm/1 inch all along its length.
4. Cut snips at right angles to the edge and about 1cm/½ inch apart, all along the folded side. The snips should just reach the fold.
5. Grease the tin, place one paper base in the bottom and grease again.
6. Fit the long strip inside the tin with the folded cut edge on the bottom and the uncut part lining the sides of the tin. Press them into the corners.
7. Grease the paper and lay the second base on top of the first.
8. Brush the base again with more melted lard or oil and dust the lined pan with flour.

❋ ❋ ❋ ❋ ❋ ❋ ❋ ❋ ❋ ❋ ❋ ❋ ❋ ❋ ❋ ❋ ❋ ❋ ❋ ❋ ❋

✻ ✻ ✻ ✻ ✻ ✻ ✻ ✻ ✻ ✻ ✻ ✻ ✻ ✻ ✻ ✻ ✻ ✻ ✻ ✻ ✻ ✻

# BREADS

✻ ✻ ✻ ✻ ✻ ✻ ✻ ✻ ✻ ✻ ✻ ✻ ✻ ✻ ✻ ✻ ✻ ✻ ✻ ✻ ✻ ✻

*Plaited white bread*
*Italian bread*
*Brown soda bread*
*Walnut bread*
*Curried pumpkin bread*

✻ ✻ ✻ ✻ ✻ ✻ ✻ ✻ ✻ ✻ ✻ ✻ ✻ ✻ ✻ ✻ ✻ ✻ ✻ ✻ ✻ ✻

**Using dried yeast**
*If substituting dried for fresh yeast when following a recipe,
halve the weight of yeast called for. Dried yeast takes
slightly longer to work than fresh yeast, and must
first be 'sponged' in the liquid, partly to reconstitute it,
partly to check that it is still active.
To avoid any beery taste, use rather less than the amount of
dried yeast called for and allow a long rising and proving
time. Using too much yeast generally means too
fast a rise, resulting in bread with a coarse texture that
goes stale quickly.
Easy-blend dried yeast is mixed directly with the flour,
not reconstituted in liquid first. Sold in small airtight
packages, it is usually included in bought bread mixtures.
One 7g/¼oz package usually equals 15g/½oz
conventional dried yeast or 30g/1oz fresh yeast.*

✻ ✻ ✻ ✻ ✻ ✻ ✻ ✻ ✻ ✻ ✻ ✻ ✻ ✻ ✻ ✻ ✻ ✻ ✻ ✻ ✻ ✻

# Plaited White Loaf

*450g/1lb warmed plain flour (preferably 'strong')*
*5ml/1 teaspoon salt*
*290ml/¹/2 pint tepid milk*
*15g/¹/2oz butter*
*15g/¹/2oz fresh yeast*
*5ml/1 teaspoon caster sugar*
*1 egg, beaten*
*milk and poppy seeds for glazing*

1. Sift the flour and salt into a warm mixing bowl. Make a well in the centre.
2. Heat the milk, melt the butter in it and allow to cool until tepid. Cream the yeast and sugar together. Mix the milk, egg and creamed yeast together and pour into the well.
3. Mix and knead until smooth and elastic (this should take 10-15 minutes). The dough should be soft.
4. Cover the bowl with a piece of oiled polythene and put to rise in a warm place for about an hour. It should double in bulk.
5. Heat the oven to 200°C/400°F/gas mark 6.
6. Divide the dough into 3 equal pieces and knead on a floured board. Form a long sausage with each piece and plait them together. Place on a greased baking sheet.
7. Cover again with the oiled polythene and prove (allow to rise) in a warm place for 15 minutes.
8. Brush with milk, sprinkle with poppy seeds and bake for about 25 minutes or until the loaf is golden and sounds hollow when tapped on the underside.

NOTE: If using dried yeast or easy-blend see page 154.

# Italian Bread

This is a basic olive oil bread which can be adapted easily by adding a variety of herbs such as rosemary or sage or by adding grated cheese or halved, stoned olives. It can also be drizzled with olive oil and sprinkled lightly with sea salt just before baking.

1. Dissolve the yeast in the warm water.
2. Sift the flour and salt on to a work surface, and make a well in the centre. Pour in the dissolved yeast and olive oil. Gradually draw in the flour and when all the ingredients are well mixed, knead the dough for 8 minutes.
3. Put the dough in a lightly floured bowl. Cover with a damp tea towel and leave to rise in a warm place. This will take about 1 hour.
4. Knock back the dough and shape as required. Prove until 1¹/2 times its original size (this will take about 15 minutes) and bake at 230°C/450°F/gas mark 8 for 10 minutes. Reduce the oven temperature to 190°C/375°F/gas mark 5 and bake for about 45 minutes. Remove to a cooling rack and leave to get completely cold.

Note: If using dried yeast or easy-blend see page 154.

# Brown Soda Bread

Many soda bread recipes call for buttermilk, but we have found that this works well using milk.

*900g/2lb wholemeal flour, or 675g/1½lb wholemeal flour and 225g/8oz plain white flour*
*10ml/2 teaspoons salt*
*10ml/2 teaspoons bicarbonate of soda*
*20ml/4 teaspoons cream of tartar*
*10ml/2 teaspoons sugar*
*45g/1½oz butter*
*570-860ml/1-1½ pints milk (if using all*

*wholemeal flour, the recipe will need more liquid than if made with a mixture of 2 flours)*

1. Set the oven to 190°C/375°F/gas mark 5.
2. Sift the dry ingredients into a warm dry bowl.
3. Rub in the butter and mix to a soft dough with the milk.
4. Shape with a minimum of kneading into a large circle about 5cm/2 inches thick. With the handle of a wooden spoon, make a cross on the top of the loaf. The dent should be 2cm/¾ inch deep.
5. Bake on a greased baking sheet for 25-30 minutes. Allow to cool on a wire rack.

# Walnut Bread

This bread is particularly delicious when served with apple and walnut marmalade (see opposite) and Roquefort cheese.

*225g/8oz strong plain flour*
*225g/8oz malted brown flour*
*5ml/1 teaspoon salt*
*15g/½oz fresh yeast or 7g/¼oz dried yeast*
*290ml/½ pint lukewarm milk*
*15ml/1 tablespoon olive oil*
*225g/8oz walnuts, roughly chopped*
*1 egg, lightly beaten*
*15g/1 tablespoon runny honey*

TO SERVE:

*apple and walnut marmalade (see opposite)*
*wedges of Roquefort cheese*

1. Sift the flours and salt into a large mixing bowl and make a well in the centre.
2. Mix the yeast with a tablespoon of warm milk. Pour into the well with the rest of the milk and oil.
3. Mix with a knife and then draw together with the fingers of one hand to make a soft but not sticky dough.
4. Knead until smooth and elastic (about 10 minutes), using more flour if necessary.
5. Put the dough into a large, clean bowl and cover with a piece of lightly greased polythene. Put in a warm place to rise until it has doubled in bulk, about 1 hour.
6. Set the oven to 190°C/375°F/gas mark 5.
7. Knock back the dough and knead the walnuts into it. Divide the dough into 2 pieces and shape into ovals. Place on a baking sheet. Slash the tops with a sharp knife.
8. Cover the loaves with lightly greased polythene and leave in a warm place until they have reached 1½ times their original size.

9. Mix the beaten egg and honey together, and brush evenly over the loaves. Bake in the oven for 30 minutes, or until they sound hollow when tapped on the underside.
10. Place on a wire rack to cool.

11. Serve the marmalade and Roquefort cheese separately.

NOTE: If using dried yeast or easy-blend see page 154.

❄❄❄❄❄❄❄❄❄❄❄❄❄❄❄❄❄❄❄❄

# Apple and Walnut Marmalade

This recipe was first cooked for us by Lesley Waters who served it with the walnut bread and Roquefort cheese.

*900g/2lb eating apples (preferably red)*
*110g/4oz unsalted butter*
*juice and zest of 1 lemon*
*225g/8oz brown sugar*
*225g/8oz walnuts, roughly chopped*
*30ml/1 fl oz brandy*

1. Quarter and core the apples.
2. In a large saucepan melt the butter with the lemon juice and zest. Stir in the sugar and add the apples. Cover with a lid and cook very gently until just soft. Remove the lid and reduce the excess liquid over a high heat. Add the brandy and cook for 1 minute. Allow to cool.
3. Add the roughly chopped walnuts and serve with the walnut bread (see opposite) and a slice of Roquefort cheese.

NOTE: This should not be made too far in advance – it does not keep well for more than 2-3 days.

❄❄❄❄❄❄❄❄❄❄❄❄❄❄❄❄❄❄❄❄

# Curried Pumpkin Bread

MAKES 2x450g/1lb LOAVES

*225g/8oz plain flour*

*225g/8oz polenta or coarse cornmeal*

*10ml/2 teaspoons baking powder*

*5ml/1 teaspoon bicarbonate of soda*

*45g/1<sup>1</sup>/2oz caster sugar*

*85g/3oz unsalted butter*

*2 onions, finely chopped*

*2.5ml/<sup>1</sup>/2 teaspoon ground turmeric*

*2.5ml/<sup>1</sup>/2 teaspoon ground coriander*

*2.5ml/<sup>1</sup>/2 teaspoon ground cumin*

*<sup>1</sup>/8 teaspoon cayenne pepper*

*10ml/2 teaspoons salt*

*20g/<sup>3</sup>/4oz cumin seeds, toasted lightly and cooled*

*1 x 425g/15oz can pumpkin purée*

*3 eggs*

*150ml/<sup>1</sup>/4 pint buttermilk*

1. Set the oven to 180°C/350°C/gas mark 4. Grease 2 x 450g/1lb loaf tins.

2. Sift together the flour, cornmeal, baking powder, bicarbonate of soda and the sugar.

3. Melt 30g/1oz of the butter in a frying pan, and add the onion, turmeric, coriander, ground cumin, cayenne pepper and salt. Cook over a low heat for 5 minutes, stirring all the time. Let the mixture cool and add the cumin seeds. Melt the remaining butter in a small saucepan. Put the pumpkin purée, eggs, buttermilk, melted butter and onion mixture into a large bowl. Whisk together.

4. Make a well in the flour mixture and add the pumpkin and onion mixture, stirring well to form a batter. Pour into the prepared loaf tins.

5. Place in the centre of the preheated oven for 40-45 minutes or until the breads spring back when touched.

6. Remove from the bread tins and allow to cool on a wire rack.

# CREATIVE LEFTOVERS

Lentil soup
Carrot and coriander soup
Simple vegetable soup
Salad tiède
Cheese soufflé
Quiche Lorraine
Creamy fish flan with burnt hollandaise
Gougère
Pork, ham or turkey pie
Fish pie
Warm turkey salad
Stir-fried turkey
Turkey in spicy tomato sauce
Turkey and Gruyère pancakes
Turkey à la king
Turkey cakes
Pulled and devilled turkey
Turkey Florentine

Mincemeat 'bombe'
'Tired' fruit ice cream
Banana cake

✳ ✳ ✳ ✳ ✳ ✳ ✳ ✳ ✳ ✳ ✳ ✳ ✳ ✳ ✳ ✳ ✳ ✳ ✳

# CREATIVE LEFTOVERS AND GETTING PREPARED IN ADVANCE

✳ ✳ ✳ ✳ ✳ ✳ ✳ ✳ ✳ ✳ ✳ ✳ ✳ ✳ ✳ ✳ ✳ ✳ ✳

*When not cooking for a special occasion over the Christmas holiday, most of us will be foraging in the fridge hoping for inspiration. This can be found most easily if you are organized and have done some advance preparation. Obviously, there will be a shopping expedition to buy all of the normal household goods: kitchen paper, aluminium foil, bread, sugar, tea, coffee, etc. Naturally, you will have wrapped and dealt with all the presents. If you are feeling on top of things, you will probably have remembered to buy a few extra presents for unexpected guests. You might even have frozen plenty of ice cubes in advance and made some French dressing. Your cupboard will doubtless be filled with much soap, washing up liquid and toothpaste.*

You also need to make a shopping list of all the other useful extra ingredients that can make creative leftover cooking easier and more exciting. We would suggest the following items for your store cupboard and refrigerator:

> *Good-quality oils, e.g. walnut, hazelnut, extra virgin olive oil*
> *Fresh herbs (these keep well, stalks down, in cold water in the 'fridge)*
> *Soy sauce*
> *Cheeses, including Parmesan*
> *Rice: basmati, organic brown, wild, etc.*
> *Pasta: all different types*

> *Dried milk*
> *Boxed juices*
> *Worcestershire sauce*
> *Sun-dried tomatoes*
> *Hoi sin sauce*
> *Canned tomatoes*
> *Canned beans*
> *Dried mushrooms*
> *Dried beans and lentils for soups*

The important thing when cooking with leftovers is not to try to be too clever – don't be tempted to use everything up together.

We have included a few recipes that use leftover meat and vegetables. You can use them as a basis for experimentation. There are some types of dishes that are particularly suitable for leftover cooking such as:

*Soups*

*Soufflés*

*Flans*

*Pies*

*Stir-fries*

*Warm salads*

*Gougères*

*Stuffed pancakes*

We have included a few examples of such types of dishes with relevant helpful hints on how to adapt them depending on what is available in your refrigerator. Fridges are always full to bursting over the Christmas holiday. It is quite easy to extend your fridge by buying and freezing some extra 'freezellas' and putting them into picnic boxes. You can also use window sills for chilling wine, mineral water and juice.

# Lentil Soup

This recipe calls for ham stock – we are assuming that you will be cooking a ham – if not, use water instead.

SERVES 4
30g/1oz butter
110g/4oz carrot, diced
55g/2oz celery, diced
1 onion, chopped
110g/4oz potatoes, diced
170g/6oz red lentils,washed
freshly ground black pepper
150ml/¼ pint milk
1.1 litres/2 pints ham stock (the liquid left over from cooking the ham)
freshly ground black pepper

1. Melt the butter in a large saucepan. Add the carrot, celery and onion. Stir over a low heat for about 5 minutes. Add the potatoes and lentils and stir well. Cook gently for 1 minute, then season with pepper.
2. Add the milk and ham stock. Bring to the boil and simmer for approximately 30 minutes, or until all the vegetables and lentils are very soft.
3. Liquidize the soup, then taste and add more pepper or some salt if necessary.

SPICY DRY WHITE

# Carrot and Coriander Soup

For this recipe we have specified carrots, but other root vegetables, such as parsnips or celeriac, could be used as a substitute or to complement the carrots.

SERVES 4
675g/1½lb carrots, sliced
1 onion, finely chopped
15g/½oz butter
1 bay leaf
1.1 litres/2 pints chicken stock or water
salt and freshly ground black pepper
15ml/1 tablespoon chopped fresh parsley
15ml/1 tablespoon chopped fresh coriander
60ml/4 tablespoons double cream

1. Put the carrots and onion in a saucepan with the butter. Sweat for 10 minutes, or until they are beginning to soften. Add the bay leaf, stock, salt and pepper. Bring up to the boil and simmer very gently for 25 minutes.
2. Add the parsley and coriander and simmer for a further 2-3 minutes. Remove the bay leaf.
3. Liquidize the soup and push through a sieve into a clean saucepan. Check the consistency. If it is a little thin, reduce it by rapid boiling; if it is a little thick, add some more water.
4. Add the cream and season to taste.

AUSTRALIAN/CALIFORNIAN
SAUVIGNON BLANC

# Simple Vegetable Soup

This recipe specifies onions, carrots, potatoes and celery, but most leftover raw vegetables could be used as a substitute or to complement as required.

SERVES 8

45g/1 1/2oz butter
225g/8oz onions, chopped
450g/1lb carrots, chopped
225g/8oz potatoes, chopped
110g/4oz celery, chopped
425ml/3/4 pint milk
860ml/1 1/2 pints water
salt and freshly ground black pepper

1. Melt the butter in a large heavy pan with 30ml/2 tablespoons water. Add all the chopped vegetables, stir and cover with a lid. Cook slowly until soft but not coloured, stirring occasionally. This will take about 30 minutes.
2. Add the milk and water. Season with salt and pepper and simmer, uncovered, for 15 minutes.
3. Liquidize the soup and pass through a sieve.
4. Pour into the rinsed-out saucepan. Season to taste, and add more water if the soup is too thick. Reheat carefully.

DRY WHITE/LIGHT RED

❋❋❋❋❋❋❋❋❋❋❋❋❋❋❋❋❋❋❋❋

# Salad Tiède

This recipe is quite delicious but none of the ingredients, with the exception of the bread croûtons, is indispensable. Any salad leaves will do. Ham can be used in place of the bacon, and shredded turkey can be substituted for the livers. Do use a good-quality olive oil to make the French dressing.

SERVES 6-8

1 small frisée lettuce
1 small oakleaf lettuce
1 bunch watercress
1 small radicchio
2 heads celery
French dressing (see page 195)
200ml/7 fl oz olive oil
110g/4oz piece of rindless bacon, diced
5 spring onions
4 slices white bread, cut into 1cm/1/2 inch cubes
salt
225g/8oz chicken livers, cleaned
15ml/1 tablespoon tarragon vinegar
1 bunch chervil, roughly chopped

1. Toss the salad in the well-seasoned French dressing and divide it between 4 dinner plates.
2. Heat 30ml/1 tablespoon of the olive oil in a frying pan and cook the bacon until it is evenly browned all over. Lift it out with a perforated spoon and keep warm in a low oven.
3. Cook the spring onions in the frying pan quickly for 1 minute, and keep them warm in the oven too.
4. Heat 150ml/1/4 pint of the olive oil in another frying pan and cook the bread until golden brown. Drain well and sprinkle with a little salt.

Keep the croûtons warm in the oven.

5. Add the remaining olive oil to the first frying pan and gently cook the livers until slightly stiffened and fairly firm but not hard to the touch. They should be light brown on the outside and pink in the middle.

6. Add the tarragon vinegar to the pan and shake the livers in the vinegar for 10 seconds.

7. Scatter the croûtons, the bacon, the spring onions and finally the livers over the salad. Sprinkle the salad with the chervil and serve immediately.

SPICY DRY WHITE

❋ ❋ ❋ ❋ ❋ ❋ ❋ ❋ ❋ ❋ ❋ ❋ ❋ ❋ ❋ ❋ ❋ ❋ ❋ ❋

# Cheese Soufflé

This is the perfect way to use up tired hard cheeses. Any mixture will do although a little Gruyère or Edam will help to improve the texture of the finished soufflé.

SERVES 2

35g/1¼oz butter
dry white breadcrumbs
30g/1oz flour
2.5ml/½ teaspoon made English mustard
pinch of cayenne pepper
290ml/½ pint milk
85g/3oz strong Cheddar or Gruyère cheese, grated
4 eggs, separated
salt and pepper

1. Set the oven to 200°C/400°F/gas mark 6. Melt a knob of the butter and brush out a 15cm/6 inch soufflé dish with it. Dust lightly with the breadcrumbs.

2. Melt the rest of the butter in a saucepan and stir in the flour, mustard and cayenne pepper. Cook for 45 seconds. Add the milk and cook, stirring vigorously, for 2 minutes. The mixture will get very thick and leave the sides of the pan. Take it off the heat.

3. Stir in the cheese, egg yolks, salt and pepper. Taste; the mixture should be very well seasoned.

4. Whisk the egg whites until stiff, but not dry, and mix a spoonful into the mixture. Then fold in the rest and pour into the soufflé dish, which should be about two-thirds full. Run your finger around the top of the soufflé mixture. This gives a 'top hat' appearance to the cooked soufflé.

5. Bake for 25-30 minutes and serve straight away. (Do not test to see if the soufflé is done for at least 20 minutes. Then open the oven just wide enough to get your hand in and give the soufflé a slight shove. If it wobbles alarmingly, cook for a further 5 minutes.)

SPICY DRY WHITE

❋ ❋ ❋ ❋ ❋ ❋ ❋ ❋ ❋ ❋ ❋ ❋ ❋ ❋ ❋ ❋ ❋ ❋ ❋ ❋

# Quiche Lorraine

This is a classic recipe. It makes enough for two people and is a 'comfort' dish. If you want to make it into a supper dish for four people, double the quantity. The bacon can be left out easily in favour of any leftover chopped ham. Any hard cheese can be used in place of the Cheddar or Gruyère.

SERVES 2

*rich shortcrust pastry made with 110g/4oz flour (see page 200)*

FOR THE FILLING:

*1/2 small onion, finely chopped*
*55g/2oz bacon, diced*
*7.5g/1/4oz butter*
*75ml/5 tablespoons milk*
*75ml/5 tablespoons single cream*
*1 egg*
*1 egg yolk*
*30g/1oz strong Cheddar or Gruyère, grated*
*salt and pepper*

1. Roll out the pastry and line a flan ring about 15cm/6 inches in diameter. Leave in the fridge for about 45 minutes to relax – this prevents shrinkage during cooking.

2. Set the oven to 190°C/375°F/gas mark 5. Bake the pastry case blind (see below).

3. Fry the onion and bacon gently in the butter. When cooked but not coloured, drain well.

4. Mix together the milk, cream and eggs. Add the onion, bacon and half the cheese. Season with salt and pepper (the bacon and cheese are both salty, so be careful not to overseason).

5. Turn down the oven to 150°C/300°F/gas mark 2.

6. Pour the mixture into the prepared flan ring and sprinkle over the remaining cheese. Place the flan in the middle of the heated oven and bake for about 40 minutes.

7. Remove the flan ring and bake for a further 5 minutes to allow the pastry to brown. The top should be golden and set.

8. Serve hot or cold.

NOTE: To bake blind, line the raw pastry case with a piece of foil or a double sheet of greaseproof paper and fill it with dried lentils, beans, rice or even pebbles or coins. This is to prevent the pastry bubbling up during cooking. When the pastry is half cooked (about 15 minutes) the 'blind beans' can be removed and the empty pastry case further dried out in the oven. The beans can be re-used indefinitely.

WHITE ALSACE

✳ ✳ ✳ ✳ ✳ ✳ ✳ ✳ ✳ ✳ ✳ ✳ ✳ ✳ ✳ ✳ ✳ ✳ ✳

# Creamy Fish Flan with Burnt Hollandaise

This fish flan is one of the most popular recipes at Leith's school, and it can easily be adapted. The fish can be leftover cooked fish mixed with a well-flavoured béchamel sauce (see page 182). You can make it equally well with a mixture of delicious leftover vegetables such as leeks, carrots and Savoy cabbage. Again, simply mix the cooked vegetables with a well-flavoured béchamel sauce and then add the egg yolk and fold in the egg white.

SERVES 4

*shortcrust pastry made with 170g/6oz flour*
   *(see page 199)*
*1 small onion, finely chopped*
*30g/1oz butter*
*30g/1oz flour*
*1 bay leaf*
*290ml/¹/2 pint milk*
*salt and freshly ground black pepper*
*1 egg*
*225g/8oz white fish, cooked and flaked*

*15ml/1 tablespoon chopped fresh parsley*
*squeeze of lemon juice*
*hollandaise sauce made with 55g/2oz butter*
   *(see page 193)*

1. Set the oven to 190°C/375°F/gas mark 5. Line a 20cm/8 inch flan ring with pastry and bake blind.
2. Reduce the oven temperature to 180°C/350°F/ gas mark 4.
3. Cook the onion in the butter until soft but not coloured. Add the flour and bay leaf. Cook, stirring, for 1 minute. Remove from the heat, stir in the milk, and bring slowly to the boil, stirring continuously. Taste and season as necessary. Simmer for 2 minutes, remove the bay leaf and allow to cool for 5 minutes.
4. Separate the egg and beat the yolk into the sauce. Stir in the fish, parsley and lemon juice to taste. Whisk the egg white until stiff but not dry and fold into the mixture. Pour into the pastry case. Bake until firm and set (about 25 minutes).
5. Heat up the grill 10 minutes before the flan is cooked.
6. Prepare the hollandaise sauce and spoon over the flan. Put the flan under the grill until the top is nicely browned. Serve at once.

CHABLIS

❄ ❄ ❄ ❄ ❄ ❄ ❄ ❄ ❄ ❄ ❄ ❄ ❄ ❄ ❄ ❄ ❄ ❄ ❄

# Gougère

A gougère is a cheese choux pastry ring which may be filled with a variety of mixtures.
We have included a recipe using cooked game, turkey or ham. This same sauce could be adapted for cooked fish, if you substitute chicken stock for fish stock (see page 179).

The cheese called for is Cheddar cheese but any leftover hard cheese will be fine, although Edam and Gruyère will make for very 'stringy' pastry.

SERVES 4

105g/3³/4oz plain flour
pinch of salt
pepper and cayenne
85g/3oz butter
225ml/7 fl oz water
3 eggs, lightly beaten
55g/2oz strong Cheddar cheese, cut into 5mm/¹/4
    inch cubes

425ml/³/4 pint filling (see below)
15ml/1 tablespoon browned crumbs
15ml/1 tablespoon grated cheese

1. Set the oven to 200°C/400°F/gas mark 6.
2. Sift the flour with the seasonings.
3. In a large saucepan slowly heat the butter in the water and when completely melted bring up to a rolling boil. When the mixture is bubbling, tip in the flour, take off the heat and beat well with a wooden spoon until the mixture leaves the sides of the pan. Allow to cool for 10 minutes.
4. Beat in the eggs gradually until the mixture is smooth and shiny and of a 'dropping consistency' – you may not need the last few spoonfuls of egg. Stir in the diced cheese.
5. Spoon the mixture round the edge of a flattish greased ovenproof dish. Bake for 25 minutes. Pile the filling into the centre and sprinkle with the crumbs and grated cheese. Bake until the choux is well risen and golden and the filling is hot (about 15 minutes).

❋ ❋ ❋ ❋ ❋ ❋ ❋ ❋ ❋ ❋ ❋ ❋ ❋ ❋ ❋ ❋ ❋ ❋ ❋

# Game, Turkey or Ham Filling for Gougère

SERVES 4

1 medium onion, finely sliced
30g/1oz butter
110g/4oz large mushrooms, sliced
20g/³/4oz flour
290ml/¹/2 pint white stock (see page 178)
salt and freshly ground black pepper

10ml/2 teaspoons chopped fresh parsley
340g/12oz cooked game, turkey or ham, shredded

1. Soften the onion in the butter over gentle heat. Add the mushrooms. Cook for 1 minute.
2. Stir in the flour. Cook for 1 minute.
3. Draw the pan off the heat and stir in the stock. Return to the heat. Bring up to the boil, stirring continuously. Season. Simmer for 1 minute.
4. Add the parsley and game or chicken and use as required.

RED BURGUNDY

# Pork, Ham or Turkey Pie

This recipe describes how to cook pork fillets in order to make the pie. If you have leftover cold roast pork simply remove the fat from the pork and mince the meat finely. It can be made equally well with leftover ham or turkey or a mixture of both.

SERVES 8-10

675g/1 1/2lb pork (tenderloin fillet)
pâte à pâté made with 450g/1lb flour(see page 204)
45g/1 1/2oz butter
45g/1 1/2oz flour
225ml/8 fl oz white stock (see page 178)
55ml/2 fl oz dry white wine
2 eggs
55ml/2 fl oz double cream
salt and freshly ground black pepper
15ml/1 tablespoon chopped parsley
30ml/2 tablespoons chopped thyme leaves
beaten egg to glaze

1. Set the oven to 200°C/400°F/gas mark 6.
2. Trim the pork fillet, discarding any fat, sinew or gristle. Place in a roasting pan and roast uncovered for 30 minutes. Remove from the oven and allow to cool.
3. Place a third of the pastry in the refrigerator. Divide the remaining pastry in half. Roll out one piece into a long strip to fit the sides of a 20cm/8 inch spring-clip tin. Press it round the sides neatly. Roll out the second piece to fit the base of the tin. Press the base and sides together carefully. Prick the base well and place it in the refrigerator to chill.
4. Meanwhile, make the filling: mince the pork fillet finely.
5. Melt the butter in a heavy saucepan, stir in the flour and stir over the heat for 1 minute. Remove the pan from the heat, add the stock and wine and mix well. Return to the heat and stir or whisk until it comes up to the boil. Simmer for 5 minutes, stirring occasionally. (If the sauce is too thick add some water, but it should be a thick panade.)
6. Remove the pan from the heat, separate the eggs and beat the yolks into the sauce with the cream. Season carefully with salt, freshly ground black pepper, parsley and thyme. Add the minced pork.
7. Whisk the egg whites until stiff and fold into the mixture. Taste and add more seasoning if necessary.
8. Place the filling in the pastry case making it slightly domed in the centre.
9. Roll out the remaining pastry for the lid. Dampen the bottom edge with water and press the lid on to the pastry case. Trim and crimp the edges. Make a neat hole in the middle of the lid. Decorate with pastry trimmings made into leaves.
10. Brush with egg glaze and cook on a baking sheet in the oven for 40 minutes. Serve cold.

LIGHT RED/ROSE

❄ ❄ ❄ ❄ ❄ ❄ ❄ ❄ ❄ ❄ ❄ ❄ ❄ ❄ ❄ ❄ ❄ ❄ ❄

# Fish Pie

This recipe assumes that you are using raw fish – however if you have any leftover cooked fish it can be used instead. Simply mix the cooked fish with a well-flavoured béchamel sauce (see page 182). A mixture of different types of fish would be very suitable. Slices of leftover tomato can be arranged between the fish mixture and the mashed potatoes.

SERVES 6

*900g/2lb fillet of haddock, whiting, cod or a
    mixture of any of them*
*425ml/³/4 pint milk*
*¹/2 onion, sliced*
*6 peppercorns*
*1 bay leaf*
*salt and pepper*
*5 hardboiled eggs, quartered*
*15ml/1 tablespoon chopped parsley*
*30g/1oz butter*
*30g/1oz flour*
*30ml/2 tablespoons cream*
*675g/1¹/2lb mashed potatoes (see page 109)*
*butter*

1. Set the oven to 180°C/350°F/gas mark 4.
2. Lay the fish fillets in a roasting pan.
3. Heat the milk with the onion, peppercorns, bay leaf and a pinch of salt.
4. Pour over the fish and cook in the oven for about 15 minutes until the fish is firm and creamy looking.
5. Strain off the milk, reserving it for the sauce. Flake the fish into a pie dish and add the eggs. Sprinkle over the parsley.
6. Heat the butter in a saucepan, stir in the flour and cook for 1 minute. Draw off the heat and gradually add the reserved milk
7. Return to the heat and stir, bringing slowly to the boil. Taste and add salt and pepper as needed. Stir in the cream and pour over the fish, mixing it with a palette knife or spoon.
8. Spread a layer of mashed potatoes on the top and mark with a fork in a criss-cross pattern. Dot with butter. Place on a baking sheet and brown in the oven for about 10 minutes, or longer if the pie has been made in advance.

DRY WHITE

# Warm Turkey Salad

This recipe can be adapted according to what ingredients there are in your refrigerator. If you have used up all your leftover turkey it can be made with large bite-sized pieces of raw pheasant or chicken that have been dipped in seasoned flour and then fried gently in sunflower oil until just tender. This will take about 8-10 minutes.

SERVES 4

*340g/12oz cooked turkey*
*salad leaves such as frisée, lamb's lettuce,*
   *gem lettuce, rocket*
*110g/4oz baby sweetcorn*
*110g/4oz broccoli*
*salt and freshly ground black pepper*
*sunflower oil*
*110g/4oz shitake or chestnut mushrooms*
*1 bunch chives, chopped*
*60ml/4 tablespoons walnut oil*
*15ml/1 tablespoon balsamic vinegar*

1. Break the turkey into large bite-sized pieces.
2. Put the salad leaves into a large salad bowl.
3. Cook the sweetcorn and broccoli in a small amount of salted boiling water.
4. Meanwhile, fry the mushrooms, then add the turkey and warm through.
5. Drain the sweetcorn and broccoli, and transfer all the ingredients to the salad bowl.
6. Toss together, season well and serve immediately.

NOTE: This recipe is truly very versatile. It is delicious with any of the following ingredients:
   *fried aubergines*
   *sun-dried tomatoes*
   *crisp pieces of bacon*
   *skinned, grilled red pepper, cut into strips*
   *mozzarella cheese, cut into cubes*
   *avocado pears, cut into chunks*

SPICY DRY WHITE OR LIGHT RED

# Stir-Fried Turkey

With a stir-fry, all the ingredients are usually raw when they are put into the wok. This recipe assumes that you have got leftover cooked turkey, but again you can adapt it according to what you have in the 'fridge. It should look bright and fresh so take care not to overcook any of the vegetables.

SERVES 4
*450g/1lb cooked turkey*

FOR THE MARINADE:
*1 small garlic clove, crushed*
*1cm/1/2 inch piece of ginger, peeled and grated*
*45ml/3 tablespoons soy sauce*
*15ml/1 tablespoon sesame oil*
*7.5ml/1/2 tablespoon sherry*
*2.5ml/1/2 teaspoon ground turmeric*
*5ml/1 teaspoon tomato purée*

FOR THE VEGETABLES:

*30ml/2 tablespoons oil*

*1 small garlic clove, peeled and sliced*

*1cm/1/2 inch piece of ginger, peeled and cut
    into sticks*

*55g/2oz mange tout, topped and tailed*

*55g/2oz baby sweetcorn*

*55g/2oz button mushrooms, sliced*

*1 red pepper, deseeded and cut into strips on
    the diagonal*

*4 spring onions, cut into chunks on the diagonal*

*15ml/1 tablespoon sesame seeds, toasted*

1. Skin the turkey and cut the flesh into strips
the size of your little finger.

2. Mix together the ingredients for the marinade
and add the turkey. Leave for 1 hour to marinate.

3. Heat the oil in a wok, add the garlic and
ginger and stir fry gently until lightly browned.
Add all the vegetables and stir fry for 2-3 minutes.

4. Add the turkey and stir fry until thoroughly
re-heated.

5. Pile into a warm serving dish and scatter with
warm toasted sesame seeds.

ALSACE WHITE

✳ ✳ ✳ ✳ ✳ ✳ ✳ ✳ ✳ ✳ ✳ ✳ ✳ ✳ ✳ ✳ ✳ ✳ ✳ ✳

# Turkey in Spicy Tomato Sauce

*400g/14oz canned chopped tomatoes*

*squeeze of lemon juice*

*salt and freshly ground black pepper*

This is a very simple sauce to make. When you
are ready to serve, simply add strips of turkey to
the sauce and reheat thoroughly. This quantity
is enough for 4 people served with 450g/1lb
cooked turkey.

SERVES 4

FOR THE SAUCE:

*30ml/2 tablespoons oil*

*1 onion, finely chopped*

*1 garlic clove, crushed*

*1 x 1 1/4cm/1/2 inch piece of root ginger*

*10ml/2 teaspoons ground cumin*

*5ml/1 teaspoon ground chilli*

*10ml/2 teaspoons ground turmeric*

*5ml/1 teaspoon ground cardamom*

1. Put the oil into a saucepan. Add the onion,
garlic and ginger. Cook slowly for 5 minutes.
Add the spices and cook very slowly for a further
2 minutes, stirring well to prevent them burning.

2. Remove the pan from the heat. Add the
tomatoes and stir well.

3. Return to the heat, and bring up to the boil.
Add the lemon juice, salt and pepper, and simmer
slowly for 20 minutes.

4. Serve with rice or pasta.

NOTE: This sauce freezes well with or without
the turkey.

SPICY DRY WHITE

✳ ✳ ✳ ✳ ✳ ✳ ✳ ✳ ✳ ✳ ✳ ✳ ✳ ✳ ✳ ✳ ✳ ✳ ✳ ✳

# Turkey and Gruyère Pancakes

SERVES 4-6

45g/1 1/2oz butter
pinch of dry English mustard
pinch of cayenne pepper
45g/1 1/2oz flour
150ml/1/4 pint white stock (see page 178)
150ml/1/4 pint creamy milk
45ml/3 tablespoons white wine
salt and freshly ground black pepper
225g/8oz strips of cooked turkey
225g/8oz Gruyère cheese, diced
12 thin French pancakes (see page 205)
melted butter

TO SERVE:
Tomato sauce (see page 196)

1. Melt the butter, and add the mustard and cayenne pepper. Stir in the flour and cook for 1 minute. Draw the pan off the heat and stir in the stock and milk. Return to the heat and bring slowly to the boil, stirring continuously. Add the wine and simmer for 2-3 minutes. Season with salt and freshly ground black pepper.
2. Heat the grill.
3. Add the turkey and cheese to the sauce. Put a good spoonful of this mixture on to each pancake and roll up.
4. Lay the pancakes side by side in a lightly buttered fireproof dish. Brush a little extra butter over the pancakes and grill until thoroughly reheated.
5. Serve the warmed tomato sauce separately.

LIGHT RED/ROSE

❊❊❊❊❊❊❊❊❊❊❊❊❊❊❊❊❊❊❊❊❊

# Turkey à la King

SERVES 4

450g/1lb cooked turkey, cut into large chunks

FOR THE SAUCE:
45g/1 1/2oz butter
1 onion, finely sliced
1 small green pepper, deseeded and sliced
1 canned pimento, sliced
110g/4oz mushrooms, sliced
45g/1 1/2oz flour
425ml/3/4 pint white stock (see page 178)

15ml/1 tablespoon sherry
150ml/1/4 pint milk
45ml/3 tablespoons single cream
salt and freshly ground black pepper

1. Melt the butter, and cook the sliced onion gently for 2 minutes. Add the green pepper and cook for a further minute. Add the pimento, mushrooms and flour and cook, stirring for 1 minute.
2. Remove the pan from the heat and add the stock. Mix well and return the pan to the heat. Bring slowly to the boil, stirring continuously. Add the sherry, and simmer for 1-2 minutes.

3. Add the milk and cream and reheat without boiling. Season with salt and pepper.

4. Add the turkey and allow to warm through without boiling. Check the seasoning.

AUSTRALIAN/CALIFORNIAN
CHARDONNAY

# Turkey Cakes

*55g/2oz butter*
*1 small onion, chopped*
*30g/1oz mushrooms, chopped*
*55g/2oz flour*
*290ml/¹/2 pint milk, or milk and chicken stock mixed*
*salt and freshly ground black pepper*
*5ml/1 teaspoon chopped parsley*
*1 egg yolk*
*lemon juice*
*285g/10oz cooked turkey, finely diced or minced*
*seasoned flour*
*1 egg, beaten*
*dry white breadcrumbs*
*oil for frying*

1. Melt the butter and add the onion. When the onion is soft but not coloured, add the mushrooms and cook for 1 minute.

2. Add the flour and cook, stirring, for 1 minute.

Draw the pan off the heat and stir in the milk. Return to the heat and bring slowly up to the boil, stirring continuously. Simmer for 2-3 minutes, season and add the parsley. Remove from the heat and allow to get completely cold – it should be very thick.

3. When the sauce is cold, beat in the egg yolk, add a squeeze of lemon juice and stir in the cooked turkey.

4. With floured or wet hands shape the mixture into cakes – rather like fish cakes.

5. Coat with beaten egg and dip into breadcrumbs.

6. Heat the oil in a frying pan and fry the cakes slowly on each side until thoroughly reheated; this will take about 10 minutes. Serve hot.

NOTE: These turkey cakes are particularly good with the spiced tomato chutney (see page 63).

SPICY DRY WHITE

# Pulled and Devilled Turkey

Jane Grigson was one of England's most celebrated cookery writers. We reproduce her pulled and devilled turkey here with no amendments.

SERVES 4

*about 450g/1lb cooked turkey breast*

*1 leg and thigh of the turkey, preferably undercooked and pink*

FOR THE DEVIL SAUCE:

*15ml/1 rounded tablespoon Dijon mustard*

*15ml/1 rounded tablespoon mango or peach chutney*

*15ml/1 tablespoon Worcestershire sauce,*
    *or 7.5ml/¹/2 tablespoon anchovy essence*

*1.25ml/¹/4 teaspoon Cayenne pepper*

*salt*

*30ml/2 tablespoons corn oil*

FOR THE PULLED SAUCE:

*85g/3oz butter*

*170ml/6 fl oz double cream*

*lemon juice*

*salt and pepper*

*chopped parsley*

1. First pull the turkey breast meat apart with your fingers into pieces about 3.75cm/1¹/2 inches long and the 'thickness of a large quill'. Follow the grain of the meat so that you end up with somewhat thready-looking pieces. Take the brown meat off the bones, and divide it into rather larger pieces than the breast meat. Slash each one two or three times.

2. Mix the devil sauce ingredients together, chopping up any large pieces of fruit in the chutney. Dip the pieces of brown meat into it, and spoon the devil into the slashes as best you can. Arrange in a single layer on the rack of a foil-lined grill pan, and grill under a high heat until the pieces develop an appetizing brown crust. Keep them warm.

3. For the pulled sauce, melt the butter in a wide frying pan, and stir in the cream. Let it boil for a couple of minutes, and keep stirring so that you end up with a thick, rich sauce. Put in the pulled breast, with any odd scraps of jelly, and stir about until the pieces are very hot indeed. Season with lemon, salt and pepper. Put in the centre of a serving dish, and surround it with the devilled bits. Serve with good bread or toast. Not a dish to be eaten with two vegetables. Keep them for afterwards, or simply serve a salad.

✲ ✲ ✲ ✲ ✲ ✲ ✲ ✲ ✲ ✲ ✲ ✲ ✲ ✲ ✲ ✲ ✲ ✲ ✲ ✲

# Turkey Florentine

SERVES 6–8

*1 garlic clove, crushed*

*6 tomatoes, skinned and thickly sliced*

*30g/1oz butter*

*900g/2lb spinach, cooked and chopped*

*salt and freshly ground black pepper*

*pinch of ground nutmeg*

*675g/1¹/2lb cooked turkey*

*290ml/¹/2 pint cheese sauce (see page 183)*

*15ml/1 tablespoon grated cheese*

*15ml/1 tablespoon dried breadcrumbs*

1. Set the oven to 180°C/350°F/gas mark 4.

2. Fry the garlic and the tomatoes lightly in a quarter of the butter without allowing the tomatoes to get too soft. Place them in a dish big enough to hold the turkey in one layer.

3. Toss the spinach in a little butter in the pan. Season with salt, pepper and nutmeg. Spread the spinach on top of the tomatoes.

4. Cut the turkey into bite-sized pieces and arrange on top of the spinach. Season with a little salt and pepper.

5. Heat the cheese sauce and pour evenly over the turkey and spinach. Sprinkle with the grated cheese and breadcrumbs.

6. Bake for 30-40 minutes, or until bubbly and hot.

NOTE: This is an excellent way of using up leftover turkey, chicken or ham. It can be made in advance and either kept in the refrigerator or the freezer until required.

LIGHT RED

❊ ❊ ❊ ❊ ❊ ❊ ❊ ❊ ❊ ❊ ❊ ❊ ❊ ❊ ❊ ❊ ❊ ❊ ❊ ❊

# Mincemeat 'Bombe'

The perfect way to use up leftover, damaged meringues.

SERVES 8

*290ml/¹/2 pint double cream*

*45ml/3 tablespoons rum*

*225ml/8 fl oz natural yoghurt*

*8 meringue shells (see page 126), crushed*

*5ml/1 teaspoon freshly grated nutmeg*

FOR THE MINCEMEAT SAUCE:

*1 large dessert apple*

*55g/2oz raisins*

*55g/2oz sultanas*

*55g/2oz chopped hazelnuts, lightly toasted*

*55g/2oz soft dark brown sugar*

*2.5ml/¹/2 teaspoon mixed spice*

*grated rind and juice of ¹/2 lemon*

*grated rind and juice of 1 orange*

*60ml/4 tablespoons rum*

1. Lightly oil and line 8 ramekin dishes with discs of greaseproof paper.

2. Whip the cream until it holds its shape. Whisk in the rum and fold in the yoghurt, the meringue and nutmeg. Turn into the ramekin dishes and freeze until firm.

3. Peel, core and chop the apple, add the remaining ingredients for the sauce, adding more orange juice or rum to taste.

4. To serve: run a knife around the ramekins and turn the ice cream out on to plates. Place in the refrigerator for 10 minutes before serving.

5. Heat the sauce until very hot but not boiling and hand it separately.

NOTE: This can be stunning made in a large pudding basin.

SWEET WHITE

❊ ❊ ❊ ❊ ❊ ❊ ❊ ❊ ❊ ❊ ❊ ❊ ❊ ❊ ❊ ❊ ❊ ❊ ❊ ❊

# 'Tired' Fruit Ice Cream

This ice cream can be made with whatever tired-looking soft fruit, such as mangoes, kiwis and bananas, you have left in your fruit bowl. This is a basic recipe that can be adapted by the addition of grated lemon or orange rind to the fruit purée. You could also try adding 4 pieces of chopped stem ginger just before freezing the ice cream.

SERVES 6

*55g/2oz granulated sugar*
*150ml/¹/4 pint water*
*450g/1lb prepared fruit, e.g. peeled bananas and kiwis*
*4 egg yolks*
*570ml/1 pint double cream, lightly whipped*

1. Put the sugar and water into a small heavy pan, and dissolve over a gentle heat. Boil for 3 minutes. Remove from the heat and cool for 1 minute.
2. Process the prepared fruit in a food processor until you have a fine purée.
3. Put the egg yolks into a large bowl and whisk lightly. Pour on the warm sugar syrup and continue to whisk, but do not allow the syrup to touch the whisk if doing this in a machine. Fold in the fruit purée and cream. Taste and add extra flavouring such as citrus rind or ginger as required. Freeze.
4. When the ice cream is half frozen, whisk again (and add the stem ginger if using). Freeze again.
5. Remove from the freezer 30 minutes before it is to be eaten and scoop into a glass bowl.

MEDIUM SWEET WHITE

# Banana Cake

*110g/4oz butter*
*55g/2oz caster sugar*
*2 drops vanilla essence*
*5ml/1 teaspoon ground cardamom*
*2 eggs, beaten*
*170g/6oz self-raising flour*
*2 ripe bananas*
*55g/2oz walnuts, roughly chopped*
*milk, if necessary*

1. Set the oven to 180°C/350°F/gas mark 4.
2. Cream the butter in a mixing bowl, and beat in the sugar until light and fluffy. Add the vanilla essence and ground cardamom.
3. Add the beaten eggs gradually, adding a little flour every time the mixture begins to curdle. Beat very well.
4. Peel the bananas and mash well with a fork.
5. Add half the bananas to the cake mixture.
6. Stir in half the flour. Add the remaining bananas with the walnuts.
7. Stir in the remaining flour. Add a little milk if necessary – the mixture should fall reluctantly off a spoon.
8. Pile into a non-stick loaf tin and bake for 45 minutes. The cake should be risen and golden. If you pierce it with a skewer it should come out clean.
9. Allow the cake to cool for a few minutes in the tin, then turn out on to a wire rack to cool completely.
10. Serve with or without butter.

✳✳✳✳✳✳✳✳✳✳✳✳✳✳✳✳✳✳✳✳✳✳✳

# BASIC RECIPES AND TECHNIQUES

✳✳✳✳✳✳✳✳✳✳✳✳✳✳✳✳✳✳✳✳✳✳✳

STOCKS AND SAUCES
PASTRIES AND BATTERS
TECHNIQUES

| | | |
|---|---|---|
| Brown stock | Hollandaise sauce | Sugar syrup |
| White stock | Beurre blanc | Shortcrust pastry (pâte brisée) |
| Court bouilllon | Fish beurre blanc | Rich shortcrust pastry |
| Fish stock | French dressing (vinaigrette) | Almond pastry |
| Turkey stock | Pesto sauce | Lemon shorcrust pastry |
| Horseradish cream | Parsley pesto | Tartlet cases |
| Uncooked pasta sauce | Mustard sauce | Martha Stewart's walnut pastry |
| Tomato and yoghurt herb sauce | Salsa pizzaiola | Choux pastry |
| White sauce | Fresh tomato sauce (1) | Filo or strudel pastry |
| Béchamel sauce | Tomato sauce (2) | Pâte sucrée |
| Mornay sauce (cheese sauce) | Red pepper sauce | Pâte à pâté |
| Parsley sauce | Black bean sauce | Hot watercrust pastry |
| Soubise sauce | Apple sauce | French pancakes (crêpes) |
| Mayonnaise | Cumberland sauce | Jointing a chicken |
| Rémoulade sauce | Maître d'hôtel butter | Boning a chicken, turkey or pheasant |

✳✳✳✳✳✳✳✳✳✳✳✳✳✳✳✳✳✳✳✳✳✳

# Brown Stock

900g/2lb beef bones
1 onion, peeled and chopped, skin reserved
2 carrots, roughly chopped
15ml/1 tablespoon oil
parsley stalks
2 bay leaves
6 black peppercorns

1. Preheat the oven to 220°C/425°F/gas mark 7.
2. Put the beef bones in a roasting tin and brown in the oven. This may take up to 1 hour.
3. Brown the onion and carrots in the oil in a large stock pot. It is essential that they do not burn.
4. When the bones are well browned add them to the vegetables with the onion skins, parsley stalks, bay leaves and black peppercorns. Cover with cold water and bring very slowly to the boil, skimming off any scum as it rises to the surface.
5. When clear of scum, simmer gently for 3-4 hours, or even longer, skimming off the fat as necessary and topping up with water if the level gets very low. The longer it simmers, and the more the liquid reduces by evaporation, the stronger the stock will be.
6. Strain, cool and lift off any remaining fat.

# White Stock

1 onion, sliced
1 celery stick, sliced
1 carrot, sliced
chicken or veal bones, skin or flesh
parsley
thyme
bay leaf
peppercorns

1. Put all the ingredients into a saucepan. Cover generously with water and bring to the boil slowly. Skim off any fat, and/or scum.
2. Simmer for 2-3 hours, skimming frequently and topping up the water level if necessary. The liquid should reduce to half the original quantity.
3. Strain, cool and lift off all the fat.

NOTE: See also the recipes for turkey stock on pages 179 and 180.

# Court Bouillon

1.1 litres/2 pints water
150ml/¹/4 pint vinegar
1 carrot, sliced
1 onion, sliced
1 stick celery
1 large sprig parsley
12 peppercorns

2 bay leaves
30ml/2 tablespoons salad oil
salt

1. Bring all the ingredients to the boil and simmer for 20 minutes.
2. Allow the liquid to cool, strain and place the fish, meat or vegetables in it, then bring slowly to simmering point.

❊ ❊ ❊ ❊ ❊ ❊ ❊ ❊ ❊ ❊ ❊ ❊ ❊ ❊ ❊ ❊ ❊ ❊ ❊ ❊

# Fish Stock

1 onion, sliced
1 carrot, sliced
1 celery stick, sliced
fish bones, skins, fins, heads or tails, crustacean shells (e.g. prawn shells, mussel shells, etc.)
parsley stalks
bay leaf
pinch of fresh thyme
pepper

1. Put all the ingredients together in a pan, with water to cover, and bring to the boil. Turn down to simmer and skim off any scum.
2. Simmer for 20 minutes if the fish bones are small, 30 minutes if large. Strain.

NOTE: The flavour of fish stock is impaired if the bones are cooked for too long. Once strained, however, it may be strengthened by further boiling and reducing.

❊ ❊ ❊ ❊ ❊ ❊ ❊ ❊ ❊ ❊ ❊ ❊ ❊ ❊ ❊ ❊ ❊ ❊ ❊ ❊

# Turkey Stock (1)

Ideally all stocks are made from raw bones. However, no one is likely to have raw turkey bones. If you are making stock before Christmas you will have to make it from the giblets.
This recipe can be used for making goose, pheasant and chicken stock as well. Never add liver to a stock pot; it will make the stock taste bitter.

the neck of the turkey
giblets, well washed without the liver
1 onion, sliced
1 celery stick, sliced
1 carrot, sliced
1 parsley stalk, bruised
1 sprig fresh thyme
2 bay leaves
10 black peppercorns

1. Put all the ingredients into a saucepan.

Cover generously with cold water and bring to the boil slowly. Skim off any fat.

2. Simmer slowly for 2-3 hours, skimming frequently and topping up the water level if necessary. The liquid should reduce to half the original quantity.

3. Strain and cool.

❋ ❋ ❋ ❋ ❋ ❋ ❋ ❋ ❋ ❋ ❋ ❋ ❋ ❋ ❋ ❋ ❋ ❋ ❋ ❋ ❋ ❋

# Turkey Stock (2)

This recipe for making stock uses the cooked turkey bones. It is important that the water is very cold; if it is hot, the fat in the turkey skin will melt immediately and, when the stock begins to boil, much of the fat will be bubbled into the stock. This stock can be used in any of the recipes that call for chicken stock.

cooked turkey bones
1 onion, sliced
1 celery stick, sliced
1 carrot, sliced
1 parsley stalk, bruised
1 sprig fresh thyme
2 bay leaves
10 black peppercorns

1. Put all the ingredients into a saucepan. Cover generously with cold water and bring to the boil slowly. Skim off any fat and/or scum.

2. Simmer slowly for 2-3 hours, skimming frequently and topping up the water level if necessary. The liquid should reduce to half the original quantity.

3. Strain and cool.

❋ ❋ ❋ ❋ ❋ ❋ ❋ ❋ ❋ ❋ ❋ ❋ ❋ ❋ ❋ ❋ ❋ ❋ ❋ ❋ ❋ ❋

# Horseradish Cream

150ml/¼ pint double cream
15-30ml/1-2 tablespoons grated fresh horseradish
10ml/2 teaspoons wine vinegar
2.5ml/½ teaspoon made English mustard
salt and pepper
sugar to taste

Lightly whip the cream and add the remaining ingredients.

❋ ❋ ❋ ❋ ❋ ❋ ❋ ❋ ❋ ❋ ❋ ❋ ❋ ❋ ❋ ❋ ❋ ❋ ❋ ❋ ❋ ❋

# Uncooked Pasta Sauce

This sauce should be served on the day after it has been made in order to allow the flavours to develop. It can be served with hot or cold pasta.

SERVES 4-6

6 large tomatoes, finely chopped
1 red onion, finely chopped
2 garlic cloves, finely chopped
60ml/4 tablespoons chopped fresh basil
15ml/1 tablespoon chopped parsley
90ml/6 tablespoons extra virgin olive oil
juice of 1/2 lemon
salt and freshly ground black pepper

1. Put the tomatoes into a sieve and drain them for 30 minutes.
2. Mix the tomatoes with the onion, garlic and herbs. Add the oil and lemon juice. Season to taste with salt and pepper.

❋❋❋❋❋❋❋❋❋❋❋❋❋❋❋❋❋❋❋❋❋❋

# Tomato and Yoghurt Herb Sauce

This sauce goes very well with hot and cold fish dishes and cold meats and poultry.

SERVES 4-6

290ml/1/2 pint Greek yoghurt
5ml/1 teaspoon Dijon mustard
15ml/1 tablespoon olive oil
15ml/1 tablespoon mixed chopped fresh herbs, e.g. parsley, mint, chervil
3 tomatoes skinned, deseeded and chopped
salt and freshly ground black pepper

1. Mix together the yoghurt, mustard, oil and herbs.
2. Stir in the tomatoes carefully and season to taste with salt and pepper. If the sauce tastes too sharp more oil should be added.

❋❋❋❋❋❋❋❋❋❋❋❋❋❋❋❋❋❋❋❋❋❋

# White Sauce

This is a quick and easy basic white sauce.

20g/³/4oz butter
20g/³/4oz flour
pinch of dry mustard
290ml/¹/2 pint creamy milk
salt and white pepper

1. Melt the butter in a thick saucepan.
2. Add the flour and the mustard and stir over the heat for 1 minute. Draw the pan off the heat, pour in the milk and mix well.
3. Return the sauce to the heat and stir continually until boiling.
4. Simmer for 2-3 minutes and season with salt and pepper.

# Béchamel Sauce

290ml/¹/2 pint creamy milk
slice of onion
blade of mace
a few fresh parsley stalks
4 peppercorns
1 bay leaf
30g/1oz butter
20g/³/4oz flour
salt and white pepper

1. Place the milk with the onion, mace, parsley, peppercorns and bay leaf in a saucepan and slowly bring to simmering point.

2. Lower the temperature and allow the flavour to infuse for 8-10 minutes.
3. Melt 20g/³/4oz butter in a thick saucepan, stir in the flour and stir over heat for 1 minute.
4. Remove from the heat. Strain in the infused milk and mix well.
5. Return the sauce to the heat and stir or whisk continuously until boiling. Add the remaining butter and beat very well (this will help to make the sauce shiny).
6. Simmer, stirring well, for 3 minutes.
7. Taste and season.

NOTE: To make a professionally shiny béchamel sauce, pass through a tammy strainer before use or whizz in a liquidizer.

# Mornay Sauce (Cheese Sauce)

*20g/³/4oz butter*
*20g/³/4oz flour*
*pinch of dry English mustard*
*pinch of cayenne pepper*
*290ml/¹/2 pint milk*
*55g/2oz Gruyère or strong Cheddar cheese, grated*
*15g/¹/2oz Parmesan cheese, grated*
*salt and pepper*

1. Melt the butter and stir in the flour, mustard and cayenne pepper. Cook, stirring, for 1 minute. Draw the pan off the heat. Pour in the milk and mix well.
2. Return the pan to the heat and stir until boiling. Simmer, stirring well, for 2 minutes.
3. Add all the cheese, and mix well, but do not re-boil.
4. Season with salt and pepper as necessary.

❋ ❋ ❋ ❋ ❋ ❋ ❋ ❋ ❋ ❋ ❋ ❋ ❋ ❋ ❋ ❋ ❋ ❋ ❋ ❋

# Parsley Sauce

*290ml/¹/2 pint creamy milk*
*slice of onion*
*good handful of fresh parsley*
*4 peppercorns*
*1 bay leaf*
*20g/³/4oz butter*
*20g/³/4oz flour*
*salt and pepper*

1. Put the milk, onion, parsley stalks (but not the leaves), peppercorns and bay leaf in a saucepan and slowly bring to simmering point.
2. Lower the temperature and allow the flavour to infuse for about 10 minutes.
3. Melt the butter in a thick saucepan, stir in the flour and cook, stirring, for 1 minute.
4. Remove from the heat. Strain in the infused milk and mix well.
5. Return the sauce to the heat and stir continuously until boiling, then simmer for 2-3 minutes. Taste and season.
6. Chop the parsley leaves very finely and stir into the hot sauce.

❋ ❋ ❋ ❋ ❋ ❋ ❋ ❋ ❋ ❋ ❋ ❋ ❋ ❋ ❋ ❋ ❋ ❋ ❋ ❋

# Soubise Sauce

FOR THE SOUBISE:

*30g/1oz butter*

*60ml/4 tablespoons water*

*225g/8oz onions, very finely chopped*

*60ml/4 tablespoons cream*

FOR THE BÉCHAMEL SAUCE:

*20g/³/4oz butter*

*bay leaf*

*20g/³/4oz flour*

*290ml/¹/2 pint milk*

1. To make the soubise, melt the butter in a heavy pan. Add the water and the onions and cook very slowly, preferably covered with a lid to create a steamy atmosphere. The onions should become very soft and transparent, but on no account brown. Add the cream.

2. Now prepare the béchamel: melt the butter, add the bay leaf and flour and cook, stirring, for 1 minute. Draw off the heat, and stir in the milk. Return to the heat and bring slowly to the boil, stirring continuously. Simmer for 2 minutes. Remove the bay leaf and mix with the soubise.

NOTE: This sauce can be liquidized in a blender or pushed through a sieve if a smooth texture is desired.

# Mayonnaise

*2 egg yolks*

*salt and pepper*

*5ml/1 teaspoon pale mustard*

*290ml/¹/2 pint olive oil, or 150ml/¹/4 pint each olive
    and salad oil*

*squeeze of lemon juice*

*15ml/1 tablespoon wine vinegar*

1. Put the yolks into a bowl with a pinch of salt and the mustard and beat well with a wooden spoon.

2. Add the oil, drop by drop, beating all the time. The mixture should be very thick by the time half the oil is added.

3. Beat in the lemon juice.

4. Resume pouring in the oil, going rather more confidently now, but alternating the dribbles of oil with small quantities of vinegar.

5. Add salt and pepper to taste.

NOTE I: If the mixture curdles, another egg yolk should be beaten in a separate bowl, and the curdled mixture beaten drop by drop into it.

NOTE II: Chopped fresh herbs can be added to the mayonnaise.

CHEESE SOUFFLÉ

WARM TURKEY SALAD

LENTIL SOUP

TUNA FISH AND PASTA SALAD

'TIRED' FRUIT ICE CREAM

STIR-FRIED TURKEY

MINCEMEAT BOMBE

CHRISTMAS DRINKS

# Rémoulade Sauce

*150ml/¹/4 pint mayonnaise (see page 184)*
*5ml/1 teaspoon Dijon mustard*
*7.5ml/¹/2 tablespoon finely chopped capers*
*7.5ml/¹/2 tablespoon finely chopped gherkin*
*7.5ml/¹/2 tablespoon finely chopped fresh tarragon*
*    or chervil*
*1 anchovy fillet, finely chopped*

Mix all the ingredients together.

NOTE: Rémoulade sauce is a mayonnaise with a predominantly mustard flavour. The other ingredients, though good, are not always present.

❄ ❄ ❄ ❄ ❄ ❄ ❄ ❄ ❄ ❄ ❄ ❄ ❄ ❄ ❄ ❄ ❄ ❄ ❄

# Hollandaise Sauce

*45ml/3 tablespoons wine vinegar*
*6 peppercorns*
*1 bay leaf*
*blade of mace*
*2 egg yolks*
*salt*
*110g/4oz softened unsalted butter*
*lemon juice*

1. Place the vinegar, peppercorns, bay leaf and mace in a small heavy saucepan and reduce by simmering to 15ml/1 tablespoon.
2. Cream the egg yolks with a pinch of salt and a nut of butter in a small bowl. Set in a bain-marie on a gentle heat. With a wooden spoon beat the mixture until slightly thickened, taking care that the water immediately around the bowl does not boil. Mix well.
3. Strain on the reduced vinegar. Mix well.

Stir over the heat until slightly thickened. Beat in the softened butter bit by bit, increasing the temperature as the sauce thickens and you add more butter, but take care that the water does not boil.
4. When the sauce has become light and thick take it off the heat and beat or whisk for 1 minute. Taste for seasoning and add lemon juice, and salt if necessary. Keep warm by standing the bowl in hot water. Serve warm.

NOTE: Hollandaise sauce will set too firmly if allowed to get cold and it will curdle if overheated. It can be made in larger quantities in either a liquidizer or a food processor: simply put the eggs and salt into the blender and blend lightly. Add the hot reduction, allow to thicken slightly. Set aside. When ready to serve, pour in warm melted butter, slowly allowing the sauce to thicken as you pour.

❄ ❄ ❄ ❄ ❄ ❄ ❄ ❄ ❄ ❄ ❄ ❄ ❄ ❄ ❄ ❄ ❄ ❄ ❄

# Beurre Blanc

*225g/8oz unsalted butter*
*15ml/1 tablespoon chopped shallot*
*45ml/3 tablespoons wine vinegar*
*45ml/3 tablespoons water*
*salt, white pepper*
*squeeze of lemon*

1. Chill the butter then cut it in 3 lengthways, then across into thin slices. Keep cold.

2. Put the shallot, vinegar and water into a thick-bottomed sauté pan or small shallow saucepan. Boil until about 30ml/2 tablespoons remain. Strain and return to the saucepan.

3. Lower the heat under the pan. Using a wire whisk and plenty of vigorous continuous whisking, gradually add the butter, piece by piece. The process should take about 5 minutes and the sauce should become thick, creamy and pale – rather like a thin hollandaise. Add salt, pepper and lemon juice.

# Fish Beurre Blanc

*225g/8oz unsalted butter*
*1 shallot, finely chopped*
*75ml/5 tablespoons very strong fish stock*
  *(see page 179)*
*15ml/1 tablespoon white wine vinegar*
*salt and ground white pepper*
*squeeze of lemon*

1. Chill the butter then cut it in 3 lengthways, then across into thin slices. Keep cold.

2. Put the shallot, stock and vinegar into a small heavy saucepan and boil until reduced to 30ml/2 tablespoons. Strain and return to the pan.

3. Keep the stock hot, not boiling. Using a wire whisk and plenty of continuous whisking, gradually add the butter, piece by piece. The process should take about 5 minutes and the sauce should become thick, creamy and pale, rather like a thin hollandaise. Add the salt, pepper and lemon juice.

# French Dressing (Vinaigrette)

*45ml/3 tablespoons salad oil*
*15ml/1 tablespoon wine vinegar*
*salt and pepper*

Put all the ingredients into a screw-top jar. Before using, shake until well emulsified.

NOTE I: This dressing can be flavoured with crushed garlic, mustard, a pinch of sugar, chopped fresh herbs, etc., as desired.
NOTE II: If kept refrigerated, the dressing will more easily form an emulsion when whisked or shaken, and has a slightly thicker consistency.

❋❋❋❋❋❋❋❋❋❋❋❋❋❋❋❋❋❋❋❋

# Pesto Sauce

*2 garlic cloves*
*2 large cups basil leaves*
*55g/2oz pinenuts*
*55g/2oz fresh Parmesan cheese, finely grated*
*150ml/¹/4 pint olive oil*
*salt*

In a liquidizer or mortar, grind the garlic and basil together to a paste. Add the nuts, cheese, oil and plenty of salt. Keep in a covered jar in a cool place.

NOTE: Pesto is sometimes made with walnuts instead of pinenuts, and the nuts may be pounded with the other ingredients to give a smooth paste.

❋❋❋❋❋❋❋❋❋❋❋❋❋❋❋❋❋❋❋❋

# Parsley Pesto

*2 garlic cloves*
*1 large handful freshly picked parsley,*
  *roughly chopped*
*30g/1oz blanched almonds*
*150ml/¹/4 pint olive oil*

*55g/2oz Cheddar cheese, finely grated*
1. Process or liquidize the garlic and parsley together to a paste.
2. Whizz in the nuts, then add the olive oil slowly with the motor still running. Whizz in the cheese quickly.
3. Keep in a covered jar in a cool place.

❋❋❋❋❋❋❋❋❋❋❋❋❋❋❋❋❋❋❋❋

# Mustard Sauce

90ml/6 tablespoons oil
30ml/2 tablespoons wine vinegar
15ml/1 tablespoon Dijon mustard

15ml/1 tablespoon chopped dill
salt and pepper

Put all the ingredients together in a screw-top jar. Cover and shake until well emulsified.

✳✳✳✳✳✳✳✳✳✳✳✳✳✳✳✳✳✳✳✳✳

# Salsa Pizzaiola

This recipe has been taken from *A Taste of Venice* by Jeanette Nance Nordio.

1 onion, chopped
30ml/2 tablespoons olive oil
3-4 garlic cloves, chopped
1kg/2¹/4lb tin plum tomatoes
30ml/2 tablespoons tomato purée
10ml/2 teaspoons dried oregano
5ml/1 teaspoon dried basil
1 bay leaf

10ml/2 teaspoons sugar
salt and pepper

1. Fry the onion in the oil until transparent.
2. Add the garlic and cook for a further minute, then stir in the tomatoes with their liquid, the tomato purée, oregano, basil, bay leaf and sugar. Season with salt and pepper. Bring to the boil and then cook very gently for about 1 hour.
3. Remove the bay leaf and check the seasoning. This sauce should be quite thick and rough but you could purée it if you wish.

✳✳✳✳✳✳✳✳✳✳✳✳✳✳✳✳✳✳✳✳✳

# Fresh Tomato Sauce (1)

1 large onion, finely chopped
45ml/3 tablespoons oil
10 tomatoes, peeled, deseeded and chopped
salt and freshly ground black pepper
pinch of sugar
150g/¹/4 pint white stock (see page 178)
5ml/1 teaspoon fresh thyme leaves

1. Cook the onion in the oil for 3 minutes. Add the tomatoes, salt, pepper and sugar, and cook for a further 25 minutes. Add the stock and cook for 5 minutes.
2. Liquidize the sauce and push through a sieve. If it is too thin, reduce, by boiling rapidly, to the desired consistency. Take care: it will spit and has a tendency to catch.
3. Add the thyme. Taste and adjust the seasoning if necessary.

# Tomato Sauce (2)

400g/14oz can plum tomatoes
1 small onion, chopped
1 small carrot, chopped
1 stick celery, chopped
1/2 garlic clove, crushed
1 bay leaf
parsley stalks
salt and pepper
juice of 1/2 lemon
dash of Worcestershire sauce
5ml/1 teaspoon sugar
5ml/1 teaspoon chopped basil or thyme

1. Put all the ingredients together in a thick-bottomed pan, cover and simmer over medium heat for 30 minutes.
2. Liquidize and sieve the sauce and return it to the pan.
3. If it is too thin, reduce by boiling rapidly. Check the seasoning, adding more salt or sugar if necessary.

# Red Pepper Sauce

1 onion, finely chopped
15ml/1 tablespoon sunflower oil
2 tomatoes, peeled and deseeded
1 red pepper, skinned (by singeing over a flame), deseeded and cut into strips
1 garlic clove, crushed
1 bouquet garni
90ml/6 tablespoons water
salt and pepper

1. Cook the onion in the oil until just beginning to soften. Add the tomatoes, red pepper, garlic and bouquet garni. Add the water and season lightly. Cover and cook slowly for 20 minutes.
2. Liquidize until smooth and push through a sieve. Chill.

# Black Bean Sauce

45ml/3 tablespoons fermented black beans
2 spring onions, chopped
15ml/1 tablespoon sunflower oil
1 garlic clove, sliced
2.5 cm/1 inch piece root ginger, peeled and sliced
30ml/2 tablespoons soy sauce
30ml/2 tablespoons sherry
5ml/1 teaspoon sugar
290ml/$^1$/2 pint water
10ml/2 teaspoons sesame oil

1. Wash the beans again and again.
2. Heat the oil in a saucepan, add the spring onions, garlic and ginger and cook for 1 minute.
3. Add the soy sauce, sherry, beans, sugar and water. Bring slowly to the boil, then simmer for 15 minutes to allow the flavour to infuse.
4. Stir in the sesame oil. Use as required.

❄❄❄❄❄❄❄❄❄❄❄❄❄❄❄❄❄❄❄❄

# Apple Sauce

450g/1lb cooking apples
finely grated rind of $^1$/4 lemon
45ml/3 tablespoons water
10ml/2 teaspoons sugar
15g/$^1$/2oz butter

1. Peel, quarter, core and slice the apples.
2. Place in a heavy saucepan with the lemon rind, water and sugar. Cover with a lid and cook very slowly until the apples are soft.
3. Beat in the butter, cool slightly and add extra sugar if required. Serve hot or cold.

❄❄❄❄❄❄❄❄❄❄❄❄❄❄❄❄❄❄❄❄

# Cumberland Sauce

2 oranges
1 lemon
225g/8oz redcurrant jelly
1 shallot, chopped
150ml/$^1$/4 pint port or red wine
2.5ml/$^1$/2 teaspoon pale mustard
pinch of cayenne pepper
pinch of ground ginger

1. Peel 1 orange and the lemon, removing only the outer skin. Cut the rind into fine shreds.
2. Squeeze the fruit juice and strain into a pan. Then add the remaining ingredients with the needleshreds. Simmer for 10 minutes and cool.

❄❄❄❄❄❄❄❄❄❄❄❄❄❄❄❄❄❄❄❄

# Maître d'Hôtel Butter

*55g/2oz butter*
*10ml/2 teaspoons lemon juice*
*5ml/1 teaspoon finely chopped parsley*
*salt and pepper*

Cream the butter, stir in the lemon juice and parsley and season to taste. Mix well and chill.

# Sugar Syrup

*285g/10oz granulated sugar*
*570ml/1 pint water*
*pared rind of 1 lemon*

1. Put the sugar, water and lemon rind in a pan and heat slowly until the sugar has completely dissolved.
2. Bring to the boil and cook to the required consistency. Allow to cool.
3. Strain. Keep covered in a cool place until needed.

NOTE: Sugar syrup will keep unrefrigerated for about 5 days, and for several weeks if kept cold.

# Shortcrust Pastry (Pâte Brisée)

*170g/6oz plain flour*
*pinch of salt*
*30g/1oz lard*
*55g/2oz butter*
*very cold water*

1. Sift the flour with the salt.
2. Rub in the fats until the mixture looks like coarse breadcrumbs.
3. Add 30ml/2 tablespoons water to the mixture. Mix to a firm dough, first with a knife, and finally with one hand. It may be necessary to add more water, but the pastry should not be too damp. (Though crumbly pastry is more difficult to handle, it produces a shorter, lighter result.)
4. Chill, wrapped, for 30 minutes before using. Or allow to relax after rolling out but before baking.

# Rich Shortcrust Pastry

*170g/6oz plain flour*
*pinch of salt*
*85g/3oz butter*
*1 egg yolk*
*very cold water*

1. Sift the flour with the salt.
2. Rub in the butter until the mixture looks like breadcrumbs.
3. Mix the yolk with 30ml/2 tablespoons water and add to the mixture.
4. Mix to a firm dough, first with a knife, and finally with one hand. It may be necessary to add more water, but the pastry should not be too damp. (Though crumbly pastry is more difficult to handle, it produces a shorter, lighter result. )
5. Chill, wrapped, for 30 minutes before using, or allow to relax after rolling out but before baking.

NOTE: To make sweet rich shortcrust pastry, mix in 15ml/1 tablespoon caster sugar once the fat has been rubbed into the flour.

# Almond Pastry

*340g/12oz plain flour*
*pinch of salt*
*225g/8oz butter*
*85g/3oz ground almonds*
*100g/3<sup>1</sup>/2oz caster sugar*
*2 egg yolks*
*30 ml/2 tablespoons very cold water*

1. Sift the plain flour with the salt into a large bowl.
2. Rub in the butter until the mixture looks like coarse breadcrumbs. Stir in the ground almonds and caster sugar.
3. Mix the egg yolks with the water and add enough to the pastry mixture to make a firm dough. Mix first with a knife and finally with one hand. The pastry should not be damp.
4. Chill, wrapped, for 20 minutes before using or allow to relax in the refrigerator after rolling out, but before baking.

# Lemon Shortcrust Pastry

*170g/6oz plain flour*
*pinch of salt*
*5 ml/1 teaspoon grated lemon rind*
*30g/1oz lard*
*55g/2oz butter*
*very cold water*

1. Sift the flour with the salt. Add the grated lemon rind.

2. Rub in the fats until the mixture looks like breadcrumbs.

3. Add 30 ml/2 tablespoons of water to the mixture. Mix to a firm dough – first with a knife, and finally with one hand. It may be necessary to add more water, but the pastry should not be too damp. (Although crumbly pastry is more difficult to handle, it produces a shorter, less tough result.)

4. Chill, wrapped, for 30 minutes before using. Or allow to relax after rolling out but before baking.

# Tartlet Cases

MAKES APPROXIMATELY 60 CASES
*225g/8oz flour quantity rich shortcrust pastry (see page 200)*

1. Set the oven to 190°C/375°F/gas mark 5.
2. Roll out the pastry to 2mm/$^1/8$ inch thick. Stamp out circles using a small fluted cutter.
3. Press the circles into tiny patty tins or barquette moulds (boat-shaped tins). Chill in the refrigerator for 20 minutes.
4. Bake the tartlet cases blind for approximately 10 minutes, removing the greaseproof paper and rice after 5 minutes.
5. Use as required.

NOTE: To make thyme pastry, add 2 teaspoons of chopped fresh thyme to the flour when making the pastry.

# Martha Stewart's Walnut Pastry

*225g/8oz plain flour*
*pinch of salt*
*110g/4oz butter*
*140g/5oz ground walnuts*
*45g/1¹/₂oz sugar*
*beaten egg*

1. Sift the flour and salt into a bowl. Rub in the butter until the mixture resembles coarse breadcrumbs. Add the walnuts.
2. Stir in the sugar and add enough beaten egg (probably half an egg) to just bind the mixture together. Knead lightly. Chill before use.

NOTE: If you have a food processor, simply beat all the ingredients together until lightly combined. Chill before use.

# Choux Pastry

*85g/3oz butter*
*220ml/7 fl oz water*
*105g/3³/₄oz plain flour, well sifted*
*pinch of salt*
*3 eggs*

1. Put the butter and water together in a heavy saucepan. Bring slowly to the boil so that by the time the water boils the butter is completely melted.
2. Immediately the mixture is boiling really fast, tip in all the flour and draw the pan off the heat.
3. Working as fast as you can, beat the mixture hard with a wooden spoon: it will soon become thick and smooth and leave the sides of the pan. Beat in the salt.
4. Stand the bottom of the saucepan in a basin or sink of cold water to speed up the cooling process.
5. When the mixture is cool, beat in the eggs, a little at at time, until it is soft, shiny and smooth. If the eggs are large, it may not be necessary to add all of them. The mixture should be of a dropping consistency – not too runny. ('Dropping consistency' means that the mixture will fall off a spoon rather reluctantly and all in a blob; if it runs off, it is too wet, and if it will not fall off even when the spoon is jerked slightly, it is too thick.)
6. Use as required.

# Filo or Strudel Pastry

*285g/10oz plain flour*
*pinch of salt*
*1 egg*
*150ml/¹/4 pint water*
*5ml/1 teaspoon oil*

1. Sift the flour and salt into a bowl.
2. Beat the egg and add the water and oil. First with a knife and then with one hand, mix the water and egg into the flour, adding more water if necessary to make a soft dough.
3. The paste now has to be beaten: lift the whole mixture up in one hand and then, with a flick of the wrist, slap it on to a lightly floured board. Continue doing this until the paste no longer sticks to your fingers, and the whole mixture is smooth and very elastic. Put it into a clean floured bowl. Cover and leave in a warm place for 15 minutes.
4. The pastry is now ready for rolling and pulling. To do this, flour a tea towel or large cloth on a table top and roll out the pastry as thinly as you can. Now put your hand (well floured) under the pastry and, keeping your hand fairly flat, gently stretch and pull the pastry, gradually and carefully working your way round until the paste

is paper thin. (You should be able to see through it easily.) Trim off the thick edges.
5. Use immediately, as strudel pastry dries out and cracks very quickly. Brushing with melted butter or oil helps to prevent this. Or the pastry sheets may be kept covered with a damp cloth.

NOTE: If the paste is not for immediate use wrap it well and keep refrigerated or frozen. Flour the pastry surfaces before folding up. This will prevent sticking.

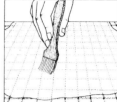

*Stretch and pull the pastry until it is almost transparent. Brush with butter.*

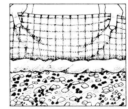

*Fill the pastry as required and then roll it up (using the teatowel).*

❋❋❋❋❋❋❋❋❋❋❋❋❋❋❋❋❋❋❋❋

# Pâte Sucrée

*170g/6oz plain flour*
*pinch of salt*
*85g/3oz butter, softened*
*3 egg yolks*
*85g/3oz sugar*
*2 drops vanilla essence*

1. Sift the flour on to a board with a pinch of salt. Make a large well in the centre and put the butter in it. Place the egg yolks and sugar on the butter with the vanilla essence.

2. Using the fingertips of one hand, mix the butter, yolks and sugar together. When mixed to a soft paste, draw in the flour and knead until the pastry is just smooth.

3. If the pastry is very soft, chill before rolling or pressing out to the required shape. In any event the pastry must be allowed to relax for 30 minutes either before or after rolling out, but before baking.

# Pâte à Pâté

*225g/8oz plain flour*
*2.5ml/¹/2 teaspoon salt*
*155g/5¹/2 oz butter, softened*
*2 small egg yolks*
*up to 30ml/2 tablespoons water*

1. Sift the flour and salt on to the table top. Make a large well in the centre and put the butter and yolks in it. Work the yolks and butter together with the fingers of one hand and draw in the surrounding flour, adding the water to give a soft, malleable, but not sticky paste.

2. Wrap and leave to rest in the refrigerator for 30 minutes. Use as required.

# Hot Watercrust Pastry

This pastry is used for raised pies, such as pork pie and game pie.

*225g/8oz plain flour*
*2.5ml/¹/2 teaspoon salt*
*1 beaten egg*
*100ml/3¹/2 fl oz water*

*35g/1¹/4oz butter*
*35g/1¹/4oz lard*

1. Wrap a piece of paper around the outside of a wide jar or small straight-sided saucepan. The paper can be held in position by tucking it in the opening of the jar or saucepan. Leave it upside down while you make the pastry.

2. Sift the flour and salt into a bowl. Make a dip in the middle, break the egg into it and toss a liberal covering of flour over the egg.

3. Put the water, butter and lard into a saucepan and bring slowly to the boil.

4. Once the liquid is boiling, pour it on to the flour, mixing with a knife as you do so. Knead until all the egg streaks have gone and the pastry is smooth.

5. Wrap in a piece of cling film and leave in the refrigerator for 10 minutes.

6. Reserve about a third of the paste for the lid, keeping it covered or wrapped and in a warm place. Roll out the remaining paste to a circle and drape it over the jar or saucepan.

Working fast, shape the pastry to cover the jar or saucepan to a depth of about 7cm/2$\frac{1}{2}$ inches. Leave to chill in the refrigerator.

7. As the pastry cools it will harden. When hard, turn the jar or saucepan over and remove it carefully, leaving the paper inside the pastry case. Carefully draw the paper away from the pastry and when it is all loosened take it out. Stand the pastry case on a baking sheet and fill as required. Use the reserved third of the pastry to make the lid, wetting the rim of the pie case to make it stick down well. Bake as required.

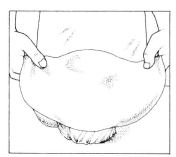 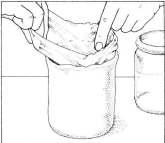 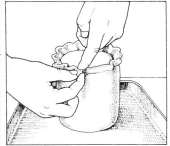

*Drape pastry over jar; when cool, remove jar and draw out the paper. Crimp the edges and bake.*

❇ ❇ ❇ ❇ ❇ ❇ ❇ ❇ ❇ ❇ ❇ ❇ ❇ ❇ ❇ ❇ ❇ ❇ ❇ ❇ ❇ ❇

# French Pancakes (Crêpes)

MAKES ABOUT 12
*110g/4oz plain flour*
*pinch of salt*
*1 egg*
*1 egg yolk*
*290ml/$\frac{1}{2}$ pint milk, or milk and water mixed*
*15ml/1 tablespoon oil*
*oil for cooking*

1. Sift the flour and salt into a bowl and make a well in the centre, exposing the bottom of the bowl.

2. Into this well, place the egg and egg yolk with a little of the milk.

3. Using a wooden spoon or whisk, mix the egg and milk and then gradually draw in the flour from the sides as you mix.

4. When the mixture reaches the consistency of thick cream, beat well and stir in the oil.

5. Add the rest of the milk; the consistency should now be that of thin cream. (Batter can also be made by placing all the ingredients

together in a liquidizer for a few seconds, but take care not to over-whizz or the mixture will be bubbly.)

6. Cover the bowl and refrigerate for about 30 minutes. This is done so that the starch cells will swell, giving a lighter result.

7. Prepare a pancake pan or frying pan by heating well and wiping with oil. Pancakes are not fried in fat like most foods – the purpose of the oil is simply to prevent sticking.

8. When the pan is ready, pour in about 15ml/ 1 tablespoon batter and swirl about the pan until evenly spread across the bottom.

9. Place over heat and, after 1 minute, using a palette knife and your fingers, turn the pancake over and cook again until brown. (Pancakes should be extremely thin, so if the first one is too thick, add a little extra milk to the batter. The first pancake is unlikely to be perfect, and is often discarded.)

10. Make up all the pancakes, turning them out on to a teatowel or plate.

NOTE I: Pancakes can be kept warm in a folded teatowel on a plate over a saucepan of simmering water, in the oven, or in a warmer. If allowed to cool, they may be reheated by being returned to the frying pan or by warming in the oven.

NOTE II: Pancakes freeze well, but should be separated by pieces of greaseproof paper. They may also be refrigerated for a day or two.

❋ ❋ ❋ ❋ ❋ ❋ ❋ ❋ ❋ ❋ ❋ ❋ ❋ ❋ ❋ ❋ ❋ ❋

# TO PREPARE POULTRY

❋ ❋ ❋ ❋ ❋ ❋ ❋ ❋ ❋ ❋ ❋ ❋ ❋ ❋ ❋ ❋ ❋ ❋

*Small birds such as quail are invariably cooked whole, perhaps stuffed, and perhaps boned (see page 209). But medium-sized ones, like chickens and guinea fowl, are often cut into two, four, six or eight pieces. Use a knife to cut through the flesh and poultry shears or scissors to cut the bones.*

### TO SPLIT A BIRD IN HALF:

Simply use a sharp knife to cut right through flesh and bone, just on one side of the breastbone, open out the bird and cut through the other side, immediately next to the backbone. Then cut the backbone away from the half to which it remains attached.
The knobbly end of the drumsticks and the fleshless tips to the pinions can be cut off before or after cooking. In birds brought whole to the table they are left on.

### TO JOINT A BIRD INTO FOUR:

First pull out any trussing strings, then pull the leg away from the body. With a sharp knife cut through the skin joining the leg to the body, pull the leg away further and cut through more skin to free the leg. Bend the leg outwards and back, forcing the bone to come out of its socket close to the body. Turn the bird over, feel along the backbone to find the oyster (a soft pocket of flesh at the side of the backbone, near the middle). With the tip of the knife, cut this away from the carcase at the side nearest the backbone and farthest from the leg. Then turn the bird over again, and cut through the flesh, the knife going between the end of the thigh bone and the carcase, to take off the leg, bringing the oyster with it. Using poultry shears or a heavy knife, split the carcase along the breastbone. Cut through the ribs on each side to take off the fleshy portion of the breast, and with it the wing. Trim the joints neatly to remove scraps of untidy skin.

For six joints, proceed as above but split the legs into thigh portions and drumsticks.

The exact join of the bones can easily be seen if the leg is laid on the board, skin side down. Cut through the fat line. With a cleaver, or the heel end of a knife, chop the feet off the drumsticks.

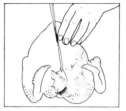
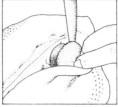
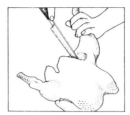

*Jointing a chicken: Stages 1 and 2 (numbers refer to text)  Stages 3 and 4*

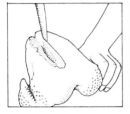
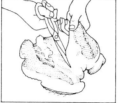
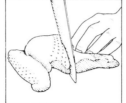

*Stages 6, 7 and 8*                                    *Stages 9 and 11*

## TO JOINT INTO EIGHT:

1. Turn the chicken over so the backbone is uppermost. Cut through to the bone along the line of the spine.

2. Where the thigh joins the backbone there is a fleshy 'oyster' on each side. Cut round them to loosen them from the carcase so that they come away when the legs are severed.

3. Turn the bird over and pull a leg away from the body. Cut through the skin only, as far round the leg as possible, close to the body.

4. Pull the leg away from the body and twist it down so that the thigh bone pops out of its socket on the carcase and is exposed.

5. Cut the leg off, taking care to go between thigh bone and carcase and to bring the 'oyster' away with the leg. (Turn over briefly to check.) Repeat the process for the other leg.

6. Carefully cut down each side of the breast bone to free the flesh a little.

7. Use scissors to cut through the small bone close to the breast. Cut away the breastbone.

8. Open up the bird. Cut each wing and breast

off the carcase with scissors. Start at the tail end and cut to and through the wing bone near the neck.

9. Cut the wing joint in two, leaving about one third of the breast attached to the wing.

10. Cut off the pinions from each wing. They can go into the stockpot with the carcase.

11. Separate the drumsticks and thighs, lay the legs skin side down on the board, and cut through where the thigh and lower leg bones meet, on the obvious fat line.

12. With a cleaver, or the heel end of a heavy knife, chop the feet off the drumsticks.

## BARDING

Poultry liable to dry out during cooking is often barded: lay fatty bacon or rindless pork back fat strips over the body of the bird, and secure or tie in place. The barding is removed during cooking to allow the breast to brown.

## BONING A CHICKEN, TURKEY OR PHEASANT

1. Put the bird breast side down on a board. Cut through to the backbone.

2. Feel for the fleshy 'oyster' at the top of each thigh and cut round it. Cut and scrape the flesh from the carcase with a sharp knife held as close as possible to the bone.

3. Continue along both sides of the backbone until the ribcage is exposed. At the joint of the thigh and pelvis, cut between the bones at the socket so that the legs stay attached to the flesh and skin, and not to the body carcase.

4. Keep working right round the bird then use scissors to cut away most of the ribcage, leaving only the cartilaginous breastbone in the centre.

5. Using a heavy knife, cut through the foot joints to remove the knuckle end of the drumsticks.

6. Working from the inside thigh end scrape one leg bone clean, pushing the flesh down towards the drumstick until you can free the thigh bone. Repeat on the other leg.

7. Working from the drumstick ends, scrape the lower leg bones clean in the same way and remove them. Remove as many tendons as possible from the legs as you work.

8. Now for the wings. Cut off the pinions with a heavy knife.

9. Scrape the wing bones clean as you did the leg bones.

10. Carefully free the breastbone with the knife, working from the middle of the bird towards the tail.

11. Take great care not to puncture the skin, which has no flesh under it at this point so is easily torn.

12. You should now have a beautifully boned bird. Keep the neck flap of skin intact to fold over once it is stuffed.

NOTE: It is also possible to part-bone a bird. Simply remove the rib cage but leave the legs and wings intact.

❄❄❄❄❄❄❄❄❄❄❄❄❄❄❄❄❄❄❄❄❄❄

# WINE

❄❄❄❄❄❄❄❄❄❄❄❄❄❄❄❄❄❄❄❄❄❄

❄❄❄❄❄❄❄❄❄❄❄❄❄❄❄❄❄❄❄❄❄❄

# BUYING WINE FOR CHRISTMAS

*Buying the Christmas drink is sometimes the only duty required of the male member of the household, and he often only does it in a rush on the way home from the office party on Christmas Eve. In order to help, here are some suggestions to stock up with to cover you for the Christmas holiday; obviously the larger the numbers, the greater the quantity of everything.*

Champagne or sparkling wine, such as Saumur or some of the very good Australian and New Zealand examples are essential to start off Christmas Day; and of course you will need more for New Year. Pink sparkling is even more festive.

A full-flavoured dry white, such as an Australian Chardonnay or a white Burgundy. These are versatile enough to accompany any of the post-Christmas collations of turkey and ham.

Some light or spicy, even medium-dry white wine, such as a Moselle Riesling, which is low in alcohol and ideal for drinking without food.

A light to medium-bodied red wine for the turkey and for Boxing Day lunch. Red Burgundy, or a village Beaujolais or a Loire Red such as Chinon, would fit the bill.

A few bottles of good hearty red, such as Barolo, or Californian or Australian Cabernet-Sauvignon or Shiraz, to accompany any game or rich stews.

Instead of port I would suggest an Australian Liqueur Muscat as the ideal accompaniment both to Christmas pudding and with the nuts and fruit.

And if you don't have the above wines just look at the following chart for alternatives within the different style categories.

Finally, make sure you have plenty of soft drinks for the children, mixers for the spirits, and sparkling water if, like most, your tap water is undrinkable. The fizz also helps the digestion!

## WINE WITH FOOD

The essential criteria in matching wine and food is that the two should complement each other. A light wine will be killed by strong food, just as a full, rich wine will overpower a light dish. A wine that is high in acid will help to cut through any oiliness in the food, yet a sweet wine will balance a sweet course. So it is important to be able to appreciate the elements in a wine so as to match the wine to the food as follows:

Dry to sweet
Light to full
Low acid to high acid
Fresh, young and fruity to mature and dry
Hard and tannic to soft and mellow

However, there are many surprising combinations that work well, the most famous being Sauternes with foie gras. So do not be afraid to experiment – you may well discover some wonderful combinations.

The following charts are intended only as a guideline, but will help those who are uncertain to gain confidence.

| Wine style | Style of food |
|---|---|
| Very dry white (Muscadet, Sancerre, Sauvignon-grape wines, Chablis) | Shellfish, salmon, oily fish |
| Dry white (Soave, Frascati, Burgundy, Chardonnay wines) | White fish |
| Spicy dry white (Alsace, some dry German and English wines) | Smoked fish |
| Medium dry white (Moselle, Vouvray, Vinho Verde) | Chicken |
| Medium sweet white (German Spätlese/Auslese, Italian Moscato) | Soft creamy cheese Fruit and fruit puddings |
| Sweet white (Sauternes, Barsac, Muscat de Beaumes de Venise) | Foie gras Rich puddings Chocolate puddings |
| Rosé (Tavel, Provence) | Bouillabaise Cold meats |
| Light red (Beaujolais, Valpolicella) | Chicken, veal, pork |
| Soft red (Burgundy) | Pork, duck |
| Medium red (Claret, Côtes du Rhône, Chianti, Rioja) | Lamb, Game birds |
| Full red (Châteauneuf du Pape, Cabernet-Sauvignon wines) | Beef |
| Very full red (Crozes-Hermitage, Barolo, Australian Shiraz) | Rich stews Venison |

| Food | Style of Wine | Suggestion |
|---|---|---|
| **Fish dishes** | | |
| Terrine | Light dry white | Chablis |
| Soups | Crisp dry white | Sancerre/Pouilly Fumé/ |
| Mayonnaise | | Burgundy |
| Buttery sauce | | |
| Smoked | Spicy white | Alsace Tokay/Riesling |
| Chinese-style | | |
| Barbecued | | |
| | | |
| **Chicken dishes** | | |
| Mayonnaise | Light, dry white | Soave/Moselle |
| Buttery sauce | | |
| Chinese-style | Full white | Mâcon |
| Roast | Light, red and fruity | Beaujolais |
| Casseroled | | |
| Barbecued/Indian/ | Fuller red | Côtes du Rhône |
| Tandoori | | |
| | | |
| **Veal** | | |
| Buttery sauce | Light, fruity red | Valpolicella |
| Roast | | |
| Casserole | Fuller red | Chianti Classico |
| | | |
| **Pork** | | |
| Buttery sauce | Light red | Beaujolais Villages |
| Spicy/Chinese style | | |
| Stewed/cassoulet | Full red | Corbières |
| Roast | Medium red | Burgundy |
| Barbecued | | |
| | | |
| **Lamb** | | |
| With hollandaise | Light to medium red | Chinon/Bourgueil |
| Stewed | Fuller red | Claret/Rioja |
| Roast | | |
| Spiced/curried/barbecued | Spicy red | Crozes-Hermitage |
| | | |
| **Beef** | | |
| With hollandaise | Medium red | Burgundy |
| Casserole | Fuller red | Rhône/Châteauneuf |
| Roast | | du Pape |
| Spiced/barbecued | Full, spicy red | Australian Shiraz |
| | | Australian/Californian |
| | | Cabernet Sauvignon |

# Mulled Wine

The important ingredient in mulled wine is, rather surprisingly, the water. Without it it can be far too rich and sickly. This recipe is just a guideline and can be altered according to individual tastes.

FOR 20 PEOPLE YOU WILL NEED ABOUT:
4 x 75cl bottles of full bodied red wine
1.7 litres/3 pints water
20 cloves wrapped up in a 'J' cloth
3 oranges, sliced
3 lemons, sliced
225g/8oz granulated sugar (you may need to add extra sugar according to taste)
2 cinnamon sticks

Put all the ingredients together in a large saucepan and dissolve the sugar over a gentle heat. Bring it up to simmering point and keep warm for at least 15 minutes. Do not boil – the alcohol will evaporate.

❄ ❄ ❄ ❄ ❄ ❄ ❄ ❄ ❄ ❄ ❄ ❄ ❄ ❄ ❄ ❄ ❄ ❄ ❄ ❄ ❄

# Champagne Cocktail

sugar lumps
Angostura bitters
brandy
champagne or sparkling white wine such as Saumur or an Australian, chilled

1. Put a sugar lump in each glass and add a couple of drops of Angostura bitters and 5ml/ 1 teaspoon of brandy.
2. Just before serving, pour on the chilled champagne to fill the glasses.

❄ ❄ ❄ ❄ ❄ ❄ ❄ ❄ ❄ ❄ ❄ ❄ ❄ ❄ ❄ ❄ ❄ ❄ ❄ ❄ ❄

# Bellini

The most cheerful drink of all – the classic of Harry's Bar.

Simply mix in equal quantities of peach juice and champagne. If you add the champagne to the juice, the bubbles will last considerably longer.

NOTE: It is possible to buy cartons or tins of 'fresh' peach juice.

❄ ❄ ❄ ❄ ❄ ❄ ❄ ❄ ❄ ❄ ❄ ❄ ❄ ❄ ❄ ❄ ❄ ❄ ❄ ❄ ❄

# Apple Punch

*1 litre/1³/4 pints apple juice*
*5cm/2inch piece of root ginger, peeled*
*2 apples (red ones look pretty)*
*1 litre/1³/4 pints dry ginger ale*
*ice*

1. Put the apple juice in a large bowl. Bruise the ginger with a rolling pin. Quarter, core and slice the apples thinly and add the ginger to the apple juice. Leave to marinate overnight or for at least 2 hours.

2. Remove the ginger and add the dry ginger ale just before serving. Chill with ice cubes.

NOTE: If a clear punch is wanted, use clear apple juice. English apple juice is cloudy but is less sweet.

# Cider Punch

This is very alcoholic despite its appearance.

*150ml/¹/4 pint brandy, chilled*
*1.1 litres/2pints dry sparkling cider, well chilled*
*2 apples, cored and sliced*
*1 orange, sliced*
*few sprigs of mint*

Pour the brandy into a jug. Add the cider, fruit and fresh mint.

NOTE: This should be served really well chilled. If a sweeter punch is preferred, use a medium-dry cider.

# Wassail Cup

This warming drink is traditionally served around Christmas time as a welcome drink. It looks wonderful presented in a large china bowl with lightly baked apples floating on the top.

MAKES APPROXIMATELY 2.3 LITRES/4PINTS
*1.7 litres/3 pints brown ale*
*225g/8oz soft light brown sugar*
*1 cinnamon stick*
*2.5ml/¹/2 level teaspoon grated nutmeg*
*2.5ml/¹/2 level teaspoon ground ginger*
*1 lemon, thinly sliced*
*350ml/12fl oz medium dry sherry*

1. Place 570ml/1pint of the ale in a large pan. Add the sugar and cinnamon stick, and bring to the boil, stirring all the time to dissolve the sugar.

2. Add the spices, lemon, sherry and remaining ale. Warm through but do not boil. Allow 150ml/¹/4 pint per person.

THIS IS THE SOMERSET WASSAIL
CAROL – many different areas have their own
versions.

*Wassail, and wassail all over the town!*
*The cup it is white and the ale it is brown;*
*The cup it is made of the good ashen tree,*
*And so is the malt of the best barley.*

CHORUS

*For it's your wassail, and it's our wassail!*
*And it's joy be to you,*
*And a jolly wassail.*

*Oh Master and Missus, are you all within?*
*Pray open the door and let us come in;*
*Oh Master and Missus a-sitting by the fire,*
*Pray think upon poor travellers, a-travelling in the mire.*

*Oh where is the maid with the silver-headed pin,*
*To open the door and let us come in?*
*Oh Master and Missus, it is our desire*
*A good loaf and cheese and a toast by the fire.*

*There was an old man and he had an old cow,*
*And how for to keep her he didn't know how,*
*He built up a barn for to keep his cow warm,*
*And a drop or two of Cider will do us no harm.*

CHORUS

*No harm, boys, harm,*
*No harm, boys, harm,*
*And a drop or two of cider*
*Will do us no harm.*

*The girt dog of Langport he burnt his long tail,*
*And this is the night we go singing wassail;*
*Oh Master and Missus, now we must be gone;*
*God bless all in this house 'til we do come again.*

❄❄❄❄❄❄❄❄❄❄❄❄❄❄❄❄❄❄

# CHRISTMAS SUPPLIERS

❄❄❄❄❄❄❄❄❄❄❄❄❄❄❄❄❄❄

*We have included here a small selection of places who we have used to send food presents by post. It is in no way a fully comprehensive list, simply a collection of suppliers that we know and trust. We are grateful to Henrietta Green for pointing us in the right direction for finding good suppliers – her book on where to buy quality ingredients will be published by BBC Publications in September 1993.*

**Chewton Dairy Farms –** Priory Farm
Chewton Mendip
Somerset BA3 4NT
Tel: 0761 241666

Traditional Cheddar cheese packed any size.

**Childhay Manor Dairy–** Crewkherne Business Park
Blacknell Lane
Crewkherne
Somerset TA18 7HJ
Tel: 0460 77422

Dairy ice cream. No additives or artificial colourings. Will make up to customer's own flavours.

**Chocolate Society –** Norwood Bottom Farm
Ottley
Near Leeds
West Yorkshire LS21 2RH
Tel: 0943 851101

Suppliers of block couverture and handmade chocolates.

**Country Cooks Ltd –** Unit 1
Great Western Court
Ashburton Ind. Est.
Ross-on-Wye
Herefordshire HR9 7BW
Tel: 0989 66868

All natural ice creams in unusual flavours. Depending on quantity, special orders possible.

**Fletchers of Auchtermuchty –** Reddiehill Farm
Auchtermuchty
Fife KY14 7HS
Tel: 0337 28369

Fresh vacuum-packed oven-ready venison. All cuts available.

**Goodmans Geese –** Walsgrove Farm
Great Witley
Hereford & Worcester
WB6 6JJ
Tel: 0299 896272

Oven-ready geese available from Michaelmas to Christmas.

**Green & Blacks –** Unit 112
Canalot Studios
222 Kensal Road
London W10 5BN
Tel: 081 970 9679

Organic dark chocolate with 70% cocoa solids sold in 100g bars. Minimum order 2 bars.

**Hales Snails –** Sulby House
North Street
Sudbury
Suffolk CO10 6RE
Tel: 0787 310800

Large variety of smoked products including game, meat, fish and shell fish. Production to specific customer requirements possible.

**Heal Farm Meats–** Kingsnympton
Umberleigh
Devon EX37 9TB
Tel: 0769 574341

Additive-free meats and game. Wonderful sausages, hams and pâtés. Special recipes for restricted diets. All can be smoked on request.

**Heritage Foods –** Springhead Farm
Barrow Gurney
Bristol
Avon BS19 3RY
Tel: 0275 393979

Specialists in wild and chemical-free salmon – can get any fish delivered the following day.

**F. Hurd –** Nelson Road
Westward Ho
North Devon
EX39 1LQ
Tel: 0237 474039

Devon clotted cream.

**Inverawe
Smokehouses –** Inverawe
Taynuilt
Argyll PA35 1HU
Tel: 086 62 446

Traditionally smoked meat, game, fish and cheese.

**Justin de Blank –** 42 Elizabeth Street
London SW1W 9NZ
Tel: 071 730 9831

Sausages, bacon and a range of bakery items. Special requirements can be organized if discussed in advance.

**The Kitchen
Garden –** Old Down House
Tockington
Bristol BS12 4PG
Tel: 0454 413605

Dairy ice creams, sorbets and sherbets. Many exotic flavours, special flavours considered.

**Leathams Larder –** 114 Camberwell Road
London SE5 0EE
Tel: 071 703 7031

Charcuterie, delicatessen, game, fish, seafood, poultry and specialist provisions.

**C. Lidgate –** 110 Holland Park Avenue
London W11 4UA
Tel: 071 727 8243

Family butcher specializing in high-quality meat, sausages and pâtés.

**Loseley –**        Guildford
Surrey GU3 1HS
Tel: 0483 571881

Frozen pork sausages. Quiches and pastry, dairy ice cream, sorbets and ice cream bombes.

**Melchior
Chocolates –**      Chittlehampton
North Devon
EX37 9QL
Tel: 0769 540 643

A range of over 40 flavoured truffles and pralines made from Swiss chocolate.

**Neal's Yard
Creamery –**      Everlands
Ide Hill
Sevenoaks
Kent TN14 6HU
Tel: 0732 461020

Unpasteurized cheeses made with vegetarian rennet.

**Real Meat Co Ltd –**  East Hill Farm
Heytesbury
Warminster
Wiltshire BA12 0HR
Tel: 0985 40436

Full range of meat, poultry and bacon all reared without growth promoters.

## EQUIPMENT SHOPS

Over the Christmas period you may need a few extra pieces of specialist equipment. These are some of the shops that we consistently use.

**French Kitchen & Tableware Supply Company**
42 Westbourne Grove
London W2
Tel: 071 229 5530

**Lakeland Plastics Ltd**
Alexandra Buildings
Windermere
Cumbria
LA23 1BQ
Tel: 05394 88100

**B. K. Mathews & Son**
12 Gipsy Hill
Upper Norwood
SE19 1NN
Tel: 081 670 0788

For cake decorating equipment and colouring.

✳ ✳ ✳ ✳ ✳ ✳ ✳ ✳ ✳ ✳ ✳ ✳ ✳ ✳ ✳ ✳ ✳ ✳ ✳ ✳ ✳ ✳ ✳

# INDEX

✳ ✳ ✳ ✳ ✳ ✳ ✳ ✳ ✳ ✳ ✳ ✳ ✳ ✳ ✳ ✳ ✳ ✳ ✳ ✳ ✳ ✳ ✳